THE OWL WAS A BAKER'S DAUGHTER

Also by Grace Tiffany

THE OWL
WAS A BAKER'S
DAUGHTER

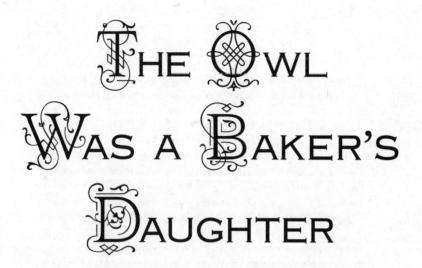

The Continuing Adventures of Judith Shakespeare

GRACE TIFFANY

HARPER

An Imprint of HarperCollinsPublishers

HarperCollins books may be purchased for educational, business, or sales promotional use. For information, please email the Special Markets Department at SPsales@harpercollins.com.

FIRST EDITION

Designed by Elina Cohen

Library of Congress Cataloging-in-Publication Data
Names: Tiffany, Grace, 1958– author.
Title: The owl was a baker's daughter : a novel / Grace Tiffany.
Description: First edition. | New York, NY : Harper, 2025.
Identifiers: LCCN 2024012042 | ISBN 9780063380530 (hardcover) | ISBN 9780063380554 (trade paperback) | ISBN 9780063380561 (ebook)
Subjects: LCSH: Shakespeare, Judith, 1585–1662—Fiction. | Great Britain—History—Elizabeth, 1558–1603—Fiction. | LCGFT: Biographical fiction. | Historical fiction. | Novels.
Classification: LCC PS3620.I45 O95 2025 | DDC 813/.6—dc23/eng/20240621

LC record available at https://lccn.loc.gov/2024012042

ISBN 978-0-06-338053-0

24 25 26 27 28 LBC 5 4 3 2 1

To Julia, who kept the faith, and to Angela, forever.

hey say the owl was a baker's daughter. Lord, we know what we are, but know not what we may be.

—Ophelia, *Hamlet*, by William Shakespeare

I.

ll the men of my family died. First my brother, then my grandfather, then Uncle Edmund in London, then Ned's brothers Gilbert and Richard at home. My father followed them into the grave. Not a year after that, we lost my baby, the son he'd asked me to name for him. That trick brought the babe no luck. He made his exit between evening and morn, his small body gone first hot as a baking stone and then all cold in the cradle. I remember Quiney's cry when he touched his cheek in the dawn.

We went on, of course. I gave birth to two more boys, and they lived to be men, but barely. Plague took them both within weeks of each other. Tom was nineteen and Rich was twenty-one. Now if God wants any more Shakespeares, he'll have to start on the women.

Rich's and Tom's deaths fell on us seven years ago. Since then the world's turned upside down. I tell Quiney to shake off his mourning, since had either of our lads survived the pest, they'd like as not have perished three years later in the fighting at Edgehill. "Which army?" Quiney says, with the ghost of a smile. His question launches a discussion which turns to a spat wherein I call him an idol worshipper and he terms me a treasonous windbag. Then I stalk off to weed my herb garden, or to gather herbs and berries in the woods, as I've done in all weathers for thirty-five years.

Quiney is fifty-seven, and I am sixty-one.

I began calling my husband Quiney when Tom was born and stole his father's name. Now that young Tom's gone, Quiney could have his name back, but he doesn't want it. I know why. It's that nothing can be what it was, anymore, in this topsy-turvy world. Life in Stratford has become a grim motley. Families who've dwelt side by side for generations no longer speak. Brothers have spilt each other's blood, and former friends stormed one another's manors. A third of the folk still rally behind the king, who chose early in the war to barricade himself in Oxford, not a day's ride from the Avon. The other two-thirds are readying themselves to seize our sovereign Charles and bring him to book like a regular man. It's a scene from one of my father's old history plays, but the players have now stepped off the stage and are arguing back and forth in Parliament house. I still wake every morning thinking life is a mad dream. It's real enough, though.

Quiney's a Royalist, like my sister, Susanna. I have always enjoyed saying the opposite of whatever Susanna says, nor am I bound to think and speak as my husband does. And I can be a windbag, it's true. But I'm not a traitor, for all my man's saying. I take no sides in this war. The fighting entirely disgusts me. The bloodshed would have horrified my late brother-in-law, John Hall, may flights of angels waft his soul to heaven, if there is, after all, such a place. It was Doctor Hall who trained me in his Paracelsian healing arts, some of which work and some of which don't, but all of which are well meant. I think the doctor's kindness taught me more than his leechcraft. To be a surgeon, or even to work in one's shadow, leaves a woman impatient with violence. The world holds so many things that can maim a body, can scar it and lop off its limbs and punch it full of holes, that men doing such things to each other on purpose begins to seem sheer madness and perversity, no matter the cause. Hands work better for healing than for fighting. Even now, in the Year of Our Lord 1646, with the good doctor nine years in the grave, I often hear his level voice in my mind, telling me where to probe a wound, how to hold a fractured arm while binding it tight, or just what amount of this or that dried, powdered plant to mix into a potion to bring down a fever. Sometimes I hear that voice in my own voice. Even in an upside-down world it's not usual for a woman to practice apothecary arts by herself, dismounting by a front stoop from a horse laden with a bag of simples, much less to tote surgical instruments in a case. But here in Warwickshire they remember John Hall, and the many seasons I worked by his side, and most of them open their doors. Kingsmen and Parliamentarians alike do it.

Still, folk are getting stranger. The old bonds are everywhere stretched to the breaking point. Godliness is on the rise, and brings with it its new superstitions, even as it mocks and sneers at the old ones. Last fall Quiney said he'd give me a year before they hanged me as a witch.

I'M NOT ENTIRELY SURE QUINEY loves me anymore. It's been a long time since he said so, and I never ask. Why should I? Would it matter? All his youthful greensickness for me, all that sappy passion that once pushed me down like a weight of wet wool, in the end was just a prologue to our real life. My father could have told it. He ended his plays with weddings, but he usually tossed in a quarrel or two at the bridal banquet, to remind folk that the flowers and kisses and dancing were only the start of the truer story. He knew. What's a marriage? The running of a shop, the keeping and paying of accounts, the two hours at a time, when other chores beckon, spent turning over feather bolsters and rummaging through drawers for a misplaced letter or a stray boot. Most of all, it's the raising of children, and sometimes, at the last, the watching, struck by horror and pain, as those children sweat and cry out and die. This, at any rate, was my and Quiney's marriage, and now we're a geezer and a crone at the far end of it, creaking about and grumbling as we perform our separate businesses. Quiney is training a new apprentice in winemaking, and I totter through the country-side practicing my craft, though we're both at an age to sit in corners, drinking mulled cider and telling strange tales and letting the younger ones do the work. That's how it should be, but it's as I said. The world's an addle-pate.

The truth. I don't totter. I ride long distances, and when the patient lies close at hand I walk, and briskly, too. Weathered I may be, but I still stand as straight as the hazel branch. I can turn a man's head in the marketplace, yet. I've got every one of my teeth, and as for strength, I can hold a lad down with one elbow on his chest while I dig a bullet out of his thigh. That is an operation I've lately needed to perform more often than I like. I still attend childbirths, of course, and can say truly that men are great babies compared to women when it comes to bearing pain. A wife will clamp her teeth on a rag, muffle her yells, and strain six hours to birth her eighth child, then wrap it in a clout and go out to skin a rabbit. Meanwhile her soldierly husband, lying at his ease in a nearby field, will howl like an infant at five minutes of knife-work done to extricate the ball he so manfully encountered. After it's done, he faints and goes off on a stretcher.

A lot of things change, but some don't.

I HAD ONLY DEALT WITH bullet wounds twice or thrice before Edgehill. The first time came when one of the Sadler boys accidentally shot another Sadler boy with a third Sadler boy's blunderbuss in the Arden Forest, when the first two were out illicitly hunting deer. That was when I learned how hot metal could tear flesh apart and lodge in the sinews, and leave a burnt and radiant circle where it entered the skin. "It hurts, Mistress Judith!" the boy squawked when I touched the wound. I muttered for him to be a man and stow it, but I probed as gently as I could. My fingers are kinder than my tongue. The lad was lucky, because the ball missed his bone, and had lodged near enough that I could see it and pull it out quickly and cleanly with forceps and give it to him for a token of the idiocy of the pair of them. If they must needs poach, bows are quieter, and arrowheads easier to extricate (so I told him). But in the past twenty years the world has gone mad for gunpowder. Where the local lords once flew their falcons for game, now those who've managed to hold on to their hunting grounds will fire in the air at a grouse. Sometimes they hit each other, without even meaning to.

So I'd seen such wounds, on occasion. But Edgehill was a Revelation. I mean not that it enlightened its beholders with new knowledge, but that it resembled the Armageddon described in the Biblical Book of the Apocalypse. We heard the ruckus before we knew what it was, some half hour before a man galloped into town and tore down Stratford High Street, his horse's metal shoes sparking on the cobblestones, crying out that the king's troops were finally facing the Army of Parliament, the hurly-burly was happening right here in Warwickshire, and to ride, ride! I think he meant ride for the king, and maybe he meant ride for your lives, but I can't be sure. Anyway, the town emptied out, with folk indeed riding or else running like demons either toward the battle or away from it. The worst fighting never reached Stratford, for which I thank God or whatever power directs this cockamamie show. But the thunder of the guns from ten miles east made the house-timbers shake, and from the smoke billowing over the hills I thought all Warwickshire was aflame. When a party of citizens rode up breathlessly, later, to fetch me to help with the wounded, Quiney said I could by no means go. But then they gasped out the names of men and boys we knew, Stratford and Shottery and Snitterfield youths now lying with head wounds or splintered arms and legs, and for all Quiney's anger, I knew I'd no choice. He knew it, too. He said nothing, just clapped both hands on his brow, turned, and went into the house. I rode off. When we came to the bloody fields, the gunpowder smell was acrid, the screams were hellish, and I couldn't see the horses or the fighting for the haze. To this day I don't know whether the camp I attended was Parliamentarian or Royalist. By 1642 it was not as easy as it had been ten years before to tell the Puritans by sight. Some of the Roundheads had let their hair grow long again. Quite a few had horses like the Cavaliers, many of them taken from their enemies, and so many different flags marked the companies that I'd have needed an officer's manual to find out who was who and what was what.

Now I would know, of course. Everyone would. But then it was all new.

And I didn't care who was who, any more than I care now. I didn't think about anyone's righteous or glorious cause, only of how to save this leg or that arm, or what final words to whisper into the ear of a lad whose life was ebbing away through a ten-inch gash in his side, a lad who would never see his dame or his sweetheart again.

"That might have been our Rich," I told Quiney when I finally got home. I sat facing him in our parlor, gaunt and shaking from lack of sleep, in my blood-crusted smock and apron and dirty hood. "It might well have been him, or Tom. Tom would always run pell-mell into any fight."

The noise in the street outside was so loud it sounded like a new battle was being waged there, and indeed a few were, though only on account of soldiers now roaming the town, looking for food and beds. I leaned forward and touched Quiney's knee. "Don't you see I am right? We might well have lost them anyway."

Quiney only stared at me like you would at a stranger who strolled into your house unasked and sat down at ease on your settle. And no wonder, I thought an hour later, when I caught a glimpse of myself in a glass. I looked like a madwoman or a stage demon, with my hair sticking out at five points and my face blackened by ash. But now I think Quiney's silence wasn't shock at my looks. I think he simply had naught to say to such cold comfort, meaning my plea that he smile at his boys' plague-deaths since, after all, they'd likely have been blown to bits by cannon fire three years down the road. I think he was thinking, *What world is this?* And, *Her heart is dead.* And I think he was partly right.

But it wasn't the last time I said it, about Edgehill, nor the last time I thought it. It solaced me to bury my special tragedy in one so vast, in the nightmare that had swept up nearly every family I knew. We find our comforts where we can.

EDGEHILL WAS THE LAST TIME tremendous fighting came close to Stratford, and now throughout the realm, if England is still a realm, there is less smoke and gunfire and killing. Last year's battle at Naseby sealed matters. There Parliament's most fearsome and capable Puritan almost destroyed the king's army outright. Nearly all the Royalist strongholds fell in the six months after. The king's men still held Oxford this spring, but with their comings and goings much circumscribed. Now, for eight months, only Parliament's forces have marched through our town demanding bacon and butter and quartering. Roundheads take target practice in New Place Garden, sending arrows and sometimes balls whizzing past my father's favorite ash tree, while my sister, Susanna, and her grown daughter, Lizzy, aim the contents of chamber pots at their heads from behind half-opened leaded glass windows. The soldiers dodge and laugh and wink at Lizzy. Quiney's and my house in town is small, and we've not yet been forced to harbor any such men. I pray the day won't come when we are. Quiney might go berserk, and lash out, and then find himself surrounded and hauled off to some makeshift cellar jail. His fuse burns long, but I've seen it reach the powder. When it does, I do not think a Roundhead's sword or even his musket would stay the explosion of Quiney.

• • •

THE FIRST YEAR WAS THE worst, for all of us. In the early up-heavals, both sides tried to outdo each other in plundering horses and oats and tallow and pewter and linen and chickens and sheep from every luckless town and village they passed through. Quiney's shop escaped ruin, though large stocks of his wines were commandeered without payment. One day in the first spring of the war, a Royalist troop under the king's nasty nephew Prince Rupert came through in the morning and took all the Spanish wines, and that very afternoon General Essex's Parliament men came into town from the other end and made off with the Rhenish. "To Luther!" the Essex men yelled as they swigged. It was remarkable how little mind that first wave of armed Puritans paid to their pastors' fervent exhortations regarding dicing, drabbing, tobacco, and drink. The outbreak of war set free the beast in all Englishmen, whether their shep-herd was Praisegod Flatcap or Archbishop Laud. (I speak of a time when that archbishop's head was still attached to his shoulders.) On that bad day we not only lost six months' worth of stock, but were forced also to watch its effects in drunken men weaving back and forth in the street outside, waving pikes and now and then firing their weapons at dogs and cats. When, in the evening, word came that another troop was marching out from Birmingham on the morrow, Quiney took down his sign. He saved the shop from ransacking by boarding up the door to make the place look as if it had been looted already. He proved wiser than the grocer.

Our stores are still commandeered, and now we have the army tax, and the Days of National Humiliation, when shops are ordered closed. But of late there's some method in the mad-ness. Over the past two years the Parliament's soldiers have shown a new and more decorous behavior. Now they march orderly through the town when they come, with their eyes straight ahead, and they topple no market carts, and do not drink wine. They pay for what they take, not enough, to be sure, but something. It's not like 1642, when the Parliament men would not only fleece the town but roam in unruly packs through the countryside, breaking into private chapels in search of altars to cleave and stained glass to smash and monstrances to melt down for bullion. There's little of that kind of thing left to ruin or steal, but they don't go looking, now. They march in file like two columns of ants, and they sing. It's a new kind of army. Their general has invented it. His soldiers eat and drink the Holy Spirit and sleep with their Testaments as pillows. "On, thou righteous band!" one of my godlier neighbors yelled from her window when some of these troops passed through three months ago, their boot-falls hard on the cobblestones and their voices joined in a hymn. I had not her zeal, and on that day I ducked behind a curtain to hide my frowning face. *Righteous band of killers*, was my thought, though even then I knew there was something about these men that eluded so short a description. The truth is, I don't understand them now, and I didn't then, and I feared them.

Still, if their virtue keeps them from Quiney's Rhenish, I am for it.

Quiney is lucky to have me, though he doesn't admit it. I've no goods to steal. I practice a craft, and that craft will bring in silver as long as women and men go about in bodies, getting pregnant and contracting the gout and stepping on live coals and hacking each other with swords and, newly, blasting each other with firearms. These are strange things to be grateful for, but, as I said, we find our comforts where we can.

2.

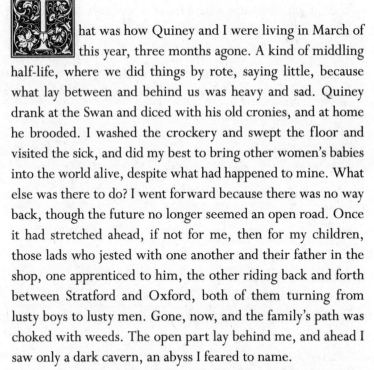

hat was how Quiney and I were living in March of this year, three months agone. A kind of middling half-life, where we did things by rote, saying little, because what lay between and behind us was heavy and sad. Quiney drank at the Swan and diced with his old cronies, and at home he brooded. I washed the crockery and swept the floor and visited the sick, and did my best to bring other women's babies into the world alive, despite what had happened to mine. What else was there to do? I went forward because there was no way back, though the future no longer seemed an open road. Once it had stretched ahead, if not for me, then for my children, those lads who jested with one another and their father in the shop, one apprenticed to him, the other riding back and forth between Stratford and Oxford, both of them turning from lusty boys to lusty men. Gone, now, and the family's path was choked with weeds. The open part lay behind me, and ahead I saw only a dark cavern, an abyss I feared to name.

At times I'd find myself standing motionless by the river-bend, tossing pebbles at the ripples or the ice, gazing at the place where my twin brother drowned fifty years ago. Gone half a century, and still I strained to hear little Hamnet's voice on the wind. Odder still, I sometimes succeeded. Now and then would come his whisper, and sometimes my mother's voice, warm and rich with laughter, and sometimes the hoots of my own boys, Tom and Rich, yelling and slipping on the bankside. I'll tell you a stranger thing. Sometimes I heard the chanting of Oberon and Titania, my father's Fairy King and Queen, and his young lovers, Hermia and Helena and Demetrius and Lysander. They spoke in the voices of the players I'd heard play them, and sometimes they spoke in my own voice. And to all of it, my lips would move soundlessly in response, speaking old lines of verse, or words of endearment to my lost boys, or to my mother, or to my brother, or to my father.

"Good morrow, Mistress Quiney," a passing angler would say, touching his cap as he strode down the bank, and giving me a curious look.

I'd jump and nod, and think, with a touch of fear, of Quiney's warning. Soon the Puritan justices of Stratford would have me for a witch, for all I was Will Shakespeare's daughter.

Or because I was.

ONION ROOT GROWS AT THE borders of the graveyard, and when crushed and boiled it can help in the passing of a stubborn stone. So when the snows are melting and the ground is soft I dig for it, after visiting my family members where they lie in earth.

In the first week of March I saw Quiney there, in the churchyard. He had left the earliest spring flowers, a few crocuses, by the graves of our sons. It must have been he who had done so. But when I spotted him he was nowhere near their resting sites, but was departing the yard from a far corner of the graves' enclosure, brushing his knees, as though he'd lately been kneeling. He didn't see me across the field of monuments, and it seemed wrong, in that silent company of gravestones, to call out for his attention. But after he disappeared I walked to that corner to see what he'd been up to. I had a dark suspicion.

I was right. I saw the footprints. He'd been praying at the grave of Margaret Wheeler and her babe. And he'd left some purple flowers on their stone.

It roiled me. That dead pair are the scandal of my life, and also of Quiney's. Thirty years ago, my weeks-old marriage was marred by Margaret's sudden claim before the church court that my Quiney was the father of her child about to be born. It might have been so. It might not. I knew Margaret Wheeler. I knew her habits, and thought it no accident that she pointed her finger at Thomas Quiney just as soon as he'd made a marriage with the daughter of the richest man in town.

I blamed her because it didn't seem fair to blame Quiney for some traffic with a willing girl done during the days when I'd held him at arm's length, mocking at his suit and telling him I'd never marry. I, after all, was no virgin when I came to his bed. He'd known it. Since I'd no bed-trick planned for a marriage night, I told him the truth, back when he was a-wooing. I'd had a lover in London once, a lover in the full sense of the word. At twenty-five I'd allowed myself that interval of passion. Though the thing hadn't lasted long, it did occur, and I thought it only just that a would-be bridegroom be informed. Perhaps I thought it would scare him off, and leave me to my brooding singleness. But, a practical man, he only said, "A bird in the hand is worth . . . Hmm." Since that proverb didn't seem to fit the facts, he changed it to "Well, the past is the past." For

Quiney's grace, then, I owed him a like indulgence. And I believe he knew nothing of Margaret Wheeler's condition when I changed my mind toward him, and in a matter of weeks, our marriage was made. After that, when we were wed and she accused him, he was caught in a pickle. He wouldn't lie and say he never knew her, and no other of her myriad swains stood up to acknowledge the coming child, so the bawdy court found Quiney guilty. I pitied him when they punished him with fines and a public chiding, but the matter shamed me, too.

It also pained me when my father, who'd been Quiney's champion for years, seemed suddenly less forgiving of him than I was myself. When I look back now, I feel sure he'd argued Thomas Quiney's suit for so long just to keep me from running off with the man I loved, a player of his own acting company by the name of Nathan Field. A shrewd observer, to say the least, my father must have guessed at the relation. And, just as I knew Margaret Wheeler, my father knew Nathan Field. He thought marriage with a Quiney would anchor me in Stratford and protect me from scandal and pain. He wasn't glad, then, when scandal jumped up at home. Nor was I joyful. But I strove to be practical and calm, and I didn't outwardly begrudge the money Quiney was fined for Margaret and her child.

As it happened, we ended up paying only for their burials. Mother and child both perished during the birthing time, and then it didn't seem to matter who the father was, anymore.

So what was this? Crocuses on their gravestone, after all these years? And what was more, when I looked closely, I could see the sodden stems of blooms he'd left before today.

• • •

I CAUGHT UP WITH HIM turning the corner into the High Street. It was not in my nature to hold my thoughts rather than spilling them as soon as they presented themselves to me, and this sometimes made our Quiney quarrels public fodder for any who cared to listen. But today I was Spartan. I forced myself to keep my peace until we were shut together in our parlor. Then I slammed my root basket down on a chair and said, "I was in the churchyard, behind you. I saw what you did. Margaret *Wheeler!*"

He looked at me with a face of shame.

"Why, Quiney? Is she a saint, that you pray at her grave?"

"Nay, nay. She was no saint. But I . . . did her wrong."

"Because you gave her a grass gown thirty years ago? At her invitation, if I may believe what you said then!" *And if I may believe my own eyes and ears,* I thought. As I have said, I knew Margaret.

"'Tisn't right that she should have died because of me. And . . ." He swallowed. "The babe did no sin."

I sat down hard on the settle beside him. "You say true." I heard the bitterness in my voice. "'Tisn't right that any woman should die bringing a man's seed to fruit, and much less the baby. There's no justifying the curse. But 'tis how we're made. Someone's bad idea."

Quiney sat silently, biting his lip, as he usually did when my speech veered toward blasphemy. He took off his cap and looked at it, turning it over and over in his big hands. His once-blond hair was now all grey, and thin, and gone at the top.

"Quiney." I made my voice kind, though inside I felt less pity than alarm. I leaned toward him and placed my hand on his arm. "What is it?"

"God doesn't forget. When the first boy died, all those years ago, I thought it was his vengeance."

I sat back, instantly angry again. My heart flared with ancient jealousy. I made a scornful noise with my tongue, and said, "You are an idiot."

I think he no longer heard such comments when I made them. Anyway, he went on as though he hadn't. "And then . . . to raise boys to manhood, and them both—"

"*Stop.*" I rose so abruptly that I knocked the table at my elbow, and my muddy new-dug roots fell to the rush-strewn floor. I stooped to pick them up, a hand to my back. "*Oof!* Next you'll be dressed in a white sheet again, beating your breast in front of Holy Trinity. Marry, if you find out that's what God wants, tell me straightaway. I've given up asking Him. Let Him send us a sign." I straightened and left the room with a slam of the door.

I was never that kind of wife who is praised in Proverbs, with the soft voice that turns away wrath.

3.

ere we dry kindling, awaiting the spark? The wrong metaphor, perhaps, but I struggle for the right one. Once, fleeing through the scullery to evade a cuff from Quiney, my eldest toppled a flask of vinegar into a bowl of yeast, and the powder bubbled and climbed like the eruption of Mount Aetna. That yeast had become something else. In the moment, my son's condition changed with it, as he and even Quiney stopped in their tracks to watch and wonder, forgetting their mischief and wrath. *Catalysis* was Doctor Hall's word for this altering of elements—though some might call it alchemy.

What began our catalysis, Quiney's and mine?

Perhaps it was our bitter spat about the blossoms he'd left to grace Margaret Wheeler's bones. Or perhaps the change began a week later, the day Jane and the Pearl first crossed our doorstep.

On that morning, I woke frowningly, having dreamt I was back in the graveyard, on my knees this time, praying to a man who sat on a tuft of grass with his back toward me. The fellow's mossy hair just brushed his collar. On his dome-ish head sat a tin crown, and in his hand was a busy quill that scratched and scratched over the surface of a flat stone that lay before him. I thought him a man of power, an arbiter of fortunes. Aloud, I begged him to give me my children back, to bring them up from the earth. I begged he would let me open my eyes and realize their plague-deaths had been the simple nightmare that, in waking life, they still seemed. Without turning, this bald, tin-crowned god stretched out his hand. "Look there!" he said in a familiar, reedy voice, pointing with his quill at a statue. "Look for the thing that was lost." I looked, and suddenly the churchyard monument was Rich, my youngest, smiling and walking toward me. But as I stretched my arms out to him, brimful of joy, I suddenly saw the sham. The walking statue wasn't my own Rich, but Richard Burbage, the famous London tragedian of my father's company, tricked up with a wig and face paint. There I stood, empty-handed and blinking like a fool. Mocked with art!

I woke on the instant, hollow and desolate and somehow angry at my quill-wielding father, though I knew my wrath to be unjustified. He wasn't, after all, in charge of *real* deaths. And as for resurrection, he'd always done the best he could with the tools at hand. He couldn't rightly be blamed for the inadequacies of pen and stage.

I sighed, rose creakily, dressed, and went downstairs. I could hear Quiney pouring new wine into the old bottles in the rear of the shop. I seated myself in the scullery. I'd begun to scan the latest pamphlet left us by a customer, detailing strange and portentous births in the fractured realm of England, which surely signified that the End of Days was at hand and the Antichrist loose, when I heard a child's voice in the front garden. Yes, it was clearly a child's, but that child was deepening its voice in imitation of a man, in a threatening intonation. "He sitteth upon the circle of the earth, and the inhabitants thereof are as grasshoppers! He bringeth the princes to nothing! Their molten images are wind and confusion!" Then the child let loose a mad, ghostly laugh. I heard a light slap and a woman's stern voice saying, "Shalt not mock at the scriptures, Pearl!" Then there came a firm knock on the door.

When I opened it, I saw planted on the stoop a woman of about twenty-five, dressed modestly in a cap and kirtle and patched smock and a worn cloak, and facing me with a blazing blue stare. She held in one hand the straps of two worn traveling bags, the larger of which swung slightly and clanked as it dangled from her fist. Her other hand was clamped onto the shoulder of a girl of some six years, whose cap sat askew and whose wheat-colored hair spilled bright from beneath it. The girl squirmed. The woman curtsied and pressed her hand down on her puny companion's shoulder till the child did me honor as well. "Mistress Judith Quiney?" the woman said. I nodded, but before giving me time to speak, she went on. "I come from Newark-on-Trent with this child of sin."

Who or what were they? I was baffled, but I heard myself, prompted by Lord knew what capricious spirit, say, "Very good. Will you step inside?"

HER NAME WAS JANE SIMCOX, she told me, and the child was called Pearl-of-Great-Price Simcox.

"Your daughter?" I asked, offering the pair of them mugs of cider and two biscuits.

"Nay. She is the spawn of my sister, a woman fallen from grace, ensnared by the lusts of an evil kinsman. Your kinsman."

"I have no kinsmen left," I said thoughtfully, munching a biscuit myself. "You err." But in my head the name tolled like a bell. *Simcox.* I remembered my sister, Susanna, saying something about a girl of that family, a maid who was sent away from her house for some impertinence.

"Wretched Master Nash, your niece's husband, is her father."

"Ah." I thought of the man, smug above his gilt buttons, possessed of a rolling eye. This tale could well be true. "But Nash is hardly kin to me. He's only a nephew by marriage. And I've no love for the fellow." My niece, Elizabeth, had married him, a vain little townsman of Shottery who was soon after converted into some type of baronet as the king's repayment for a hundred pounds spent to help raise him an army, once Parliament took away the one he'd thought was his own. Now the pair of them—Lordling Nash and Elizabeth, not Nash and King Charles—lived with Susanna in Stratford, at New Place, my father's old house, almost a mansion, which had gone, when he died, to my sister and her husband, my good Doctor Hall. In time the house would be Lizzie's, or rather, her husband's, and then Master Nash would swell up grander than ever. Meanwhile he made himself much at home at New Place, even to the point of chasing scullery maids into the bedchambers. Mistress Simcox had been one of those unfortunates. From Susanna I only knew that Elizabeth had caught the pair of them tussling on our parents' old bed, and had called the girl baggage and whore and thrown her out of the house within the hour.

"She should have thrown the husband out," I'd remarked, and had gotten the feeling that Susanna agreed with me, for a rarity, though she hadn't said as much.

As for young Simcox, when bounced from the house she'd traded some insults with her mistress from the yard, then sneaked into the stable, stolen a horse, and ridden off to God knew where.

To Newark-on-Trent, it now seemed.

"The prodigal daughter came back to us. To our home," said my visitor, Jane of the piercing blue gaze. "Let the wages of that man's sin be his death. She was ravished by your pleasant fiend in fine brocade."

"He's not *my* pleasant fiend. I told you. He's no real kin to me, in blood or manners."

She nodded, looking satisfied. "I have no wish to beg a place in *his* fine manor."

My sister's *fine manor*, I thought, while wondering if she'd misconstrued my last word. *Anygates, Lizzie would likely slam the door in your face.*

It seemed she'd drawn the same conclusion when she chose my house as her destination. She said, "I'd heard that you, Mistress Quiney, were more charitable than your niece to the hapless victims of the lusts of men."

I frowned, considering what ancient bits of Quiney-related gossip might have inspired her judgment. I wasn't inclined to ask. In any case, she was charging on. "For behold!" She pointed. "From my sister's sorrow and travail came this Pearl of Great Price."

"But you called her spawn. And dark flower of sin, or something like."

The child in question had dropped to the floor and, inspired by our grey tabby's yawning entrance into the room, was pretending to be a cat. She made a fair job of it.

"Aye. The devil is strong in Pearl." Jane Simcox gazed down at her fondly. "Off the floor, child."

Pearl began to roll and mew.

"Do you see? She wrestles with the Old One, with the valor of a saint."

I must have looked doubtful of this interpretation of Pearl's antics, because Jane quickly changed her theme. "We seek work," she said bluntly. "We are become laborers. My parents are with God. My brothers are fallen at Newbury, and the Royalists seized my family's bakery. Now the Scots have besieged the town, and when they gave us the chance, we fled. They held their fire and let the women out."

I nodded, feeling an inward shudder of compassion. All Stratford knew of the Scottish Covenanters, as those militant Presbyterians now called themselves, and their bloody siege at Newark-on-Trent. "But what of your sister? Your Pricey Pearl's dam? Her name was Hannah, was it not?" I wrinkled my brow, trying to remember her. I could summon up only the vague image of an auburn-haired girl of sixteen or so, humming and scrubbing a banister with a rag. She'd been a youngster, a mere maid, in a fresh cap and apron. I recalled her cavorting in the garden with Tom and Rich on one of our visits to the manor. From the house I'd watched as Tom pushed the girl in his cousin Lizzie's old swing, and then the girl pushed Tom, and then Tom pushed Rich, all of them far too old for such play, and laughing because they knew it. I recalled Elizabeth putting a stop to it, calling for young Simcox to get back in the scullery and mind her plates and cups.

My guest's face took on a look of ardor. "Hannah has lately gone to glory."

"Do you mean she's dead?"

"Aye. Two years ago she caught swine fever delivering pigs to General Balfour's troops, on their holy trek northward."

"Pigs' or troops'?"

"Say?"

"Nothing. Pray continue. Your sister died. I am sorry."

"She was bringing succor to God's Army. Surely He will welcome her into the company of angels!"

Lord, I thought, my suspicions more than confirmed. *A poxy Parliament zealot.* Quiney wouldn't have her in the house.

The moment I thought it, he came through the door.

"Who's this?" he said pleasantly enough, wiping his wine-stained hands with a clout. He looked down at Pricey rolling near his feet. "And what's this?"

I rose. Before Jane could start speaking, I did. "Mistress Jane Simcox here has heard I seek someone for help with the surgery and the house."

"*I* hadn't heard it."

"But I *do*. I'll pay her a fair wage, and she'll help me cook and tend the garden and gather the cures. She and her Pricey can sleep in the lads' old room." *If she'll limit her preaching*, I thought.

Quiney looked resentful. None had slept in that room for seven years, save the occasional visitor. Sometimes I would see the door standing open and, through it, him inside, sitting on the edge of the old bedstead with his eyes closed, as though the room's four walls housed a shrine. It made me want to scream, though, at the same time, it broke my heart.

"They can help clean your jugs, Quiney."

This was a blunder. I saw Jane start to puff up in a godly way. Before she could spout out a verse about wine-pots and drunkenness, from Genesis or Saint Paul, I pulled at her arm and said, "Come, Jane, let me show you the room." I left Quiney in the parlor staring at the Pearl-of-Great-Price, who had now joined our tabby in scratching her claws on the settle.

4.

It was one of the more rash acts of my life so quickly to agree to bring Jane and her Pearl into our household. I could see Quiney wasn't well pleased, even before Jane started gospelling over the wine barrels. But the truth was, I did need help in the scullery and with my apothecary calls, and the further truth was that in our house, noise and life of some kind would be welcome. With the mad comings and goings in the countryside due to the sequestrations, and the shifting movements of the soldiers, which it seemed would never subside, it was hard to keep a housemaid or even a contracted apprentice for long. All the youth were running, some to join the remnants of the king's troops, most to swell the ever-expanding New Model Army. Or they were returning home from service to try, in their raw greenness, to manage small farms that had lost all the family's older men, or to succor a widowed mother or sister. Some of the girls went off also to follow the armies, finding more sport or livelihood in this wise than could be got in Stratford town. We were becoming a town of elders.

So I took these young ones in.

For a little over a fortnight, life carried us on in its stream, its course not too much altered, as far as I could see. Sharing rooms with a gospeller and a mad hoyden of six was part of the new order, or the new disorder. I was done fighting fate. *Come what may!* I thought. But Quiney continued to be quietly displeased at the subtle disruption of his habits, and there was little I could say to change his mood. Once, I had arts to persuade my husband to good humor, but now a sour distrustfulness presided in our chamber. Something had been lost.

Quiney might have steeled himself to abide Jane's ceaseless good cheer, whose most frequent expression was the singing of the most joyful psalms. And he tolerated the chatter that was not always reminders of what the prophets Jeremiah and Ezra had said, but was quite often speech about ordinary things, like the best way to shoe a horse and the state of last year's harvest and the price of wool in Tewkesbury. Quiney didn't care much about any of it but found such talk easy to ignore. It was when Jane began on God's kingdom coming to England and her brothers who'd died for the cause at Newbury and the casting down of graven images that he could not bear it. He would not argue the matter with her; he would simply leave the house. Twice during her short stay in our home he came home late, to wend with an uncertain step through the hallway and up the stairs, after an evening spent grog-pounding in the Bear or the Swan. Both times I turned my back to him when I heard him sink down on our bolster, even with ears plugged with wax against his snoring. (I hate a drunken man.) And then the next day, each time, things were worse, because Jane had heard him stagger up the stair, too, and while scrubbing the floors she regaled all hearers with the story of Noah and his addiction to the grape, and a tale of foul doings in Sodom and Gomorrah. The peculiar thing was that even in these Biblical recitations she didn't seem angry or scornful, only rapt in some kind of exaltation produced by the need to recount the various sins of man. The first time, she ended by raising her hands toward the thatched roof and bursting into song. The next, she cried out, "God our Redeemer be praised, who washes us in the blood of the Lamb and takes away our iniquities!" And Pricey, helping her scrub, gleefully echoed her words.

I have always had small patience for gospellers, since most of the ones I've known have been like perverse little boys who delight in smacking eels with sticks. The godly call *Down, wantons, down!* when a vice raises its head, their eyes peeled for every transgression they can see and denounce. But Jane intrigued me. She wasn't like that at all. Her speech was no slavish recitation of platitudes, and it was far from grim. She considered things, and reached conclusions. Behind her every denunciation was a recipe for joy.

"Wine is a devil," she announced, pointing through the window at our vintner's sign, "because it turns wise men into quarrelsome babes. After your breakfast beer, drink clear, clean water and love thy neighbor!"

"But, Jane, your brothers—"

"God welcome them into his eternal army!"

"—loved *their* neighbors by firing at them with long-barrelled flintlocks."

"And as sober as owls were they when they did it!"

"But how is this love? Not only to quarrel with a neighbor, but to blow his head off? Sober or no, this seems something uncharitable."

At this she rocked back on her haunches and waved her dirty rag like a battle flag. "Ah, my dear mistress Judith, you think death is the worst thing that can happen to a man. What if it were the best?"

"The *best*? So your brother did a grand kindness to some Cavalier by shooting him off his horse? And then another Royalist rode by and returned the favor by—" I stopped short. I couldn't finish. I knew what it was like to lose a kinsman. I wouldn't jest about her brothers' battlefield deaths.

But Jane was unperturbed. She looked up at me with her round face shining under her cap. "Aye! You have it! So I contend! Or at least I say there is no sin in the killing when a weapon is raised in justice. For thy last act on earth to be a righteous one, is glory! Glory!" She raised both hands skyward. Then she dropped them abruptly, and with her rag scrubbed furiously at a stain on the wall, her face clouding in godly indignation, or as if she brooded on some ancient injury. "And as for the unrepentant one, the idol worshipper, who rides only to wreak havoc in the pride of his heart, yea, on the field he meets God's beadle."

I'm sure my face reflected my doubt. *What a cock-brain*, I thought. Yet I could not help admiring her thinking. Or rather, the simple fact that she *was* thinking. In truth, I was amazed at the philosophy this wench had derived from her family Bible. Four years into the war and all I had ever heard from my neighbors were slogans. *King and country! The sacred throne!* from one side, and *The golden calf to the furnace! God's voice through the will of His people!* from the other. I was sick of the phrases. But Jane was no parrot. I couldn't agree with her; I thought a live vintner or farmer or even an idle lord worth more than any number of dead Cavaliers or Roundheads. Still, I was grateful to find, so unexpectedly in my kitchen, not only hands but a mind at work. If Quiney disliked it, he could go elsewhere.

But in the end it was we—Jane and I—who went elsewhere. And it was Quiney who made us do it. I couldn't have foreseen the reason, even though Quiney had.

THE TROUBLE STARTED A FORTNIGHT after Jane and Pearl's hiring, when the pair of them accompanied me on a birthing call. I barely knew the chandler's wife, who had come to Stratford recently from Snitterfield, but I'd delivered hundreds of babies in Warwickshire by now, and most of them had lived, so my name as a midwife was unbesmirched, and the call didn't surprise me when it came. As for Jane, she told me she'd assisted at the childbeds of two cousins, and she seemed, when I quizzed her, to know something of the craft. So I brought her into the house with me, and charged her with boiling the water and sitting close by the bed with clean towels to swathe the child when it came out all new and slippery.

I took care to wash my hands with soap before I touched the woman, a custom whose oddness prompted stares and whispers from the maids peeping in through the doorway, though I would swear that this practice, taught me by Doctor Hall, is the ground of my success in keeping not only babies but also their mothers alive. Her labor was brief—it was her sixth—and the boy yelled lustily when I bit the cord. Her eyes on the infant, the woman seemed undismayed by my new servant Jane's loud praising of God, as I saw to the afterbirth and Jane mopped and wrapped him; praise for sending us one more Christian warrior to increase His Kingdom on Earth and speed us toward the Millennium. As for me, seeing that Jane's hands did good work, I let her mouth run, and only bit my lip and hoped it were no Royalist household. These days you asked before going anywhere, but this call had come suddenly, awakening us at daybreak, and in my rush I'd forgotten. But the mother remained absorbed by her new son. She seemed spent and weak but hale as she held her babe to her breast.

And then we heard the growling.

The mother started and let go the babe, which set up a weak wailing as it slid down the counterpane. Quickly I restored the infant to her arms and her nursing, then looked tensely around to see what dog had entered the room. What I saw sent a shock of fright through me. I jumped backwards, stumbling over a stool.

We had forgotten Pearl. Left in the garden to play with a rag poppet, she had thrown it in the dirt and crept or crawled into the birthing room. Now she was pushing herself up gradually at the end of the bed, her hands on the frame, so that only her eyes and the top of her head could be seen from the mother's perspective, and from mine. She had lost her cap, and her hair, like her eyes, was wild. As the chandler's wife stared, Pearl changed her growl to a bark, then began snapping her teeth. "I will eat you, my pretty!" she said between snaps. "Yum yum yum yum, give it me, give it me—"

The chandler's wife shrieked and clutched her new boy so hard it lost the nipple and began its crying anew. I grabbed Pearl by the arm, hauled her to her feet, and dragged her to the door, where I all but threw her down the passageway. The two female servants scuttled from our path, exclaiming in horror, and the little girl slid parlorward on her arse, yelling "Plague on this house!" She said it in that same strange imitation of a man's voice I had heard her use outside my door on the day we met. I looked back at Jane, who, oblivious to the ruckus, had placed her hand on the baby's head and was speaking some kind of blessing, though it was unlike any blessing I had ever heard, something about the child growing to observe the covenant made by Moses with the children of Israel in the land of Moab. From the terrified expression on the chandler's wife's face, I could tell she thought this some satanic curse.

"Get out!" the woman yelled, more heartily than a woman lately delivered is wont to be able to call. "Hands off my child!"

I yelled at Jane to cease her chanting and hastily gathered up my soaps and cloths. Thinking it best not, at this moment, to introduce the matter of my fee, I hurried us both from the room. I'd brought some boiled eggs for the mother to nibble on, to restore her strength, and these still lay in my bag, but no matter, she'd done this five times before and could see to herself, she and her goose-like maids. Outside we scooped up Pricey Pearl, who was now humming and spinning about in the front yard while the silly girls peeped from the windows. "*JesuMaryJoseph*," I swore as we hustled down the lane, dragging our short prisoner by the arms.

That afternoon Pearl suffered the beating of her life from her aunt Jane, who, as she smacked, shared with her niece much godly invective concerning wicked offspring. Her memory was marvelous. With the voice of a prophet, she quoted fluently from both the Old Testament sages and the Apostle Paul. I left her and her hard hand to it, hoping only that my decades-old good name as a licensed Warwickshire midwife would prove a charm against any tales the chandler's wife and servants might tell, about the apparition of Satan's spawn at the good woman's childbed.

But I couldn't keep it from Quiney, who was expecting the money (which, by the way, I never got). I made the tale as humorous as I could, even barking like a dog to mimic Pearl mimicking the devil, but he only looked at me in frowning dismay. "They will bring us to ruin," he said. "That child is possessed."

"You may call it the devil," I said coldly, disappointed in him. There'd been a time when my tales could make him spit his ale in laughter. "You may call it what you will. I call it imagination."

SOME FIVE DAYS AFTER THE unhappy episode at the chandler's house, a strange thing befell me at the Market Cross. Standing before a stall, a townswoman and I reached at the same moment for a cabbage. When our hands met, she snatched hers back as though she'd touched a hot coal. She looked at me with a face of fear, then averted her eyes from mine and scurried away. I looked down at my hand, then touched my hair to see if something was amiss with it as I watched her fleeing back. She stopped to say something to another dame, and the pair of them looked over at me, frowning. When they saw I was staring boldly back at them, they both dropped their eyes.

I bought the cabbage and walked home briskly, standing as straight and looking as youthful as a woman of sixty-one can, and cursing the luck of the old. I knew what the woman had meant. There are folk who think any hag who has cunning with herbs is a witch, and this woman didn't know me. She had no inkling that I was the wife of a respected townsman or the sister of the proprietress of New Place. Or the daughter of William Shakespeare.

But as I discovered later that day, it was worse than that.

Because she did know.

Strange news about my household was abroad in the town. And it had reached the ears of the aldermen.

Quiney and I had just finished our supper of roasted fowl and boiled potatoes when a messenger knocked on the door. Quiney answered it. He was handed a letter, which he opened with a curious look. When he read the contents his face darkened and he swore.

"What is it?" I asked. "A new requisition for the army? I thought they had gone sober."

He looked at me with anger. "I *said* they'd be the ruin of us."

"Who, the Parliament?"

"Judy, hide. Go into the pantry."

"What?"

"*Go!* And bring the woman in there, too. And the mad puny one, if you care for her life."

What in the name of God? I thought, but I scrambled to find Jane and Pricey, who were washing spoons in the scullery. I bustled them into the bread room. Quiney followed at our heels.

To this day I marvel at how much better than we three he understood what was happening, and what we needed to do. He told me, a long time after, that he had lain awake many fearful nights planning what action to take in such a time, while I lay dreaming mournfully by his side.

In the pantry I tried to grab the paper from his hand, but he waved it aloft. The cramped space was dark and windowless and I couldn't have made out its lettering, anyway. "What *is* it, man?" I held his arm. "Tell me!"

"I will not tell you what this letter says. But I will tell you what I heard in the shop today, from a man who does not even know you or what arts you practice. The chandler's new son has gone yellow and will not eat."

"That's jaundice. 'Tis common enough. Tom had it, remember? Black hellebore will—"

"The last thing you must do is visit the woman with your black hellebore. The very name of it!"

I went silent. For a wonder, Jane stayed quiet, too. I could hear Pricey Pearl's quick breathing at her side. We were all standing very close together.

Then I said, "Is that a summons—"

"You don't know what it is, and you will not. Let me be the scofflaw. I will saddle my horse and yours while you bundle your clothes. Stay away from the windows. I'll give you all the money in my strongbox. You have cousins in Banbury. Perhaps they're in need of a visit. In forty minutes the sun will be down, and then you can set out. You know the road."

"Oh," I said, in the smallest of voices.

"Mistress Jane, can you ride?"

"Bareback on a draft horse!"

"You'll have a saddle, but you'll need to hold the child before you."

"And there went out another horse that was red: and power was given to him that sat thereon to take peace from the earth, and that they should kill one another!" Pricey chanted happily.

In less than half an hour we three females were booted and spurred and cloaked and leading our two mares through the back garden gate. We did not dare the High Street. Quiney gave me a quick embrace. He whispered, "Write me from Banbury, from the house of your cousin. If the babe lives, nothing will come of this."

"And if it doesn't?"

"Perhaps naught will come of it then, either. But better if you're away, and better still if, when you return . . ."

He let the sentence hang, but I knew what he meant. I was a crone with a bag of simples, a common-enough sight in the end, in a country town. But Pearl: she was odd. Everyone who saw Pearl thought her possessed by a demon. She had cursed a woman's house while her guardian, a stranger, had voiced an unintelligible prayer. When I came back, I should come back alone.

I kissed Quiney. "Farewell."

5.

We flew by dusk, when the ways out of town were empty. Not until we had crossed Clopton Bridge and the Avon did Jane and I speak together about the reason we had sought the southward road.

She knew. It was she who broke the silence, hissing, "I said a blessing for the babe! From the Book of Numbers. That he might partake in the covenant—"

"No one reads that part of the Bible."

"None of your town merchants and Pharisees may, but—"

"Jane! Don't work yourself into a holy lather. I beg you, speak lower! Who knows what travelers we'll meet on this road?"

She quieted. In a moment she said, in a chastened voice, "Forgive me. I came to you because Hannah said you Shakespeares . . . that you reminded her of me. I meant no harm to your family."

"Reminded her of you!" I knew not what to make of this; I'd barely known her sister, Hannah. I knew Jane had done no wrong, but I felt anger breaking through the shock of it all. Why should I, at a grandmother's age, because of some random acquaintance be made to bounce my bones on the hard road? I said, "Why could you not train the child to act seemly?" I could hear my strict grandmother, Mary Arden, speaking through me, and remembered that when she'd chided my mother in this wise all those decades ago, the topic had been me. But I was too ireful to stop. "Pricey put a curse of the *plague* on that house!"

"She knows not what she does," Jane said humbly.

"What's more, she stole that curse from one of my father's plays." I stopped myself short with that, though the horses jogged on. For a moment, I gave myself up to thought.

I had never wondered at the circumstance when people recited lines from my father's scripts. Some of those lines were nearly as well known in England now as the Bible, and I hadn't been surprised when even a six-year-old child could come out with a malediction from *Romeo and Juliet*, which might indeed have been the best-known of all his works and deeds. But this thought of my father reminded me of something I'd seen the month before; an unheard-of sight: a folio copy of his plays half charred in a neighbor's ash-pit. Other partly burned books of poetry had lain near it.

My neighbor, that day, stood by, poking the ashes. When he saw me self-halted and staring, and noted at what, he said in a voice of shame, "It's foolish, Mistress Quiney. And all honor to your father. I knew him when I was a boy, a kind gentleman he was. He always looked on me with sympathy when I passed him with my Pliny, trudging to the grammar. But my wife won't have these in the house."

"Why?" I'd asked in a strangled voice, thinking, *That folio is worth a laborer's yearly wage.* I spotted a smoldering copy of Chapman's *Iliad*, keeping my father's works company.

"Well. The spells and the witches and the . . . whatnot."

"Dunce!" I strode past his house and his ash-pit, cursing his tradesman's soul.

Remembering the scene now, it came to me that Jane and her Pearl were not the sole targets of Stratford's suspicion. The summons to court which Quiney had kept from me, wisely, lest I be knowingly fleeing the law . . . Who, exactly, had it named? Most in Stratford knew me not only as an apothecary, a dealer in simples and odd remedies, a wanderer of the forest— all suspicious-enough trades and activities, to the gullible mind—but also as she who'd been darkly involved, as a child, in her own brother's drowning. And as the leftover twin (and ah, twins were strange) who in her mad youth had sneaked off to London for a few weeks and played parts in her father's plays.

The devil's spawn? It wasn't only Pearl. It was I.

"I'M TIRED, AUNTIE, AND THE horse is bumping my arse."

"Hush, poppet. We'll stop soon."

I had no confidence that Jane was right. We'd been riding three hours, and had already passed through two Parliamentarian garrisons. We'd no official passes, but I'd showed the guards some papers and said a vague thing or two about a friend in Banbury who was nearing her time. Because of that, or because Jane quoted Leviticus, or simply because we were women, they let us through. The moon was high and so full and bright it cast shadows from the trees and bushes that lined the road, and we saw lights in the windows of some of the taverns and post-houses we passed. But all the houses that weren't shuttered and dark were full of beery shouting, and we saw no place where we dared stop.

Once we stood to the side of the road while a very large troop of soldiers marched past. The men looked dusty and non-descript. Even with the moon's help it was hard to see whether they wore tawny or buff and scarlet. They seemed too road-weary even to grumble amongst themselves, and their flags were carted and furled, so there was no guessing their allegiance. At that point we were near enough to Oxford, where the king kept his doomed, festive court, but these were infantrymen mostly, their few horses lashed to creaking carts bearing guns and powder-sacks and crates that I guessed were filled with victuals. I reckoned they were Parliament, like the garrisons. They tramped by and paid us no mind. We returned to the road at a distance behind them, keeping our pace de-liberately slow, and they soon disappeared into the shadows, their hard footfalls fading to naught.

That slight entertainment had passed from view an hour before. I could hardly blame the child now for bewailing the tedious, comfortless ride. "If need be, we'll sleep in the shade of the trees, girl," I told Pearl. "Our cloaks are wool."

I knew the road to Banbury well. We had already covered most of the distance. That town was not walled, and I knew how to find my cousins' dwelling.

But we weren't going there.

I'D BEEN PONDERING THE MATTER since we left the hearth lights of Stratford behind us. If the town council truly meant to question me for a witch, likely Banbury wasn't far enough. The chandler's wife's poor jaundiced babe might not get bet-ter, and . . . I fretted, wondering if anyone with a brain in her head would think to give the thing fluids and coax it back to

the breast, since what it needed most was food. As I'd tried
to remind Quiney, black hellebore, crushed into warm water,
usually worked. I hoped the babe would fight through, for its
own and its mother's sake, but mostly, I will confess, for mine.
Infants die all the time, of course, in Stratford like everywhere
else, and customarily no one but God is blamed. But these were
strange times. New customs were seen. These days the devil was
often given dark credit for happenings my mother and her
gossips would have simply called bad luck.

So with the chandler's wife. If she lost her boy, the stark
memory of our odd threesome, crone, woman, and child,
would loom even larger in her mind. Recalling the weird scene
after the birth, I could almost forgive the woman for bringing the charge, now that her baby was sick. Pearl's creeping
and growling had proved a startling-enough sight even to me,
though I've witnessed old men raging like Lear against the
death-dark, and a pregnant woman drop to the ground and lick
dirt, and a lad kick his aunt in the face rather than swallow an
emetic. I have never confused these human outbursts with the
workings of demons or sprites. I've long been familiar with
odd behaviors, given the father I was blessed or cursed with.
I could see my da now, as from the perch on the stairs where,
as a girl, I used to peep. He would jump suddenly up from his
writing desk and race twice or thrice about the room, roaring
Once more unto the breach or something like it, then drop back
into place on his stool and placidly pick up his quill, as though
nothing unusual had happened.

So I knew the difference between demonic possession and
a teeming mind, as I'd told Quiney several days before, when
Pearl was our subject. But fewer and fewer in England seemed
to allow such a difference nowadays.

Quiney had warned me of something else during our scramble to leave the house that evening. "The shop customer who spoke of Jane and Pearl today," he'd said. "He's the chandler's neighbor." Quiney was rifling through his strongbox papers for my apothecary's licenses and pulling out every coin he saw there while I rushed to throw petticoats and skirts and stockings and even, for some reason, an old jerkin of Tom's into a leather traveling bag. "He told me one of the maids who helped at the childbed has grown listless and sickly of late," he added.

I laughed shortly. "None of *them* helped at the childbed. They were gossiping in the hall. I'm not sure Pearl even saw them when I pitched her out the door and she yelled her ridiculous curse. The maids weren't the target. The hussy just wants attention. Anyway, what folly! A lass of seventeen feels listless, or claims to, and this is a witch-borne malady?"

"You need not make the case to me. I'm not your judge. I know 'tis mostly tomfoolery and superstition." Quiney opened a drawer. "Now. You'll need a tinderbox on the road. Here."

I'd grabbed the box and a candle and stuffed both in my sack, thinking that for a man who held no superstitions, he'd been fairly free scattering crocuses on a dead woman's grave to save himself from God's punishing wrath. But for once, I'd held my tongue.

So, I thought now, as we plodded the night road. I was reconsidering his warning about the maid. *So.* Girls were in it. And silly girls, too. They might say anything, bring any charge, and a mother in grief might believe them. A young girl might make up a thing out of whole cloth, or otherwise embellish the facts. I knew it (*Margaret Wheeler!*), and I knew that the maidservants' wagging tongues were increasing my danger threefold.

That being the case, Banbury was too close for me, at only half a day's ride from Stratford. Since it was known the Shakespeares had kin there, it would not be hard for some zealous citizen deputy to follow and find me. Pricey, Jane, and I had to go farther.

Much farther.

It would be best, I thought, to skirt Banbury tonight and bed down in some shrouded copse off the roadway. It was balmy for the start of April, and we had warm cloaks and wouldn't freeze if we huddled together. I knew a brook south of the town. We could drink there, and our mounts could graze, and we'd saved some biscuit for breakfast.

Just as this thought passed through my mind, a horse and rider galloped out of the trees and blocked our passage forward. We shrieked and our horses shied, but the rider quickly dismounted and grabbed their reins before they could bolt. "Off," he said gruffly, pushing and pulling at Jane, who nearly fell to the road, staggering, her arms still tightly wrapped around Pearl, who'd been dozing. He kicked Jane in the throat. She let out a strangled cry and collapsed sideways.

I yelled, "Jane!" But he was at my horse's side and blocked me from dismounting. I raised my hand to chop him in the neck—he could see how he liked it—but he turned and pulled me from the saddle. I landed on my feet and kicked at his legs, but he hit my face so hard I fell back against my horse with a cry. Immediately he began groping inside my cloak, pulling it from my shoulders. "It's fine enough wool," he said gruffly. "But I'll leave you with it if you show me where the money's sewn."

No money was sewn anywhere. We hadn't had time. My silver was stored in a leather purse tucked inside my belt. He found and grabbed it almost immediately and held it aloft, crowing. But I took advantage of his avaricious distraction to throw myself forward and bite his bristled cheek till I tasted blood. He let out a cry and tried to punch me again, but I ducked, and suddenly he fell in the road, yelling, "Stay thy dog!"

In the fitful moonlight, I saw the small, ferocious outline of Pearl. She had thrown herself against the man's legs and bitten his thigh hard through his breech-cloth, and was now crawling around dangerously close to the horses' hooves, a piece of that cloth in her teeth. As soon as she heard the word *dog*, she spat out the cloth and started barking. Had I not known Pricey for weeks I might have thought she was a hound myself, and a vicious one, too. I stooped to grab her by the arm. I dragged her away from the horses, who were now tossing their manes and trotting forward and back, whinnying. The highwayman was up in a trice and had me by the shoulder again, gripping hard. I threw Pearl from me and struggled with him, scratching and kicking wherever I could reach. "Keep still!" he hissed. "You'll give me thy horses, hag, and whatever they carry!"

"We are three and you are one, and why will I do that?"

"I've a pistol on my saddle."

"*Have you, then?*" There came a click.

At the sound of the wheel lock the man dropped my arm and spun. By the moonlight I saw terror wash over his face as he gazed at the barrel of his own weapon, aimed straight at his forehead from not a yard distant. Jane was holding her neck with her left hand, but her right bore the pistol, and it did not waver.

The man reached out toward the gun. "You know not how to use that, bitch."

She shot him in the elbow, where the bones met. The horses bolted into the trees at the sound. As he fell to his knees with a cry, Jane bent down to him, grabbed the bags of powder and shot that hung from his belt, and with marvelous strength ripped them free while, cursing in his pain, he tried to fend her off with his good arm. In seconds she'd reloaded the gun and was aiming again at his face. *"Flee from the wrath to come!"* she yelled. Pearl, now a small hopping shape in the starlight, echoed Jane's words from the roadside, her voice a fife. *"Flee, sinner, from the wrath to come!"*

He fled from it, clutching his shattered arm as Jane fired after him shouting, "Glory! For the Lord shall rise up, that He may do His work, His strange work!"

I was still panting for breath and my face was sore and swelling where he'd hit me, but for all that, I was hard put not to laugh like a madwoman, at Pearl, at Jane, and at my own crazy surgeon's impulse to ride after the man and demand that he allow me to splint his elbow. For all the lout's violence and ill will, I hoped he'd find help for the bone-break. Not from me. I stumbled toward Jane and grabbed her shoulder. "Strange work indeed!" I gasped. "Woman, *where* did you learn to fire a pistol? Nay, hold, I can guess——"

"From David and Mordecai, now mustering in God's regiment!" She rubbed a finger along the hot barrel and shook the gun as though it were a sword, and she a fierce Bellona in the starlight. "And now this is mine. Also a fine bag of shot, and I have *balls*."

"I'll ne'er gainsay that. Let me see." She held out her hand, and I fingered the bags. "I've seen this kind on the belts of Prince Rupert's soldiers. Belike the man was some deserter."

"Let him flee from the wrath of God," she said grimly, and stuffed the gun in her belt.

It took us twenty minutes to find the horses and coax them back to the road, but when they came, the rogue's mount came with them. Its saddle was laden with a bag of florins and a wicker cask of ale and bread and dried beef. Pearl named the new horse Glory, and it came along with us willingly enough, loosely tied by its reins to Jane's mare, our own bags now hanging from its saddle. Our drowsiness was fled. Pearl seemed especially elated. We rode ten miles more before my own heart stopped racing and Jane finally heeded my pleas that she cease flourishing her new pistol and threatening the innocent moon.

WE SPENT TWO MORE DAYS traveling, and during that time had to make our way past three more garrisons. Jane kept her new wheel lock hidden, and the soldiers gave us no trouble. That first night, when we'd ridden off our and our horses' excitement, we slept among the trees well away from the outskirts of Banbury, our three cloaks piled as blankets, and us huddled together for warmth. Jane's throat was bruised, and I heard her cough with discomfort many times before we heard a cock crow. As for my face, at my direction, Jane had treated it with a rag soaked in cold water and spread with marrow mud from the stream bank. When I rose, though my left eye was puffy and bruised, I could see through it, and the swelling went down as the day wore on.

The second night we tied ourselves to the fringes of a soldier's camp ten miles west of Aylesbury, joining the women who were cooking and washing clothes for their husbands and sons. There'd been a skirmish in the area, and for an hour or two I helped bandage and cauterize wounds, even pressing a whiskey-soaked rag between a private's teeth as a surgeon sawed at his wrist, below which the bones of his hand were splayed, ball-splintered beyond repair. Blessedly, the man fainted during the operation, and I helped the surgeon tie off the arm after. A few men lay dead in a field, and to those who moved or moaned, Jane and Pricey brought water. Afterward, Jane irked me by handing our evening meal of cold beef and bread to a group of beggarwomen who hung at the edge of the camp. "God will provide," Jane said of our empty food-sack. But it wasn't God but one of our highwayman's florins that purchased us a loaf of bread, some cheese, some dried salmon, and ale from a group of soldiers. We took this back among the tents, found a sheltering tree, and for the rest of the night kept alone.

We were bone-tired, but I did not welcome the end of the day's activity and conversation. One of the dead young men in the field, scarred and scored on the face and body, had resembled Rich with his neck and shoulders mottled by the marks of the plague. While the leaves above me rustled, in the middle time between waking and sleep, the memories of my son's dying drifted into my thoughts.

I am sorry, he'd said, before he slipped into cloudy oblivion. I was barefaced then, seated by his sweat-stained bed. After the sage and lavender had failed, while his fever still climbed, I'd pulled off my apothecary's mask so in his delirium he might see me, his mother, who loved him, not a frightening bird-thing, beaked and predatory, hovering at his side to carry him off to Hell. What matter if the pest struck me now? *I am sorry*, he'd whispered then, looking into my teary face. Sorry for the petty crimes of his childhood, for making a mockery of my medicines, for failing to stay alive. Sorry for dying like his brother Tom had only a fortnight before. Sorry for leaving me and his father to our desolation.

• • •

JANE KNEW NO GEOGRAPHY BEYOND the road between Newark-on-Trent and Stratford, half of which territory she and Pearl had traversed in a cart with other citizens who had fled her town in the dark, weeks before, and we were risen and mounted in the light of the third day and far south of Oxford before I told her we'd taken a southeasterly road and avoided Banbury entirely.

I told her why.

She wasn't dismayed. In fact, she seemed delighted. "The farther south we go, the godlier it gets," she crowed.

I knew not whence she'd got this strange notion, but it suited my purpose not to argue. "Well," I said. "Very well."

"Will you take a new name, then, mistress? Win-the-fight Praisegod? Jerusalem Newborn?"

"Lord! Do you think these up yourself?"

"They come to me. They crowd my brain. What of Ancient-of-Days Manassas?"

"Ancient of Codfish! Marry, I may be old, but I've teeth in my head, and sharp ones, too. Pearl and I can bite!" Pricey snapped her teeth in agreement. "Pearl's pearlies!" I said approvingly, and essayed a doggish howl. "*Woo-woo-wooo-woo!*"

My black mood of the prior night was gone. Away from the late scenes of death, feeling our health and wholeness, we were giddy.

"But your new name, mistress?" Jane persisted as our horses plodded southward. "A good holy one. Though Judith *was* a woman of God, 'tis true, for all that she's in the Apocrypha and not the true Bible. She slew her an Assyrian." She thought for a moment. "There is also Deborah. You might call yourself Deborah Justice."

"Or Hecate."

"What's she?"

"No matter." The sun had climbed high, and I wiped the sweat from my forehead. "Jane, once, long ago, I stole away from my home and I gave myself a new label. But things are different now. We may not be going back home for some time. Where we find ourselves, we may lack friends. I may need to work, and to work I'll need to show my licenses. I'm too old to change my name now."

"But Glory bears gold on his saddle," Pearl piped up. "We're rich as kings!"

"Lay not up your treasure on earth, child," Jane cautioned. "And that money isn't truly ours. God knows who that man stole it from."

"And lucky for us we don't know, so we can't give it back." My face bent in a grim smile. "I'm glad we have the money. But it won't last forever, where we're going."

We rode in silence for another minute or two as Jane's baggage clanked against Glory's flank and Jane hummed a tune I recognized as "General Leslie's March to Marston Moor." Then Pearl said, "Where are we bound, grandmother?"

Grandmother. I smiled at the little straw-haired sprite. "To the moon," I said gaily. "Everything costs more there."

"Nay, but where? Where?"

"I will tell you." I had a destination in mind. But, to say truth, the plan wasn't real to me until I named it aloud to the child. "My Pearl-of-Great-Price, we're going to London."

6.

es. London.

Because . . .

Because . . .

Because London!

Compulsion, not reason, was drawing me forward.

Not that our journey lacked logic, or could not have been so justified. I'd not visited London in decades, but during my brief residence there as a boyish girl, and again as a youngish woman, I'd seen it was a beehive, or rather, something less orderly: a gallimaufry of neighborhoods, a forest of buildings, an ocean full of strange fish. The town may have grown Puritanical of late, but still it was London, ever growing, adding boroughs as fast as a tree sprouted branches, its streets full of folk too busy to care about strangers, or too used to a constant stream of new faces, from all parts of England and Holland and Ireland and everywhere, even to notice the three of us. Yes, logic served me here. London would be a fine place to hide from Midlands witch-hunters.

But it wasn't my brain that had chosen our route. It was something in my heart. I couldn't have said what it was; I can't now. I only know that some vibrant energy in Jane and in Pearl had worked on me on the road, yes, and even in the weeks before our flight. *Catalysis.* Some spark had lit in me a vague yearning for . . . what? Crowds, and new faces, and music, even if the music was not the wild pipings and catches of revelers but the martial trump of massing soldiers. I knew I was Judith Quiney of Stratford. This couldn't change. But I wanted to be some earlier Judith. Or at any rate I wanted my name, for a while, to become meaningless, and thus usable for some new value I could bestow on it. My feelings on this score were as sharp as my plans were vague. And I was almost as scared to go south as I would have been to turn about and go north again. But I must tell the truth. With every step our horses took away from Stratford, my heart was lightening.

I glanced leftward at Jane and Pearl. Both their faces were radiant. For a rarity, they were too thrilled to speak.

THE COUNTRYSIDE AROUND LONDON WAS unrecognizable. Earthworks and trenches were everywhere, and new walls created mazes. We wound our way through numerous detours, presenting identity documents to a series of brusque soldiers at checkpoints, a process which greatly lengthened our travel through the suburbs, and put me out of temper. We were exhausted by the time we reached Westminster, hard by the busy, boat-laden Thames, and squeezed into one chamber in an inn that cost thrice the price of a room at Stratford's Swan. I remembered the Westminster place from my father's day, when it had been called the King's Arms. It was now the Pike and Powder, with a fresh new sign, though not else much changed. The new hostess, like the old one, knew how to pinch her guests for a profit, especially when those guests spoke with the broad vowels of the Midlands. To stall our three horses, we spent nearly as much as we had to for a bed. In our weariness we paid what was asked. Jane and I knew little of the scale of wartime London prices, now decades after my last visit to the capital. (Within the week, though, we'd learned to look sharp and make better deals, and had nick-named the Pike and Powder the Gouge and Squeezer.)

In our room we opened our dusty bags and aired out our clothing. Jane had brought all she had, which was little more than two smocks each for herself and Pearl, two caps and sets of small-clothes, and a dead brother's armor. That, she had told me on the road, was what clanked so rhythmically against our new horse's side. Standing by the large bolster, she pulled out a metal back and breastplate and a pot-shaped helmet with sharp front and posterior edges. She laid all these things reverently on a table. "Mordecai's gun and his shoes were gone before he was found on the field. But his fellows brought these things back to us. Nay, I have said! You may not touch them, Pearl."

I folded my arms and looked at her narrowly. "Jane, why do you cart this stuff around? I know you revere your brothers. But 'tisn't practical. Relics are heavy, and they take up space."

"Relics!" She bristled. "These are none. We'll have no relics in the New Caanan. Our grandfathers had done with the saints' bones, and now we'll have done with their images, and with all the gold crosses in the sanctuary. Nay. These be no relics. This is armor."

"Your brother's in glory. You said it. What's the gear good for?"

She stroked the helmet fondly, rapped the breastplate, and didn't answer. I chose not to press her. A memory had suddenly come to me of my own brother, dead so many years gone, and of how, for months, when a child, I'd stowed his clothes under my pillow and sometimes slept with them in my hands, inhaling their fading scent in the mornings when I awoke. And even here, among my skirts, lay my youngest son's jerkin, which I'd kept for seven years and then unthinkingly seized on when packing so hurriedly for our journey. Placing my hand on it now, I thought of my Tom, who stole his father's name, as well as many other things throughout his childhood, including rashers of bacon from my kitchen, and paper from our account book, to despoil it with mad pictures, and, when he was eight, his father's burgess's gown and cap so he could parade through the yard before an audience of his puny friends, delivering mock speeches and dragging the velvet hem in the mud. When Quiney came round the house corner and saw Tom speechifying, he pulled him down to the woodshed and thrashed him so hard his howls spurred the neighbors' dogs to join the chorus. I, spying the scene through the window, had failed to move quickly enough to warn Tom of his father's approach. First I was laughing too hard, and then I was off and rushing to the scullery so I myself wouldn't be caught and tried as a fellow conspirator.

I stole a glance at Jane, who was tucking an already sleeping Pricey into the middle of the bed, which was, happily, near the size of the Great Bed of Ware, since we'd all need to share it. Jane's back was to me. I buried my face briefly in my son's jerkin, smelling old leather and a faint trace of tobacco. Tom's laugh, his spirit, his very self were with me on the instant. But his face was a blur. It tore my heart that I could not see him clearly. I closed my eyes and tried as hard as I could to summon up his eyes, his nose, his mouth. What came to me instead were the elfin features of the child in this room, the face of our tagalong puny, Pearl. So I stopped searching, and simply breathed in his scent.

Grief fills the room up of my absent child, lies in his bed, walks up and down with me, puts on his pretty looks, repeats his words, remembers me of all his gracious parts, stuffs out his vacant garments with his form. From a play, that. How could my father have known?

Ah, but yes. He knew.

I hid Tom's jerkin under my folded traveling cloak. I'd no call to mock Jane. Her dead brother's armor was useless to us, but use wasn't everything. Anyway, in a month's time, if our bread grew scarce, Jane might be willing to sell Mordecai's kit.

Now Jane took a box from her traveling bag, opened it, and shook out an apron. A gold ring fell from its folds to the floor. She picked it up. "Ah! My sister's only treasure."

"May I see?"

She dropped the ring into my palm. My eyes opened wide. For I knew the piece! It was engraved inside with a posy, *Love Eternal*, and the rough outline of a marigold, my mother's favorite flower. She'd left monies in her will for two such rings to be made in her memory, for each of her daughters, me and Susanna. I was not the sort to use even the simplest jewelry, and had kept my ring in a drawer, only wearing it on special days of memory, like her birthday, or my brother's. I think no one else in my household had ever even marked the gold thing before it finally dropped out of sight, on one of those days, years ago, when I was treating a visiting patient for piles. It had been, in fact, the anniversary of the day of Hamnet's drowning. I'd taken my mother's ring off in my surgery to grease my hands for a surgical purpose that's best left undescribed. I never mourned its loss. I missed my mother every day of my life, and I long for her still, but the keepsake made after her death meant far less to me than the old patched quilt that once lay on her bed, and now graces mine. That—like my son's jerkin—I will cherish forever.

But now, this mystery. "Who gave this to your sister?" I asked. "Why did Hannah have it?"

"Faith, I know not." Jane took the ring back. "Someone in New Place, by my reckoning, but she never said. It's a puzzle of twisted letters now. When Pearl is old enough not to lose it, it shall be hers."

I watched as Jane packed the ring away lovingly in a cheap little cloth pouch she kept inside her box. She pulled the pouch's drawstrings tight. It was clear to me that for all her scoffing at tokens and relics as priest-craft and trumpery, the shining piece of metal kept her sister's memory close. I would say no more about it.

I could guess how it had come to poor, dead Hannah. Unlike me, Susanna had kept her ring safe for years, then passed it on to her daughter, Elizabeth, upon Lizzy's marriage. But the ring was too plain for my niece. I'd never seen her wear it. I could well imagine her husband, wily Master Nash, rummaging through his wife's neglected baubles for something to please Hannah Simcox the maidservant, the better to beguile and entrap her. A crafty plan. She was a young girl who, unlike her sister, Jane, had left a Puritan household to earn her bread in a Royalist one, in the rawness of youth, to boot. Having grown up among wooden bowls and bare walls, why mightn't she crave a small piece of the finery she saw all around her? And

Master Nash, though a weasel, was a well-dressed beast, and
fair of face, and could doubtless trot out a sonnet or two. Had
the poor girl fallen in love with him? Was it seduction rather
than rape?

All the more pitiful, if so.

THE MORNING CONFIRMED MY GUESS that there'd be plenty of
call for a well-kept armor in London, should Jane wish to part
with hers. Before sunrise we were woken by the *rat-a-tat-tat*
of drums and the harsh bawling of men's officers, rising from
the drilling in nearby Finsbury Fields. When we went down
into the street after our porridge breakfast, it seemed we had
entered an armed camp. Soldiers were quartered in all places,
even in the yards of Parliament Palace. The scarlet and buff
were everywhere, and few women were to be seen.

Well. *We* would be seen. We left our horses in their stable
and, laden with one bag of our clothes and necessaries, help-
fully shouldered by Jane, we walked eastward, toward the
metropolis.

AS IT HAPPENED, JANE WAS right. The south was godlier than
the north. I can hardly begin to describe the changes wrought in
London since last I'd been there during the reign of our Charles's
father, King James. Suffice it to say that decadence had diminished. It was not just the legions of soldiers, either drilling or
milling and staring (at us), and their officers, no feather-capped
lords but rough-handed fellows with tradesmen's accents. Such
was the New Model Army, and they were a spectacle for our trio.
Still, it was the sights on the river that most caught my eye. Back

in my father's day the Thames was crowded enough, dotted with penny wherries and oyster boats and barges and the finer sloops of the rich. All those craft were still there, but now they were joined by giant gunboats with cannon and culverin anchored at bankside wharves, this though all the fighting I knew of had happened on land. The mark of the military was everywhere, along with the mark of money. A gabble of tongues filled the air by the bankside, and we saw well-dressed men in dark woolen capes walking right alongside the meaner sort who still peddled their fish, the finer ones clasping hands with one another or signing slips of lading. I never saw so many silver-buckled Dutchmen. And among the many boats rode galleons with Dutch flags, and others flying the notched Cross of Burgundy, and one big ship, just docking, which, alongside its Union Jack, bore a red-and-white flag picturing a pine tree. I'd never seen that emblem before, not in any books of maps and colors. When I couldn't forbear stopping a bustling citizen to ask him what it was, he laughed and told me, as though speaking to a child, that it was the flag of New England.

"New England!" Jane's eyes shone. "The new flag of England!"

"No, ninny!" I told her. "That ship comes all the way from the New World, across the sea."

I've never seen a face more wonder-filled than hers grew then as she stared at that trim gunboat and its colors. She went goggle-eyed, as might a lass who'd grown up hearing tales of a far fairyland full of virtuous, black-hatted elves bearing Bibles, and then had come upon its embassy in creaking wood with its sails unfurled. She strained toward the ship as though she would head for the gangplank and dash aboard, but I gripped her elbow firmly and walked her on, with Pearl in our wake. "Some other day for that, Jane."

We saw all these vessels in glimpses, in gaps between buildings, because the bankside had grown so crowded with new wooden shops and houses, some full three stories high, that for streets at a time you could forget you walked near the river. I still heard, more faintly, the hawkers advertising skate and mussels and oysters, those cries of women that had met my first awakening in London, so many years before. But now most of the voices were male, and there were fewer strolling sellers, as well as fewer ragamuffins darting through the lanes ahead of shouting folk whose purse-strings they'd lately cut. As my eyes swept the lanes, I could clearly see that regulated establishments had supplanted most of the strolling buyers and sellers, the fishermen's wives trading their husbands' catches. The barterers were fewer, and the prices were higher, too.

From this omen I might have guessed how it would go with my own attempts to practice my profession. But that revelation came later.

JANE AND PEARL WERE NEARLY speechless with awe at the city. Partly because we'd skirted the towns on our journey southward, they'd never seen anything like it in size or bustle. Like the ship from New England, London itself was the stuff of legend, come to life. Jane seemed to grow more vibrant with every troop of foot or horse we passed, or that passed us, and with every cannon shot she heard in the distance. Ceremonial gate-openings, arrivals of ships, or ordnance tests, they were all, for her, a summons to glory and a harbinger of England's New Jerusalem.

"And this is not even most of the army," she crowed to me as we scuttled through the muddy lanes. "Wait until they come south and march on the town!"

"Hush. Why should they?" I asked, something crossly. "The Parliament owns the army already." I was preoccupied. I'd a paper in hand on which I'd scribbled the names of some streets where apothecaries practiced their trade and many midwives dwelt. But the town had altered almost beyond recognition, at least to my eyes, with its new turnings and new shops, and my memories of the old ones were in any case faded, and then again, my knowledge of the city was never very extensive in the first place. On my longest prior sojourn, I'd lived and worked, for a brief and scandalous time, in what was properly Surrey, across big London Bridge on the south side of the river, where the playhouses stand. I mean to say, where they stood, before, in 1642, the godly Parliament pulled them all down.

However, I could still see the dome of St. Paul's Cathedral shining down on the city. In the end Jane and I walked toward that beacon, hauling Pearl, who, of course, wished to stop and gawk at everything. I couldn't blame the child, and even felt sorry that, for all the great buzz and traffic of this newer London, there were not so many things to thrill a child as once there were: no puppet shows, no mechanical birds at market stalls, no young men striding by dressed gaudily in wide slops and tight hose of peacock blue or orange tawny. There were soldiers, and citizens, and some women now, as well, in this part of town, walking in twos or sometimes in threes, just as we were. And I saw finery enough, especially as we approached St. Paul's. But the colors were dark, apart from the soldiers' scarlet, and as for men's legs, they were no longer on display for their fineness of shape, but shrouded under boots and long breeches.

"Come along, Pearl," I said, walking faster.

ONE THING THERE WAS NO less of in London was books. Paul's Yard was still crowded with bookstalls, and pamphlets were also everywhere, though most of their titles made me yawn. Still, we browsed. "*The Task of the Commonwealth*," I read. "*A Godly Plan for the Limits of Monarchy.* And this one. *Trade News from Amsterdam.* And I see Bibles over there. And there."

Jane had spotted them already. Now she leafed through the pages of a new King James edition. Then she put it down and picked up a penny ballad sheet from the corner of the same stall. She shook it at me. "See this ballad, Mother Judith!" (It seemed being "Grandmother" to Pearl had made me "Mother" to Jane.) "Look! *The Woman Warrior!*"

I took the page from her, scanned the text, and laughed. "'*From ladies down to oyster wenches, we labored like pioneers in the trenches.*' 'Tis about the siege of Lyme, and the women who worked with the men to defend the town from the Royalists." Jane, looking over my shoulder, was staring, entranced, at the etching of a helmeted woman carrying a flag, her image stamped inkily above the clunky verses. Jane seemed to want the ballad for this drawing alone, so I shrugged and bought it for her.

All this while, Pearl stayed unusually quiet, walking among the books and touching them gently, stopping to gaze long at an illustrated page of a child's primer, looking curiously at the black letters.

I took Pearl's hand and pulled her over to Jane. "What we must find are the notices for houses to rent, or rooms. One thing I am sure of. Westminster's too costly for us, when we don't know how long our stay will be. But closer to Shoreditch, perhaps . . ." I assumed a thoughtful look. I didn't know much of what I was talking about, but I wanted to give Jane and Pearl the faith that we wouldn't simply lose ourselves and end up as beggarwomen at the town gates. Yet I don't think, in fact, that this possibility had crossed any of our minds but mine, so enthralled were the pair of them with the sights and sounds of the Yard. They barely listened to me. They looked at the stalls and the people, and I looked at recruitment notices pasted on pillars, until in the end a gentleman took pity on my frowning perplexity and guided me toward the east cathedral door on which were stuck the notices I sought. He told me which houses-to-let stood near the apothecaries' street, though he looked at me doubtfully when I told him that this was the craft I practiced.

BY NIGHTFALL WE'D SECURED THREE decent rooms above a cheese seller's shop in Milk Street, with the use of a stove in a rear kitchen below us. We found a mews nearby for our horses. We'd a table, four stools, and two beds, and Jane tacked her penny ballad to the wall for decoration. The cheese seller's wife owned a bouncing young mousing cat who raced from room to room and could be heard through the floorboards, but his antics didn't keep us awake that night. We were exhausted. We slept long the next morning, then rose to take the long walk back to Westminster to claim our mounts. Jane offered to do it and to let me rest at home with Pearl, but I feared for her on the streets full of soldiers; and the bargaining for and paying of the fees, not to mention the control of three horses, was something I thought would be beyond my servant—though now, after all that has passed, I do not doubt she could have found some way to manage all of it.

So the trio of us set forth again, for the horses. When we had them, my feet's soreness made me glad to rest and ride on the journey back to our new dwelling. But on the way, in response to a hanging sign, I insisted we stop at an inn, where I sold one of the mares. We wanted the money, and we didn't need the animal, and I'd been told that stabling space in town was scarce with so many soldiers afoot.

At first I proposed selling Glory, our newest addition, but such were the grievings of Pearl that I relented. In truth, he was the finest of the lot—I wondered from whom he'd first been stolen—but that meant he'd fetch the highest price, and we needed no stone-horse. In the end, though, we only sold one of the mares, and stabled Glory in the Milk Street mews, and paid a fee also to have him exercised daily in the yard, which was grumblesome. Pearl beamed, and, looking at her, I wondered at myself, going as soft as any real grandmother.

All this bustle of buying and selling distracted me from certain important questions which, on our way back at last to our lodging, now pushed themselves rudely into my brain. Exactly how long would we—or at any rate I—be staying in this city? If danger in Stratford had sent me here, how would I know when that danger had abated? And—the most uncomfortable question of all—what would Quiney say or do when he knew how far I had traveled from him?

Might it be best—safer for him and for me—if he *didn't* know it, at least for a while?

Tomorrow, I thought to myself. *Tomorrow for the conundrums.*

I think even then I knew I would solve no riddles on the morrow, or on the day after, or on the day after that. I would just stop pondering them, in the hope that in time they would sort out themselves.

In the meantime, I reckoned we had money enough for the nonce, and that if our gold did dry up quickly, I could earn enough to feed us for as long as we needed or chose to be here. I burned for more activity, and I knew where to find it. The streets of London might now be commanded by men, but there were women in the houses, and women had babies, or would have them. And I had my licenses. With Jane as my apprentice, and perhaps a muzzle for Pearl on our household visits, no one could stop me from plying my skill.

Or so I thought.

7.

uiney and I weren't rich. My father had seen to that. He left nearly everything to Susanna. Just after his death, when we heard his will read, I thought he had chosen thus because she was eldest, and had already cropped, giving him a granddaughter, little Elizabeth, who'd bounced on his knee and shown few signs of the full-grown bitch she would one day become. I remember him with Lizzie in his lap, he placing her pudgy little forefinger on pictures in a book, teaching her the names and the meanings of animals: the fox for craft, the lion for valor, the owl for wisdom. He saw in her the seed of an endless line of Shakespeares, marching into eternity, like a parade of kings across a stage. How sad he'd have been to see Lizzy now, forty, sharp-tongued, and still barren, despite all the doses of powdered white ginger I'd supplied her with for years, as an aid to conception.

I was always dubious of ginger's power to induce fecundity. So many things can balk a woman from bearing (including a man who wields a powderless gun. Though I must say that in my whole life I've never heard a single husband take the blame for a barren house, not even when put to the proof with three childless wives in a row). I hadn't hidden from Lizzy my doubts about the ginger treatment and, later, the abdomen plasters and the coral amulets. Still, she wheedled and begged until I administered what she wanted. None of it helped, and now in middle age she'd none but her husband and herself on whom to waste her ample inheritance. We were all past child-bearing now, mother, aunt, and, apparently, niece. My father would have been heartbroken to know his line had petered out entirely. He hadn't foreseen it, when he packed into his will all those codicils directing his fortune to secondary and tertiary male heirs, first through Susanna, then through Elizabeth, and lastly through me. If we can judge by dowries, he clearly had more hope for Susanna's house than for mine. Though perhaps he channeled the money thus because he simply discerned, even in dainty three-year-old Lizzy, a taste for costly goods that might one day match her mother's.

Doubtless he also wanted to reward Susanna's husband, the kind Doctor Hall. John was my father's own physician for years, and often tickled his fancy with his wild Paracelsian lore. John had even cut my father for the stone one painful Eastertide, after which successful operation and his recovery my father insisted on dancing a morris before him. We all loved John.

As for Quiney, his sire was my father's old friend, and my father cherished other members of the Quiney clan who'd moved to London to become wool-traders in the capital. He was indeed godfather to young Philip Quiney, a London fellow who was my own Quiney's nephew. My father loved all Quineys. But still, it was easy to guess that my bridegroom's folly with Margaret Wheeler played a part in my father's choice to halve my own particular Quiney's wedding gift. Dying men have inspirations. My father's last brilliant thought was to play

Lear, while casting Quiney as France to my Cordelia, hoping Quiney would prove his faith by vowing I was in myself a dowry. Which thing Quiney, to his credit, did hold to be true, though he'd never have said it iambically.

Such, I am sure, were the thoughts my father distilled into the dry terms of his will. But as Quiney's and my married life wore on, I began to think there'd been still more to it. My father had left Susanna money because she cared about money, which I didn't, and because she spent it well, which I couldn't. And I believe he wanted me to work. Not to punish me, but to keep me from dwindling into a wealthy wife: a well-dressed matron who hired servants to raise her children. Better I should always be close to my young ones' hearts, mired in worry for the state of their clothes, winding and wearing myself in chasing them about the garden with a switch. Better, as well, that I should keep on with my herbs and simples and midwifery, and be daily abroad in the town, speaking to folk and practicing my wit and my craft. That, after all, was why my father had said "Welladay!" the morning my mother told him their odd duck daughter had found, at the age of one-and-twenty, a new channel into which to pour her passions. No longer bellowing out Oberon's speeches alone in the greenwood, young Mistress Judy was now trailing the new Paracelsian doctor about town, applying poultices to gouty legs at his instruction, and even stitching up young Master Evans's latest head wound, God 'a' mercy! And getting paid silver for it, too!

"Welladay!" said my cackling father. I heard his rough laugh from the kitchen, where I was practicing splint-craft on our neighbor's dog. Perhaps the man reached for a quill that very moment, to scratch me out of his final testament.

Or perhaps that came later, after Quiney's disgrace.

At any rate, I didn't guess all this at once. What my father's likely thoughts had been came to me gradually over the years that followed our loss of him. I wove flashes of insight together piecemeal, not patching rags into a quilt, but fitting threads into a whole tapestry, which perhaps is now nearly finished. It has taken me decades to complete it, because, as my father himself used to say, the owl of Minerva flies by dusk. This meant, he explained, that you never can understand anything till 'tis long over and done with and the bodies well buried with their slit throats bleeding into the English loam.

He had a ghastly cast of mind, did my da.

Mostly, as regards me, he was in the right. I would have gone as mad as a Bedlamite with no constant excuse to flee from my smoky house into the woods and fields, to cull flowers and roots and herbs and stones from the earth, gathering the materials of a trade that brought us the coin that helped pay for our bread. And now, though no child of my own any longer needed me, those same trees and meadows gave me respite from an aging husband's heavy grief, and his silence. My father's will had seemed ungenerous to some. I'd heard the talk. But it allowed me some freedoms gold couldn't have bought.

Still, if my father had visited us more during my childhood, or spent any of his time when he did come home observing my mother at her labors instead of hunching, ever-scribbling, over a writing table, he might have seen flaws in his plan to make way for a daughter who was both mother and town healer. He himself played the jack-of-all-theater-trades in London, being poet, scene-painter, player, and company sharer, but it wasn't as easy for a woman to juggle her ten balls in the air. Many was the day I'd have welcomed more help. Quiney worked hard and was as successful a vintner as his father had been, at least until the world began to tilt four years ago, and the trade in tobacco and spirits fell off. Whatever befell us, we'd always had coin enough to pay the odd maidservant (none so odd as Jane). But with all that needed doing in our house and garden, the pair of us, Quiney and I, were stretched thin, both in time and in money.

And even my father did not foresee that one day his own townsfolk would confuse the fancies of his plays with the lives of his family, and see in the art of a country cunning woman the dark conjurings of Hecate.

SO QUINEY SAW SOME THINGS my father had not, though, of course, Quiney now had the advantage of having lived thirty years longer into the new century. Towns change, and with them countries. As I've said, folk go mad. And so here I was, a witch fled from the Midlands to London, and the bag of silver Quiney had handed me during our flight from the house was less heavy than what Susanna might have taken from New Place, had she found herself in my situation.

Which she never would have. There. A pun for my father.

Still, I now harbored some worries for Susanna. Her husband Hall had been of a Puritan stripe, but his faith had never affected her own stubborn Royalism. And now John was dead, and rich widows like her were fast losing their manors to the sequestrations of the New Model Army. New Place was no castle, of course, nor any nobleman's estate, but it was a proud house, with aspirational inhabitants. It had hosted Queen Henrietta Maria once, when she paraded through our town many years ago. Elizabeth never tired of telling me how Charles's queen had praised its tapestries. In contrast, what seemed chiefly to impress Cromwell's commanders, as they themselves had passed through, was its size. If Parliament and the king could not forge some kind of peace soon, and pay the army to disband, New Place might find itself an absolute barracks. The Roundheads might indeed make the move I feared, and jump from billeting in the yard to camping in the parlor, and whither Shakespeare's daughter and granddaughter then? For all our years of quarreling, Susanna was my sister, and I'd never turn her away. Perhaps I'd even take Elizabeth in. But for Master Nash, I would not pledge such charity. Especially not with Jane and Pricey in my house.

Which at the moment was no house, but three small and dingy rooms in Eastcheap.

In which I felt safer and freer than I had in Warwickshire.

Yet I didn't want Quiney to follow me.

And the moment I saw clearly that I was running from him, too, and from the grief in his face, I shut the door on thoughts of Stratford. I would not think of my town today.

I need work, I said to myself. And I set out to get it.

WHEN I VISITED THE GUILDHALL to inquire about the practice of midwifery in London, I got, however, a rude shock instead. There an affable official told me that while midwives no longer needed licensing from the damnable bishops (those were his words), each woman was expected to undergo an apprentice-ship with one of a company of London doctors before she could lawfully practice her art in the city. And even then, she might only be called into service as an assistant, or sent to perform deliveries among the destitute, where small or no fees could be collected. These in itself were outrageous requirements and conditions that, if observed throughout the countryside, would have put a stop to the businesses of thousands of she-citizens, and perhaps brought a whole wave of them southward to storm the gates of Parliament, scattering all its New Model soldiers in their wrath, like Pharaoh's soldiers in the Red Sea. But since, as it happened, I'd for many years worked by the side of Doctor John Hall—who'd been happy to leave the birthing part of the business almost wholly to me—I thought I could bypass the training requirement, and then perhaps talk my way into a bit of decently paying work. I produced the documents to make my case, and was amazed when the man brushed them away with barely a glance at Hall's signature. "A *London* doctor," he said, in a tone that suggested: "A doctor anointed by God." I knew it was barely worth asking whether this restriction of trade to London doctors extended to other apothecary and curative work, but I did ask. The man stared at me incredulously, then said, "Of a certainty!" He then nodded. "Good day, mother."

I said, "You might ask your true mother whether a man's hands or a woman's helped *you* into the world."

"Yes, that's often the response," was his cheery rejoinder.

I wanted to throw something at his fat head, a book or a paperweight, but none was to hand, and besides, I knew I'd stand even less chance of earning a wage lodged in a cell in the Clink or in Bedlam, and what then would become of Pricey and Jane, who knew nothing of life in a city? So I only stamped away with my head held high. Outside, on the muddy street in the rain, I stopped and considered.

All those years ago, when I'd sneaked away to London at the raw age of fourteen, I'd found employment on the edges of the town, in the places where no one asked for a license or questioned the name you said was your name, whether they believed you or not. I'd gone south of the Thames, across the river, where stood bawdy houses and the lower sort of taverns, and bear-baiting pits, and, most scandalous of all, the public theaters. There, doors had opened to me because I could do what was needed: roll a barrel, start a fire, and, finally, recite a passage of sad verse as though my heart were breaking, because, at that time, it was.

Of a certainty, I'd been dressed as a boy then, in my dead brother's clothes, and had carried the disguise off passing well. I'd fooled even my father for a time, or so I'd thought. In later years, piecing together his stray remarks and looking back on it all, I came to think he and some of his fellows had suspected my identity, or at least doubted my gender, from the start, and had simply allowed to be true what they wanted to be true. They were masters of pretense, after all.

Now I was old, of course, and in no wise fit to practice this same deception. And now all those lively places were gone, destroyed by the order of Puritan city councilmen even before the Parliament's new laws banned such loose entertainments from the whole of the country. The brothels, the bear pits and cockfighting yards, the playhouses, even the rowdiest of the taverns had been razed. I didn't have to go to Southwark to confirm this. All England knew it.

But I knew something else as well. Laws might be laws, but folk were folk. Somewhere even in General Cromwell's London lived women who dwelt on the shady side of the law, women who plied whatever dark trade they plied and birthed their babes without asking to see a surgeon's documents. And men, furthermore, who might be happy to pay an old trot who could treat a sword or gunshot wound without asking its cause, or the source of the silver they handed me once I'd bandaged them up.

I had a skill to trade on, and London had its markets. The task was to find those markets.

I STARTED THAT VERY AFTERNOON. Though Pearl whined to come with me, and Jane fretted for my safety, I thought it were best that the pair of them stayed nearer to home. "There's flour to be bought, and you might bake some loaves in the ovens," I said. Jane was the worst cook God ever made, but a fair enough hand with pies and cakes and loaves of bread, which was reasonable, given her family's trade. When she looked unhappy at my suggestion, I added, "Perhaps there's a service where you can be preached at, at St. Clement's Church, hard by." I pointed to its spire, standing sharp over the rooftops. "Or outside it, at the door. There may be prophecies! I hear these are a daily entertainment this year." And may I be damned if her eyes didn't start to glow. She and Pearl walked with me as far as the mews, and then on toward the church, while I went to secure one of our horses.

I would have welcomed Jane's company as I traveled through London, but I also feared it. I guessed she'd come out with whole passages from Jeremiah to condemn the places I planned to visit, and that would mar my errand. And none of those places would be fit for a child to play in.

I went first to a house I knew in Gracechurch Street. I knew it still stood from a notice I'd seen tacked on a wall in Paul's Yard. I must even then have felt some foreshadowing of my coming trouble at the Guildhall, because I'd paid keen attention to the bill, which stated in bold print that a new city ordinance placed a fine on any man who sang, in any tavern or alehouse, "a song called 'Three Men's Song'" that was "heard lately at the Cross Keys, in a common play."

"Perhaps a woman might sing it, lawfully," I'd jested to Jane.

"Or sing 'Three Women's Song.'" She'd smiled radiantly. "That would be our song!"

My father's laugh rang like a chime in my head when I saw the tavern sign with its golden door keys, pictured in a perpendicular cross. *Look, Da!* I wanted to cry. The Cross Keys had been a hallowed site to him and his London friends. It was among the first places to stage plays and interludes for the common London crowd since the time of the old Bible plays. It was indeed the very first place my father had found work, when he'd journeyed to the great city as a young man, after being knocked nearly flat by the skills of professional players who'd passed through Stratford, speaking poetry in character. My father had told me of his small-scale triumphs at the Cross Keys, mock-sword-fighting and mock-kinging it in the muddy courtyard, while the watching drinkers (whom he called the drinking watchers) cheered and hooted from the galleries, and horses in the adjacent stable neighed at the noise. Even after standing playhouses began popping up in Shoreditch and Southwark, and playing got restricted to licensed companies, the Cross Keys still staged plays.

But now? Fifty years of Puritan preaching against the lust and bloodshed peddled on the scaffolds of London had finally destroyed the vocation of playing, for all I could tell. No public sports. Public stage plays did not well agree with our seasons of national humiliation, our exercises of sad and pious solemnity. Cleopatra and the Duchess of Malfi had been slain for good, not by the bite of an asp or the hand of a strangler, but by Deuteronomy. Pastor John Field and his like did them in, railing against all spectacles of pleasure and lascivious mirth and, most of all, against the abomination of young men dressed as women on the stage.

But the fine against the Cross Keys, for a song in a common play? Where there was smoke, there must be fire. Perhaps Cleopatra was not dead entirely.

The inn was bustling, even in mid-afternoon. The place seemed less frequented by the soldiery than other establishments I'd passed, more a haven for ordinary London folk, mostly leather apron men, but also a few of the wealthier sort. Professions were hard to distinguish now in the city. All men seemed to dress alike in drab woolen cloaks and dark breeches. Lawyers no longer went gowned, and apprentices had shed the blue caps they all wore in my youth. Here and there, however, I spotted a bright feather on a man's hat, which signified, if nothing else, that he liked some color in his life. And I even saw a sprinkle of women raising mugs of ale alongside their men. It cheered me. This was something of the London I remembered.

The proprietor was wary of my questions, and I thought this no wonder. Who was this outland dame, well struck in years, inquiring about forbidden entertainments? Was she an agent of the Parliament or the Church or the city, feigning her country accent? Of a certainty, no plays were done here, and no bawdy countenanced, and the only songs sung in his courtyard or rooms were ballads of great English victories.

"And hymns." I winked. "I am sure that your patrons gather in the evenings and sing psalms."

He looked at me shrewdly. His eyes began to dance a bit. "How did you come hither, madam?"

"On a horse's legs, and then on my own."

"Ah. And your name, once more?"

He was decades younger than me, but his own name was the same as that of a man who had owned the inn when my father lived, and I knew his family had made its fortune not only serving ale and meat but also staging entertainments. I was sorely tempted to mention the names of some of the players I'd known, names he would have recognized even if the men who'd owned them were dead. I even thought of telling him who my father had been. But I didn't. I would like to say what stayed me was my man Quiney's voice, warning me to be cautious and wise, but truly, it was the fear that he wouldn't believe me.

So I told him another part of the truth. I said I was Judith Quiney, a midwife and an apothecary, late of the English Midlands, displaced by the war, and now balked in my profession by the city laws. I showed him my documents, which he perused, and to allay his skepticism, perhaps because of my age and his notion of my likely feebleness, I said I had a servant, an apprentice or assistant, who was strong and discreet. (I would deal with Jane's zealous tongue when I needed to.) His manner grew warmer. He not only thanked me, and noted where I was to be found, but pointed me toward two other establishments wherein, he said, there might sometimes be accidents or maladies to be attended to, small scrapes or unhappy incidents for which it were best not to call in a doctor who owed his license to a city official. Even babies to be birthed, as it might fall out, with a call for some discreet mother-midnight, and no paperwork required.

I visited these places all, said who'd sent me, and was welcomed. One merry inn host even offered me board and a room in exchange for my services. That gratified me. It put me in mind of the time when I, a green girl, briefly lived and worked at a bawdy riverside house—what was it, the Cardinal's Hat?—as I schemed to find work at my father's new white-walled theater that shone like the sun a few streets away. The Globe. I almost said yes to the host, on the strength of the memory, before I remembered that we were three. A vision of Jane railing against dicing and drinking and card games at all hours made me shake my head regretfully.

And besides, Pearl was a child.

My interviews and travelings amongst public inns took me hours, though none of these sites was far distant from my new dwelling. By horse, the journey back to Eastcheap seemed short, and I felt lively rather than tired. It was dark when I climbed the stairs to the candlelit rooms where Jane and Pearl were arranging our meal. The smell of freshly baked bread and burnt fish wafted down the stairway, and I heard them both singing their favorite ballad, "General Leslie's March to Marston Moor."

London, and furtive playing places, and none knowing whose daughter I was.

It felt almost like a homecoming.

8.

We were three days in London before I sent word to Quiney. Indeed, I am ashamed to say it was that long before I forced myself to admit his right to know my whereabouts, if not to control my steps. He was thinking I'd gone to Banbury and no doubt expecting I'd write him from there. What would he think now? Reluctantly, somewhat fearfully, I purchased ink, quill, paper, and wax. But when I sat down at our little table to scribble a message, I didn't know what to say.

I thought back on the near-eternity of our life together. Thirty years, the pith of which we'd spent in the swamp of boy-raising, where the channels of passion get child-choked. Like other houses on the lane, ours was filled with crying that called to be stilled and messes that needed mopping. The time of nursing gave way to the time of bickering, me telling Quiney to get out of the house and leave me in peace, as I'd enough to do giving harried instructions to the puny ones not to fall into cooking fires or toddle into the stream of traffic on the High Street. That fraught phase was followed by years when it seemed all Quiney and I did was swing back and forth between swatting the boys for their mischief and nagging at them to see to their chores. These included the stocking of wines and the cutting into marketable squares of hanks of imported tobacco, which Quiney sold along with his wines, and which Tom and Rich filched and smoked behind the outhouses, as though we didn't know. Tom, our youngest, was a rogue who'd lay hands on anything that wasn't nailed down. When he was five it was sweetmeats, and when he was fifteen it was the Virginia weed and any stray cask of Madeira. And throughout all these phases of our family life ran the incessant searching for some item that was lost, be it Rich's hornbook or Quiney's favorite pipe or one of my vials of mercury, a roly-poly substance that Tom and his friends liked to play with. It seemed half my life was spent looking for some misplaced thing that I clearly remembered but could no longer find.

And of course there was the lads' schooling, Quiney and I taking turns in the evenings helping them with the grammar and the figuring and, in later years, the Latin, of which I only knew the names of medicines, and which neither Quiney nor Tom nor Rich was ever much good at, no more than any male in my family ever was, including my father. And the nights, which, far more often than Quiney liked, were given over to exhausted sleep, me as often as not evading his needy hands and kicking him to the far side of the bed. This was our life, and it was the same as the lives of most of the folks we knew. It was like my own family life when I was a child, although there were some notable differences. For one, Quiney was unmarked by the guilt and horror of a child's drowning, on a summer night when a game of two twins, me and my brother, turned deadly, resulting in the never-to-be-forgotten tragedy of my youth. For another, Quiney was there. My children's dwelling was his. When a youngling, I was rich in uncles, but nearly fatherless. My sire lived in London and sent my mother money, money, money, to pay for the sins he did there.

My father was a ghost in the days of my girlhood. By contrast, Quiney was solidly present in our house, filling his shelves, trading with the townsmen, once even serving as a Stratford burgess. And instructing his boys, at times the kind tutor, at others the grim disciplinarian.

But for all our work and care, we lost them.

So now, from my table in London, I looked back on a rich land turned to waste. Why should I have bothered admonishing the boys to stay clear of the river when it swelled with the rain? Why take care they learned to swim in case, when they ignored my warnings, they fell in? Why watch through nights treating each fever? The scores of times I bandaged scrapes and cuts, the hours Quiney spent teaching both of them his trade, the money we saved and the money we paid, in the end, after Rich begged for half a year, to send him to Oxford . . . It had all come to naught in the end. That house back in Stratford was a haunted one, where my husband and I faced each other across an empty parlor, and more than half the time did not speak.

When the lads died, the church sent its miserable comforters. "Pray," the pastor told us, as if the thought hadn't occurred to us—as if we hadn't tried it. I'd prayed with every fiber of my being when Rich lay sweating and crying out with the fever of the pest, his skin marked with buboes, his brother not cold in the grave. I prayed that God would leave us just one.

Let it go, all, I'd thought, when they lowered Rich into his grave.

Pray again? For what?

THE CURFEW CALL ROSE FROM a neighboring street. I sharpened my quill and sighed, staring at the blank sheet before me.

I think, had Quiney been with me in the room, I could have spoken to him of the fears that had spurred me to ride south. I could even have told him of the suffocating Stratford sadness I'd seemed to break free of while on the highway with Jane and Pearl. It was all clear to me in the moment. But to write it in a letter, rather than say it to his face, seemed a kind of cowardice. Not to mention that to put all the facts down on a paper that might fall into the wrong hands seemed altogether reckless.

I finally wrote that I was well and safe with our servant and her niece in London, having thought it a good time to travel hither to visit dear friends in this city. I named no one, and said nothing of any date of return, or of my having leased rooms for the three of us and set myself up for the meantime as an apothecary and midwife to the punks and players and cutthroats of the town. How could I have explained all this? I would have had to tell him, and, through telling him, tell myself, that I wanted to start a new life, or to start life anew. That I'd come to London in my old age as I'd once done in my youth, hoping to drown a sorrow by playing a part, by becoming another person who was somehow still me, indeed, *most* me.

I said none of that. I knew he would guess that I wrote in a kind of code, but I hoped he might understand the better part of my motives without my saying more. That is, I hoped he would somehow see that I came here out of fear for my well-being, as well as for Jane's, and Pearl's, and even his. If I'd had other motives—if the heavy air of our house had pressed on me, if the walls were plotting to murder me if I stayed—this were best left unspoken.

And I thought, with an anger both sudden and ancient, that if Quiney were aggrieved, he might always stroll to the graveyard and offer a prayer to Saint Margaret Wheeler.

Are we ever wise before we are old? For was it not folly, to be jealous of a woman so dead?

I sealed the letter. The next day I posted it from the Cross Keys Inn.

REVISITING THE GREAT CITY WAS, as I've said, a kind of home-coming. But, of course, it wasn't the London I'd last tasted several decades before, when I'd come there a second time, a young woman in the company of my aunt, and stayed for a week in the company of . . . another. Now, everywhere was talk of the war and the sound of marching feet. In the streets, in the taverns and ordinaries, arguments raged about the shape the new commonwealth was to take. If there were Royalists here in the city, they held their peace. This was Parliament's town, and the question was not how far to side with the king, but how to bring him to justice for his pomps and tyrannies, how to punish him for calling his powers, and the army, and the people's coin, his own possessions, when his rights came only from Parliament. The question was even—aye, it was said openly—whether a godly sovereign nation need harbor a king at all.

We were a month in London, in all. In the scant weeks of our sojourn—weeks in which I barely acknowledged to myself, much less to the folk I encountered in the practice of my craft, that I'd another life in Stratford—I avoided political talk. I was, after all, a witch in hiding. The people with whom I now dealt in backstreets and taverns were not likely to care if I trafficked with Beelzebub, but when buying cabbages from the greengrocer in Eastcheap, or perusing the pamphlets in Paul's Yard, I strove as far as I could not to make myself memorable by any action or utterance. I'd been right in one thing. In some ways a woman could disappear into London like a drop into a sea, so vast and crowded were its lanes and thoroughfares, so many its shops and dwellings, so numerous its boroughs and parishes. But in other ways this wooden wilderness was less private than Stratford, where I could grow herbs in my own garden and find the leeches and the savage plants and stones I needed in the fields and woods. Here, I had to buy all that. I earned some peculiar gazes at market stalls and shops when I asked for borage and bugloss and red sage and inquired about powder mills for sulphur. Ginger was common, as was oatmeal, since both were used for cooking as well as for the itch; and malmsey, spice, and nutmeg might as easily make a warm grog in the evenings as be mixed into a paste and spread on the forehead to allay a fever. But the first apothecary whom I asked for a vial of mercury looked at me as though he would call in General Cromwell and all his officers and have me jailed as a counterfeit wizard.

"Do you not know," he said, "that mercury can cause madness?"

Indeed, this thought had occurred to me now and then over the years, and I'd even voiced my worries ten or twenty times to Doctor Hall. There were herbs that worked as well as mercury to forestall infection. But more than one of my patients had heard of Paracelsian cures, and it seemed a good thing to have mercury in my kit, if only to increase people's faith in my powers. This apothecary, however, either had none or wouldn't sell it to me, and he began to inquire about my licenses, at which moment I feigned the deafness of the aged and made my exit.

• • •

BY MID-APRIL I HAD THE lie of our London geography, and could walk two miles in any direction from our rooms without getting lost. Age is an armor, and I could move about more freely alone, without danger of molestation, than ever I could have when I was a young woman on my own. That, of course, had been the reason, or one of the reasons, I dressed myself as a boy on my first visit to London, back in the century that was forever gone. I'd no need for disguising now, partly because my face no longer invited so many men's attentions, and also because here and now, among soldiers and citizens, a somber, almost menacing call to duty and godliness seemed to order men's actions and words, even when it couldn't command their eyes. And in truth, though inclined all my life to mock at the Puritans and other virtue-mongers, I felt some stirrings of admiration for the new order. I cannot explain it, but though in some ways the laws against dicing and drabbing and swearing and dueling hemmed a spirit in, still, in other ways, they made us women feel free.

Jane was no beauty, but she was fresh and young. Yet she encountered no more trouble than I did in London, no more interference than a gallantry or two from a youth or a soldier. This may partly be because she usually walked with Pearl, who if not growling like a bear would be rolling her eyes back in her head and reciting verses from Ezekiel. I saw armored soldiers fly like geese from the path of Pearl, scurrying to step into shops and peeping from doorways until she and her aunt were safely by. And then when the brave fellow stepped back into the street, Pricey Pearl might turn and point and cry, "*Thou!*" then whip about again as before, leaving him quaking and white as a flag of surrender.

The pair of them accompanied me on many of my errands, after I strictly warned them not to bark or prophesy. Pearl proved less outlandish when given a task to perform, like pounding juniper berries or washing dishes or towels, and Jane was a help to me in lifting the heavier patients. I took care not to bring either of them along when something contagious, like smallpox, was feared, and in such cases to wear my beaked mask stuffed with onion and lily root. This was my only London disguise. Pearl thought it a costume. One day of our London sojourn I found her flitting around our rooms with the plague-mask clapped to her face, screeching like a Fury. But Jane wouldn't wear it.

It is hard to describe how greatly London increased Jane's already remarkable vigor. She would not bide at home, even when I'd no need for her help on my sick-calls or errands. There were open-air pastors to be marked, and Hallelujahs to be shouted in the vocal crowds that gathered to listen, and New Jerusalem pamphlets in the bookstalls, and the tread of soldiers' boots everywhere. Even early in the morning, before our day's activities were well begun, Jane would stand at the window with her face intent, straining to hear the distant calls of the troops' officers that wafted over the rooftops from Finsbury Fields. And I thought, *She is remembering her brothers.*

9.

As I've said, in our brief time in the city, I did my best not to enter with Londoners into conversations about the king's wrongs or his troubles, or the powers of Parliament. But I cannot claim the same for Jane, who'd read little more than the Bible but could listen and speak; who delighted in the London talk, and had no sense of a servant's place. She would argue with anyone. This was likely because of her Independent Protestant upbringing, but also because she'd never been anyone's servant before she was mine. Though her sister had been sent to Stratford to work at New Place, Jane had stayed in Newark-on-Trent to knead dough and bake bread with her family, and to sell their wares to buyers whom they considered no better than they were themselves, if no worse. And in truth, this new London, where pastors preached that we were all a community of saints, and noble crests were idols to be broken and cast down . . . Well, it was a good place for someone like Jane.

Though I never met anyone else *quite* like Jane.

In our rooms I would catch her staring raptly at the etching of the Woman Warrior in the ballad sheet, bought in Paul's Yard, that she'd now tacked to the wall. Jane was lettered—her father, steeped in the family Bible, had made sure of that—and she scanned the text of her warrior song over and over until she knew it by heart. With the help of my rudimentary note-reading skills, she approximated the melody, and she and Pearl added the ballad to their musical repertory.

"Jane!" I would chide. "Are you a Christian? You sound as if you would blow somebody up, with your pioneers and your trenches and your bullets."

Of course, she had her answer. "I sing of the armor of righteousness, Mother Judith! I sing of the fight! *Put on the breastplate of faith and love; and for an helmet, the hope of salvation.*"

"But this is a metaphor."

"A what?"

"A kind of poetry." I thought of fit words to make the thing plain to her. "'Tis a sign. As when Jesus said he was bread, though he was flesh and blood. And we eat communion bread as a sign of his resurrection, not as the Papists do, who hold the bread to be Christ himself, magically."

Her eyes flashed. "As did wicked Archbishop Laud, with his popish ways. And all the banned bishops with their groves and high altars."

"You have it. *You* know Christ's words were a metaphor. And so are Saint Paul's, when he speaks of the breastplate of faith, and the weapons of righteousness, and all of it. He doesn't mean Christians should go out and kill other folk. Not for *any* righteous cause. How can you think it? He means that our hearts should be steeled against evil and wrongdoing."

Jane smiled broadly and pounded her fist on the table. "*Life* is a metaphor!"

This was perplexing. I had hoped to change her militant mind, not inspire her to some new zealous conviction. "Life is *life*, Jane. The child in your arms, the bread in your mouth, the ground that you tread—"

"It is *all* a metaphor! Do you think that these clothes of flesh, these bodies that fail, these teeth that rot, these hands that grow palsied and shake, are real? Our very *brains* decay." She leaned over our table and grasped my shoulder. "Mother, I tell you what you need to know. Our *souls* are real, but the flesh is naught but a picture. What matter death? Do you not sense the presence of saints who have crossed to the realm where there is no dying, where God dries every tear? Do you not hear their voices?"

I only looked at her, unspeaking, my eyes suddenly full. I couldn't bring myself to say yes, I had heard my missing loved ones talk to me, I heard them every day of my life, but I didn't believe they were real. I'd never been able to think their words anything more than echoes, endlessly returned by the walls of my own longing. The people I'd lost were ghosts, just as a whisper is the ghost of a voice.

Jane sat back, very sure of herself. "The *body* is a metaphor. It withers as the grass." She held out her arms and smiled mysteriously. "When the Assyrians came to burn my home, to put my old kin to the sword, and to challenge my flesh—"

"To challenge . . . Jane, did they—"

"Hush, mother! 'Tis no matter." She rose and turned to kneading bread. "The body is naught but a sign and a shadow."

I looked at her strong back, at her muscular arms, at the gingham cloth of her blouse rolled up above her elbows. I could see the edge of her flour-smudged face as she worked the dough. "Jane, has some scholar at one of your assemblies been speaking to you of Plato?"

"Who?"

I smiled. "No one. At times you seem mad. But other times you seem as wise as an owl. I might call you Minerva."

"Who's she? She's not in the scriptures." Jane wiped flour from her cheek, and shook her head dismissively.

THE NEXT DAY OR TWO I spoke little and thought much. I tended to a scullery maid's burned arm and diagnosed a case of the pox and, in a back room of a Cloak Lane tavern, stitched up an arm that was slashed in a duel over a wench, or the price of an ale, or some such thing into the details of which I made sure not to inquire.

On my way out of the tavern I caught sight, through a half-opened door, of a group of ten or so folk in a room. They were behaving so strangely that I paused to stare. An equal division of men and women, garbed simply in dark or dull colors, as most people were nowadays. They had no ale in hand, and no food stood on any tables before them. Instead they sat grouped in a rough circle about the room, straight-backed on benches and stools, holding themselves quiet and still. The woman who had opened the door to enter the room, and exposed them to my view, saw me staring, and gestured at me to follow her in. Without thinking, I did so. I still can't say why. I sat beside her on a bench. Then I rested my bag on my knees and waited.

Silence. Blessed, restful silence. No one said a word. From the lane outside I could hear cartwheels turning and men's voices calling, and from behind the closed door came the muffled rumble of ale barrels rolling and tapsters ferrying beef and drink to the tavern's patrons. But that noise was all muted. The room was quiet.

I closed my eyes and sank into the calm. After what might have been ten minutes, or an hour, something in my chest gave way, and I felt tears starting. Why? Who can say? I had a thousand reasons to weep, and yet none at all.

Quiney, I thought. *Quiney.*

It was now a fortnight since I'd ridden from Stratford, and ten days since I'd written, and I'd kept thoughts of him mostly at bay. Now something slipped, and I felt his presence in my mind like a burden. I saw myself struggling to swim with him in my arms, his body listless with grief and pulling me down into a bottomless dark well. I longed to let go and swim upward. But a voice whispered, *Hold fast.*

I suddenly wished Quiney were here, seated at my side, his hat in his hands, suffering the silence, as I was.

After a moment I sat up straighter, to be like the others, and wiped and opened my eyes.

I don't know how many more minutes passed before a slender, clean-shaven man stood and held out his arms, for all the world as Jane had two days before, when dazed by life's metaphor at our little parlor table. He wore a white linen scarf knotted about his neck, and held a broad-brimmed hat in one hand.

"We welcome to our circle all seekers of the light," he said. Then he sat back down on his stool.

I looked at him in anticipation. Now would come the homily. But he'd no Bible, and no one else seemed to expect anything more from him. Religion was afoot here, it must be, but their pastor seemed not yet to have arrived.

Then, to my amazement, the woman I'd followed into the room stood too, and started to speak. "God hates the sword and the pike and the gun. Lay them down! Beat them into plowshares. Love one another."

She sat. Her words rang in the silence like a chime.

We sat for another half hour. Then the clean-shaven man with the linen scarf rose again and said, "The service is ended."

Though I hid in my hood and tried to slip out unnoticed, that man caught up with me at the door. I feared I was due for a session of proselytizing from the viewpoint of whatever strange stripe of Covenanter or Leveller or Anabaptist or Fifth Monarchist or Brownist or Muggletonian I had stumbled upon. But the man only looked into my eyes, squeezed my hand, and said, "I am Brother George. We meet on Wednesdays and Fridays at six of the clock, just past sundown. Come to us again, sister."

In the yard outside the tavern I stopped a porter. "Who *are* those Godsters in that room there?"

"Which Godsters?"

"The quiet ones who tote no Bibles."

He shrugged. "I know not. Their leader lodges here, and they've been coming for six months. First two or three came, then more. They only say they are a society of friends."

I WAS HOMEWARD BOUND AND two streets from my house, proceeding on foot, when I saw a boy come racing toward me. His appearance was striking. He'd a black eye, a knob nose, an overlarge, flapping, and rather soiled shirt, and hair that stuck out horizontally at four points from beneath his cap. Catching sight of my leather apothecary's bag as he loped by, he wheeled and trotted back toward me, calling breathlessly, "Mistress Quiney?"

"Aye, slow ye down," I said to this grisly urchin. "What's the catastrophe?"

"Apocalypse at the Cross Keys Inn! There's a man with his head stove in!"

As we hurried to the stable for my horse, the lad explained, with many thrilling gestures, how a mid-day performance of a comical play called *General for a King* had ended abruptly when a culverin cannon wheeled onto a makeshift scaffold had fallen through the floorboards, taking down with it the players who had brought it and were pretending to light it. One of the men was only bruised, but the edge of the wheeling mechanism had struck the head of the other, and he lay barely conscious in one of the inn's inner rooms, bleeding from a gash in his pate.

"The watchers all scattered before we could even pass a hat, and they were all a-gabble. If the city guard hears how it befell—"

"They won't if thou'lt stow thy chatter!" I threw some coin at the boy for his trouble and turned my mare's head toward the Cross Keys. It was already dark, but I knew the way well by now, and my horse did, too. In the yard outside the inn I handed my reins to a groom and went in. The fretful proprietor led me to a small room in the back.

The victim was conscious now, and sitting up with a tankard of ale, which I straightaway snatched from his hands. The fool was going to drink himself back into oblivion. I set the ale on a table, called for a lamp, and perched on a stool to examine him. The injured player's fine cambric shirt had got ripped at the sleeve, no doubt when his arm caught a split floorboard's jagged edge. Someone had wrapped a tapster's cloth about that arm. With the hand of his other, the victim was pressing a blood-soaked towel to his forehead, near the hairline, and some blood had already dried on his powder-dusted cheek. Despite his misfortune and evident pain, he wore a wry smile. "Come, Mistress Apothecary! That dose of huffcap is my sole wage for all this trouble. Have it here again. You'll drink, too."

I peered at the man closely. Even by lamplight, I could see his eyes sparkling green.

JesuMaryJoseph. This couldn't be why I'd come to London. I'd not allow that to be true.

But whatever I allowed or didn't allow, I had to say something. So I said, "Good e'en, Nate."

10.

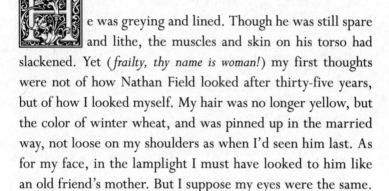e was greying and lined. Though he was still spare and lithe, the muscles and skin on his torso had slackened. Yet (*frailty, thy name is woman!*) my first thoughts were not of how Nathan Field looked after thirty-five years, but of how I looked myself. My hair was no longer yellow, but the color of winter wheat, and was pinned up in the married way, not loose on my shoulders as when I'd seen him last. As for my face, in the lamplight I must have looked to him like an old friend's mother. But I suppose my eyes were the same. His were.

At any rate, time's ravages to my complexion must not have been too severe. It only took two seconds of brow-wrinkling and squinting for those green eyes to flash with recognition. And that was less time than he'd taken at an earlier reunion, which, in a trick of fate, had also taken place behind a stage, back in old King James's time. Then, he'd given me a long minute's gaze, just before he undid my heartstrings by calling me beautiful.

Back in the dark abyss and chasm of the past.

"Jesus Christ my Savior," he said now. "I sleep. I dream. This knock on the crown has flipped my brain like a pancake. I think you be Judith Shakespeare."

"And so I am." It did not even come into my mind to correct his saying. For I was now, of course, Judith Quiney. That fact seemed suddenly very remote.

He leaned in to gaze at me more closely, and I pushed him back lightly with my fingertips. I hadn't come to stare into an old player's eyes, but to stitch up a gash on his forehead. I am a human woman, and I confess, had I known the identity of the man I was riding to succor, I would at least have combed my hair. But I'd not have done more, I swear. A crone is a crone. The ladies of King Charles's circle cloak the damage of years with their paints and their powders, disguising their skin like actors in a masque, but plain folk don't do it, and Charles and his circle are fast becoming the clowns of the commonwealth. Not even Susanna paints her face now, and to speak true, few women of Stratford ever did. Why hide what you are? Time divides a female into three selves, girl-child and prime woman and old mother. There's naught to be gained by feigning to be something you once were, and are no longer. When you try, you stop being a person, and start being a ghost.

None too gently, I gripped his chin and tilted his head to the lamplight. His brow was still bleeding. "Are there no clean towels in this place?" I asked, turning impatiently to the Cross Keys' host. "Why do you stand staring, sir? Your mouth could trap flies."

"Shakespeare?" This man, too, seemed to have been smacked in the head. "Shakespeare?"

"A playwright of the sinful old days, yes, I've heard of the fellow. This man's had a blow to the noggin. He's addled. Next he'll be calling me——"

"Viola." Nate winked. He wasn't addled at all.

"Yes, or Cleopatra. Please, now, good sir, fetch me boiled water and some clouts that haven't been used to wipe grease from a skillet."

The man turned tail and went. I brought out my own clean bandages, needle, packthread, and, yes, a small vial of mercury from my kit. Mad-making? Life couldn't be madder than it had suddenly become. Within the minute, I was stitching Nathan's wound closed, and dabbing it with this spirit, against infection. It wasn't as difficult as it might have been. His grey hair was cut shorter than a Roundhead's, the timeless custom among players, for their wigs, and that made it easier to clean the wound before pinching and sewing. He winced as I worked, but he didn't cry out, though he muttered, "Why *can* I not have my ale, Mistress Surgeon?"

"For you must keep still."

"Nor even a grin? I cannot keep from it. I'd heard years ago that you'd shrunk into a dutiful wife, Viola, though something adventurous in the way of leechcraft. And now here you be, escaped southward once more, and haunting the old playing places—*Ow!*"

"Quiet you, then. And I'll need to clean and re-bandage your arm as well. No doubt it's full of splinters."

He irked me, as of old. I could not believe that any friend of my father's, gone from London to Stratford and back again, and then spreading the Shakespeare news, would have described my wifedom in such belittling terms. These were Nate's own.

WE SHARED A TANKARD OF huffcap after all, once his bandaging was complete and he'd washed the blood and powder and paint from his face. Scrubbed clean, that face was even more the face I knew, though now scarred across the nose. Doubtless some angry husband had marred it. I told him, shortly, of my companions Jane and Pearl and, briefly, of the misfortune that had sent us to London and Milk Street. I wasn't halfway through the tale before he had his head in his hands, and was laughing. "Oww." He straightened, with a grimace. "It hurts."

"I'm glad it hurts. My plight is no laughing matter."

"Oh, is it not?"

"'Tis a jest to be hanged, then." But I was smiling, too. In his company, I couldn't help it. I took a swig of huffcap and squinted at him. "You've shed your pearl earring."

"None wears one now outside the court of the king. I am a virtuous citizen."

"Marry, you——"

"A tuppence fine for that oath."

I laughed outright. "Nathan Field! How is that you still play, and in such a year? Rotten floorboards and hat-passing at the Cross Keys Inn? You were a liveried King's Man for years."

"That was a different king. He was allowed his players."

"Still, you should be rich. You should have money enough for a house and garden."

"So I did have."

"Then where is your wealth?"

He shrugged. "At the start of the end times, I invested most of it in a new playhouse in Golding Street."

I frowned. "When did you so?"

"In January of 1642."

I choked, laughing, and sprayed ale on his sleeve. "The year the theaters were closed!"

He shook the wet cambric gracefully. "Yes, as it happened. Now the place houses the Ministry of Charitable Works. I've lately striven to pay more mind to the shifts in Parliament."

"If that were true, you'd have chosen another profession altogether."

He smirked. "I? Impossible. I will never stop playing. And writing! The times are rich for satirical pieces." He tapped me familiarly on the wrist. "This one today, Jude. You should have been there! The crowd roared at it. 'Twas the tale of a godly general who eliminates king and nobleman and then steals the crown for himself."

"You're mad."

"They roared, I say. Roared. And so would you have."

"I'd have liked the part where you fell through the floor."

He winced. "That was painful. I should have known by now not to bring a cannon on the stage."

"Thou shouldst not have been old till thou hadst been wise."

He winked and pointed at me. "Good! But you know, I thought if we only feigned to light it, we'd be safe. Not so. You are in the right, Jude. A man in his fifties—"

"Fifties!"

"Well, inclining to three score."

"I am sixty-one, and you are sixty-three."

"Am I so old, indeed? Ah, well." He took a new swallow of ale and sat, looking meditative under his bandage. "'Tis a long year since I played Hermia. Or Joan of Arc." He wiggled his eyebrows at me. "And long since you were Viola. Ah, Judy!" He winked. "Why did you not marry me?"

"You didn't ask me to."

"Did I not?" His smile grew wider. "I thought I did."

"Well, I learned one thing from my father's plays. Men who seem to be all tongue usually are."

He stuck his tongue through his teeth.

"Ah, clever. Are you eight yours old?" I steadied myself. "And you? Did you never marry?"

He wrinkled his brow thoughtfully. "Did I? I think not. Though I could have had a wealthy widow, or two. Still could."

"Indeed." I folded my arms. "I reckon you think you're still handsome."

"I know I am."

And he was, in a ruined sort of way. His hair was still thick, for all it was grey and chopped short, and though he'd lost a tooth or two, his smile shone white in his beard. His face was scarred, as I've said, but it wasn't pocked, and though he'd lines in his forehead and deeper ones around his mouth, still, he looked more like the man of fifty he claimed to be than like a *senex* two years older than me.

And his eyes.

I looked away from them. "Nathan, I thought you were dead."

"Why?"

"Because someone like you likely would be, by now." I leaned to pick up my bag of surgical stuffs. "And now I must go."

"But why?" He tapped my half-empty tankard. "Stay for another."

"Nay!" I lifted it for one more swallow, then set it down with a bump. "I've patients to visit in the morn."

"Come visit *me* in the morn. They'll give me a bed here for the night."

"No." I stood up, raising my hood. "I've finished with you now. So spend that smirk on some bawdy-basket tap-wench. I spotted one or two downstairs."

I felt as though I'd last seen Nathan yesterday.

This, of course, was illusion. It had to be. I wasn't the person I'd been. The years had pummeled me into the shape of an old married dame, and given me the heart of one, too. The heyday in the blood was tame. Nor could he be that man I remembered, after more than three decades. Not in truth.

Though he seemed unaccountably like him.

"You should lie low," I warned as I tied my hood. "After your illegal playlet."

Nathan slapped his hands on the scarred wood of the table. "I'll be safe e'en if they do come a-questioning. I'll be a private in God's Special Army who got grazed by a ball down Plymouth way. I keep my ears open now, I told you. There was a scuffle there last week. If I can't concoct a name and a story, call me a knave."

"I do call you a knave. But the danger's real, Nate."

"Then I will accompany you home," he said gallantly, and rose. "Oh." He put both hands on the table to steady himself.

"I've a horse, so nay."

"Neigh!"

"And you've a head wound."

He looked a jot glad of these obstacles, but said, with perfect memory, "Then I will call on you and your Jane and your Pearl tomorrow, in Milk Street." He kissed my hand.

I rode home alone, feeling exhilarated and strange and altogether at sea. The day seemed to have lasted a month. More things had happened to my heart in the space of twelve hours than in the seven years before.

In my old age I'd come to think more and more like that Greek sage who thought the world was composed only of tiny bits and pieces of matter colliding against one another, devoid of purpose or reason. Randomness reigned. And this is one way to read a life. But there is another way, the way Jane saw, whereby matter was mere metaphor for spirit, and good battled evil, and demons were real. Now, looking back on this day, I recall the long minutes I spent in the afternoon, in Cloak Lane, just before I was summoned to the Cross Keys. I think of a hard bench in a room full of quiet folk who, when they spoke, spoke of love and peace and the laying down of arms. I think, too, of my fancy—or vision?—that I was fighting to swim with Quiney in my arms, and the strange inner voice that said, *Hold fast*.

And I marvel how closely on the heels of that vision and voice came the accident that brought me, once more, to Nathan Field. I ask myself if it were, after all, an accident. *Satan seeks to enlarge his kingdom*, thunders Jane. A dead heart, he already owns. But what of a heart that, steeped in silence, hears itself being whispered back into purpose? Did the devil throw Nate in my way to divert me from that whisper, and from what it was telling me to do?

If that were the case, then I toast the devil. He could have devised no more brilliant distraction than Nathan Field.

II.

I was stopped once by a guard on my way back to Eastcheap. I said I had ridden to see to a birth, and that babies cared nothing for curfew. He squinted at my papers in the light of his torch, and seemed to think them slightly amiss, but the truth is I think he could not read them, and the fact that I had any papers at all were, for him, sufficient to distinguish me from the common lurking scamp gone abroad to do nightwork. That, I suppose, and my age. My living past sixty had helped make me a target of suspicion in Stratford, where the older, uglier, and poorer a woman got, the more she seemed likely to go galloping through the night sky on a broom. But Londoners were less leery of sorcery than country folk. This was a comfort to a female apothecary.

Jane and Pearl were asleep when I reached our rooms. In a corner of our tiny parlor I lit a candle and gazed at myself in a three-penny mirror I'd bought for Pearl in Paul's Yard. I grimaced at my gauntness. I looked hollow-eyed and dead-tired. I tilted my face to view it in profile. Yes, my nose was as sharp as a pen, and the fat from my chin had melted away so its tip seemed to cant upward. I might easily play a witch on the stage, with very little need for putty. Nathan could never have found in this face more than a trace of the beauty that had once made his heart quake like an egg in aspic, as he'd put it back then.

But then I remembered the look of him tonight, and his ridiculous playing accident, and his absurd tales of his foolish investments, and I grinned in spite of myself. And right away, there was my old self, the Judith of yore, beaming back at me from the glass. I don't think I'd stopped smiling—smirking, perhaps—for a single moment during Nathan's and my conversation tonight. So, wasn't that the face he saw?

Not that it mattered a pea. I slapped myself for a ninny, then blew out the candle and went to bed.

NATHAN DIDN'T APPEAR THE NEXT day. I was half sorry and half glad and wholly unsurprised. Our new interlude had been entertaining, though I felt a little sad that the seasoned dame of our night-time encounter would now have replaced his prior last image of me—a passing romantic one, it must have been, with my fine twenty-five-year-old self striding briskly away from him, my head high, my cloak blowing in a hard breeze off Thames. I'd always liked to think of him remembering that, and him feeling a twinge of heartache as he did so. But, no matter. Things were as they were.

I had now been three weeks in London. I wrote a second, short letter to Quiney, speaking of my experiences in a general way, and again saying nothing of any scheme to return north-ward. I would postpone all planning, even in thought.

· · ·

AS THE DAYS PASSED, WE busied ourselves in the town like regular citizens. I said little about Nathan to Jane. "A roisterer got hit with a cannon," was my only word. She took this event as a matter of course, perhaps as one more sign of the justice of God. But when I told her of the quiet meeting I'd gone to, by chance, at the tavern in Cloak Lane, she showed more interest. "These are folk who speak as the Spirit moves them?"

"So it appears. Their pastor did not even carry a Bible."

"Not a Testament?"

I shook my head.

She frowned in puzzlement. "The Word is our armor."

"Well, that is another thing. These folk seemed to think we English could do with less armor and weaponry altogether."

"What! In the time of Armageddon——"

"I think you should hear them yourself, Jane. But if you go with me, we cannot bring Pearl. Once she sees folk standing up to speak whensoe'er they're moved to do it, she'll be jumping atop a stool and singing one of her sailor's sea chanties about Willing Kate or Ten-Inch Teddy."

"And why should she not speak nonsense, and sing?" Jane sniffed, and wiped a knife on her apron. She was cutting cheese and apples for our midday meal. "Why not Pearl, if any fool can babble what tripe slips into his head, and call it God's voice?"

I laughed. "How can I know that's not what you do?"

"Because I have the scriptures to guide me!" She laid her hand on the Bible she always kept close. "I know the Word."

JANE INDEED HAD MORE SCRIPTURE by heart than anyone I knew. She certainly had more than I, perhaps more than my

father had had, which was plenty. Both Jane and I wanted to
teach Pearl to read, and I had even bought, in Paul's Yard, an
illustrated abecedarium for the purpose. When I had time, I
vowed, I would sit with Pearl and show her the letters. But
we had all been mightily busy. Jane and Pearl herself had been
earning pennies by helping to strain cheese curds for our
neighbors, and with all our activity, Jane and I had never found
a moment to corral her and begin. The child was not wholly
unlettered. She knew some of the alphabet, and could write
her first and last name. Since she loved stories, I thought it a
fine idea to get her a book of simple fairy tales, if such could
be found nowadays, but Jane bristled at the suggestion. Besides her woman-warrior ballad and, of course, her worn
King James, the only printed text which Jane found fit for
perusal was a book of godly prophetic anagrams she'd seen in
a bookseller's window and bought at the dear price of a half-
shilling. The anagrams thrilled her, and she concocted her
own, using, for a start, her own name, JANE SIMCOX. She
became convinced, like the pamphlet's author, that names
were riddles which, unfolded, revealed God's secrets. She
would sit for hours with a pencil and a sheet of foolscap,
combining and recombining letters. She did it with my name,
too, when I wrote it for her, and with Pricey's. Sometimes
she'd join our two names and surnames with Pearl's. This
yielded "YEA, QUOTHD I! JUN! RIPE! AMEN!" though
this invention left an extra *J* and an *X*, a problem she simply
ignored. To me her result was mysterious, not illuminating,
but Jane declared the meaning to be as plain as day. "In June
we are ripe for victory."

I looked again at her words. "Well. With better spelling,
we might *rip* something in June."

She said nothing, busy with another reorganization of her name's letters, which turned out to be "SIN, COME AX," though the sentence still left a pesky superfluous *J*.

"Perhaps you could change your name to 'Ena,'" I suggested. "Or 'Ane.'"

She glared.

"I beg pardon," said I. "Would that break the rules of the game?"

"Game!" she scoffed, tapping her pencil against her lip. After next converting "CROMWELL" to "HOWL, ROME!" by changing an *L* to an *H* and ignoring the *C*, she sharpened her lead with a kitchen knife and set to work on "CHARLES STUART." That yielded "LET US CHAS RAT," if, once more, the prophet were not finicky about spelling and was willing to jettison an *R*.

"Jane!" I chided. "Do you call our sovereign a rat?"

"I do. He is an Absalom, who makes wars against his people. Let him hang from a branch by his lousy long hair."

This was so clever, even for Jane, that I hugged her for it. But I said, "Now, then, dearest. Absalom was a rebel, but Charles *is* our king."

Her chest inflated like a bellows. "King? He is a golden calf. He is the false god of the Assyrians!"

"Come, Jane, this is only the windy pulpit-stuff of a flat-capped pastor in Newark-on-Trent."

She seemed not to hear me. She had risen and was striding the floor, well launched now, her sails filled. I settled back to enjoy the jeremiad. She cried, "And may he tax the folk to buy silks and a thousand comfits for his papist wife? Nay! The hammer of God will fall, and the veil will be ripped—"

"In June?"

"Aye, mayhap in June! God will burn off the curtain that shrouds the sins of the mighty, they who hide their evil behind their luxuries, sitting prettily in their manors, vaunting their trinkets and titles and ravishing their innocent servants. *Robes and furred gowns hide all.*"

That made me stare. "Speak that line again."

She raised her arms heavenward. "*Robes and furred gowns hide all. Justice rails upon the simple thief, while the gilded dog's obeyed in office.*" She lowered her arms and said, in a calmer voice, "This is scripture."

With a great effort I kept my face straight. "Say you so? What scripture?"

"Proverbs, methinks."

I nodded. "Proverbs. And your flat-capped Newark pastor preached this."

"Aye, he did, of a Sunday. But he did not write it. God wrote it."

Now I had to laugh. "Well, then God's a playwright."

"Nay! You blaspheme!"

"Jane, those lines come from a famous tragedy. One of those vice-ridden outlawed London entertainments." She looked so dismayed that I rose and took her hand. "Ah, Jane! God speaks through many mouths. Sometimes God even speaks in silence."

She looked dubious, but a little shaken.

"Will you come with me to the Friends?"

RELUCTANTLY, JANE CAME WITH ME to a meeting of that strange society. We left Pearl in the care of the cheesemaker's wife, for a groat. As we shut the door, the poor woman was wrestling with Pricey, trying to dislodge from her grip one of the bigger cheese molds, which Pearl was attempting to don as a crown.

And, of course, despite Jane's fears of being forced to listen in silence to other folks' nonsense, it was she herself who popped up at the meeting, twice or thrice or at any rate more than anyone else, to voice her godly indwelling insights into the state of the realm and the lance of justice and the armor of righteousness. Yet she could follow the Friends only up to a point. Jane could not sit easily with the notion of turning swords into plowshares. She thought too well of pikestaffs and guns. Indeed, I considered afterward that I'd narrowly escaped her sharing with that peaceful group her anagrams about the rat king and heaven's ax.

After that visit, she did not return to the quiet ones, preferring the zealous pastor of St. Clement's and his militant assembly, whose weaponry clanked when they walked in and out of the church. She attended St. Clement's twice the next week, dragging Pearl by her side. I think they went unarmed, though she had chosen not to sell our highwayman's wheel lock.

I went to church on Sunday, too, so as not to pay the stay-at-home's fine. But on the following Wednesday and Friday I went back to the Friends, where I sat in the silence, and listened.

SO, THERE WE WERE ON Milk Street, householders, churchgoers, industrious females. We might have settled in to become real Londoners, townswomen and payers of the local army tax. Yet the truth is that we were in London a little less than four weeks, in all. When we first came to our rented rooms, we'd hidden our twice-robbed gold coins behind some loose wall plaster, thinking to use them in some vaguely imagined future time. But before we even began to need that bandit's money, and despite my willful indecisiveness about the future, we suddenly found we were actively plotting a return to the north.

Because of Nathan.

For he paid us a visit, after all.

ome ten days after I'd stitched and wrapped that prodigal player's torn grey head, the cheesemaker's wife stopped me on the stair. "A man was here this morning, about eight of the clock, in search of you, Mistress Quiney."

"Ah?" I felt my heart quicken. "What manner of man?"

She shrugged. "Middling tall. Of middle years. He said he sought the daughter of the playwright, from Stratford." She peered at me curiously. "Would this be you?"

"What did you tell him?"

"That I knew naught of your folk, but that your name was Quiney. And I will say he described you to the life."

I refrained from asking her just what the description of me had been. In truth, I preferred not to know. But what matter? He had been here! Surely he had! "Did he say who he was?"

The wife looked chagrined. "I asked the name, but just then our mouser knocked a cheese pan to the floor, and it made such a racket I could barely hear, and then I must dash to see what the beast had ruined—"

"Will he come again, think you? Said he so?"

"Within the week, he said." She frowned, straining to recall. "So I think."

My fool of a heart was singing as I mounted the step.

In fact, Nathan called the very next day, and surprised me. When he came up my stairs his bandage was hid under a wig, and he was clad in a coat of fine brocade, so when a knock sounded and I peeped through the keyhole, I thought we'd been visited by some wayward Cavalier seeking a remedy for the pox. Feeling himself stared at, he stooped to put his green eye to the hole. "Jude," he said in a stage whisper. "'Tis I, Captain Lovelocks. Let me in!"

WE MET NOW IN FULL day rather than lamplight. But I was too proud to shy from the sunlight that spilled through the window and showed, I knew, the wreck time had made of my face. I can't say the light did Nathan much credit, either, although nothing could much alter his rogue's smile, nor the depth of those verdant eyes. He might have been sixty-three, but his hard gaze could have made a new bride set fire to her orange blossoms.

"Judy!" He dumped a canvas sack on my table. "Now that you've run away from your husband—"

"I have not."

"—you'll be free to enter into business with me, and none better than you to do it. Have you boiling water?"

"The kitchen's below."

He looked around at our plain rooms, devoid as they were of tapestries or moveables, but scrubbed clean as a brook-washed stone, thanks to Jane. "You've a maidservant, you said?"

"More like a friend, in our new circumstances. She's out gospelling, or being gospelled at."

"Ah, one of those." He pointed at the ballad with the drawing of the Woman Warrior, which Jane had affixed to the wall. "Is that she?"

"It looks something like her, to speak true."

"We shall wait for the water."

"What need have you of—"

He laid a finger to my lips. "*Pauca verba.* Time to listen." He seated himself comfortably on our one chair. Reluctantly, I lowered myself onto a stool and faced him.

"Jude," he said. "I am in haste. You are the best friend I have in the world—"

I snorted. "Until ten days past I'd had nary a sign nor a letter from you in thirty years."

"And whose fault would that be?"

"Thine, I would think."

He looked thoughtful. "Well. I grant ye. But here we are again, you in London, by the hand of Providence, in my hour of need." He grasped my hands and stared into my eyes. "Judy, I have a part for you to play."

I laughed, none too merrily. "Not in this day and age. I came here to escape a witchery charge. I'll not jump from frying pan into fire by creeping about on an outlaw scaffold, feigning to be God knows what."

Nate still clasped my hands, though I kept mine stiff and unyielding. "Ah, but this is a part on the *world's* stage. Would you not play a rôle to save a kingdom?"

"I wouldn't." I pulled my hands away and stood. I felt his eyes on my back as I rummaged among the items in a cupboard, pretending to be seeking some lost thing, though my true aim was to hide the flush that had risen to my cheeks. "We've seedcake, and a jug of ale hereabouts. My friend won't have wine in the rooms."

"Ah, she is wise. Seedcake, yes, but no ale, not now. I've something better. Judy, sit. I say it again. A part to save a kingdom."

"My word was no." Avoiding his eye, I plunked some dry cake on the table and reseated myself. I held my tongue as long as I could while he sat squinting and grinning at me like an aging imp. After ten seconds I surrendered. "Right, fool. Say what you mean."

He slapped a ringed hand on the table. "The king cannot win his war by force of arms. All know it. The English aristocracy have forgotten how to fight. *Miles gloriosi.* With drawn swords they couldn't defeat the unarmed House of Commons."

"Well." I bit my lip, recalling the tales I'd heard of the bloody battles of Newbury, and Jane's descriptions of the savage violence in Newark-on-Trent. "I think in four years they've learned a trick or two from their enemies."

"They'll not topple New Model men with a trick, or with a crowd of banners painted with the name of Henrietta Maria. The sight of that only makes a plain Englishman angry, and then he enlists with Fairfax or Cromwell for another year."

"You *have* paid mind to Parliament talk."

"I keep my ear to the ground. What's needed is—by St. Charity, it's no jest!"

I covered my mouth, and tried valiantly to keep its corners down. "Only take off the wig, Nathan. And the curled moustaches."

Grudgingly, he laid his peruke to the side, then touched the tip of a moustache with a mix of self-mockery and pride. "But these are my own. I dyed and waxed them this morning."

"What an idiot you are, to walk the streets in that gear."

"I'm never the dunce you confuse me with. I capped me with the wig and put on the coat on your stairwell. I meant to show you these disguises, for they're an unshakeable part of the plot. They, or something like them. I'll need a far better wig, of course, and as for a coat—Ow!"

I had stood to lift his bandage and lightly touch his wound. "'Tis healing well," I said. "I might take the stitches out."

"Do it, then."

"Do it! I do what I choose, not what some jack-in-the-box tells me."

"Pray do it, milady."

I fetched my instruments and pulled my stool over to his side. He winced as I worked, but kept on with his tale and his schemes. "A fortnight past came a letter to me from a Frenchman named . . . Never you mind what his name was."

"I don't care what his name was."

"He met with me at the Mermaid Tavern—"

"That place still stands?"

"Aye, and you can still dice in a back room between two and three of a morning. The long and the short of it is, he said, on behalf of his government—"

"France's?"

"Aye! He's met with two Presbyterians from the Commons, who've met with a general of the Scots Covenanters, who've met with some men in Oxford, who've met with Charles Stuart himself. They've a plan to get him out. Hold, are you trying to kill me, you country—"

"Call me slut and you can roll down those stairs in your wig, with your sack, and ne'er bang on my door again." I held my surgical scissors suspended in air. "Be manly. 'Tis only a few more pinches. Then I'll slap on some liniment."

"No slapping."

"I'll be gentle. Now, on with your lies. And hold *still*."

He relaxed a trifle, saying, "Not lies, my fine lady. I am friends with the king. And why not? I played for him oft, back when playing was licit. He gave me a watch. He liked me as Giovanni in *'Tis Pity She's a Whore*. Now he's going to slip out of Oxford, and I am to join in the game."

"There. That's the last of it." I slipped my scissors into my apron and unscrewed the lid from a jar of liniment I kept on a shelf. I could feel his muscles slacken, giving up their tension, as my fingertips rubbed the lotion into his skin. After a moment, I spoke, partly for fear of this silence, which seemed pregnant with memory and meaning, but mostly because he had made me intolerably curious. "Is any of this true, Nathan?"

"All of it is."

I capped the jar and reseated myself across from him. "Then go on."

The plan he sketched was madder than the plot of my father's wildest romance. Nathan was to slip through the Parliament's garrisons using a pass forged for him by certain London Presbyterians who apparently thought alliance with the king would give them purchase over their Dissenting rivals, the new Independents in Parliament. Then Nathan would make his way to a farm outside Oxford to meet with a Royalist spy or two. With a new set of passes, they'd enter Oxford by night, and there meet with the king. Charles Stuart was then to change clothes with a servant, and with the help of Oxford's governor—who, overjoyed to see his royal guest leave, would happily unlock the town gates— the king would cross the Magdalen Bridge and move south on the London road, posing as his own servant's man.

As for Nathan—he rubbed his hands in the telling of it—he was to stay in Oxford a week, masquerading as Charles in public appearances. "Else the spies in that town will straightaway get news to Parliament that he's flown the coop. This way, he'll have time to get to the Scots Army at Newark-on-Trent—"

"But why should he? The Covenanters hate him as much as the Roundheads do. They're fighting his defenders at Newark."

"But everyone tires of the war. And the Scots may be calling themselves Covenanters now, but they are still Presbyterians."

"Meaning?"

"They're a thought less newfangled than Cromwell's Independents. More sane and politic. At least at this stage of the game, they're more willing to bargain, without cutting everything short by jumping up and speaking in tongues. This plan *comes* from the Covenanters' generals, in league with their friends in London. Or at least the Scottish Lord Chancellor's agreed to it." He frowned. "To speak true, I'm not entirely sure whose idea it was first."

"*Nathan.* It might come from the French!"

"No. It savors too much of wit. I'd wager it came from Charles himself. He knows the Presbyterians see advantage in treating with him. He knows he can't win with his Cavaliers. But he can make the Covenanters a few promises, and with twenty thousand Scots behind him he can strengthen his hand against Cromwell. And if Old Noll softens, so will Parliament." Nate beat the tabletop like a drum. "Or perhaps our man will evade the Covenanters *and* the Roundheads, and flee to France and his Henrietta Maria, and then sail back with a navy—"

"You see? You may be selling us to France. But you don't care, because this"—I pointed to the wig—"and those foolish moustaches are not meant to mimic a random Cavalier. You will get to parade as the Stuart himself."

"Do I not resemble him?" He put his wig back on his head and struck a pose, his right fist on his waist, his left arm extended before him, grasping imaginary reins. "Imagine me in armor, with a sash, astride a stallion."

"That knock on the head has addled your brain. He is fifteen years younger than you." I could not resist needling him, though, as I've said, Nathan did look a hale fifty, far better than my father had when he died at fifty-two. And I couldn't deny that Nate's stance and expression caught, to the life, the careless hauteur that marked England's sovereign's attitude in every copy I'd seen of his famous portrait. It was a marvelous success, though I'd have bitten my own tongue off before telling Nate so.

He dropped the pose. "Come. You know I can do it."

"Why do you tell me all this? I might run to the House of Commons right now and spoil your game. Surely not all their Presbyterians know of this plan, and the Independents would have your head on a pike." I shuddered to think of it.

"You won't do that. And 'tisn't as mad as it sounds. I know 'twill be no pleasure ride to pass through the garrisons around Oxford. But I've done it before."

"*Say* you so?"

"Aye. I played for the king there, last year. In a comedy I wrote myself. I got in as a surgeon's assistant. Cromwell's not pitiless."

"I'd heard otherwise."

"Well, his officers let a few doctors and midwives go by, if they can prove who they are."

"Ah." I squinted at him. "I see."

"I slipped in, but it was a trick, and I almost couldn't. My medical nomenclature was gibberish. As I say, the soldiers aren't pitiless, but nor are they stupid. At any rate, the one who questioned me wasn't. For the coming plot, I'd thought to perfect my disguise and pose as an apothecary himself, but with you, I couldn't fail. You'll teach me what to say——"

"Thirty-five years of my lore in half a day, aye."

"No need for that. Playing is not quite the same as life."

"*You* say that!"

He clapped his hands. "And *you* are the life. So if you hear me go off my track and I begin to sound like a fraud, you can speak over me like the shrew you are, from your sure and certain knowledge, and . . . Jesus Christ my Savior, what is *that?*"

I turned quickly to follow his startled gaze. On the floor, inching toward us on its belly through the open bedroom door, crept a small form covered with a blanket, its head shrouded by a pillowcase, over which it had tied my beaked plague-mask. The thing hissed as it crawled.

I sighed. "Pearl. I thought you were napping. Come here."

The monster sat erect. Its pillowcase and mask slipped off and revealed a flushed face under a mass of unkempt yellow curls. "I be Snake in the Garden."

"Well and good, but come over here. Use your feet."

Pearl stood and came dutifully.

"Tell me what you heard."

"That the gentleman is a doctor who has a lady in France and a Coven."

I smoothed her hair. "Excellent. But he's only telling an old wives' tale. It's fancy." I looked sidelong at Nathan, who was still staring curiously at Pearl. Or at the pair of us. "Master Field is not a real gentleman," I said.

She made her curtsy anyway, and stayed, swaying slightly back and forth, and gazing at Nate with interest. "I know a song of Willing Kate and Ten-Inch——"

"Pearl. Go wash your face in the bowl in the bedroom. And walk, don't crawl."

Nathan looked sidelong at me as she padded away. "Your granddaughter?"

I smiled sadly, shaking my head. "Nay. She calls me so, but she's the niece of my friend, who lives with me here. And her aunt must not hear a word of your plan."

I thought now, since a living child had popped up between us, Nathan would ask me what my children in fact were, and where they were, and how many grandchildren I had. But he didn't. And I was glad. I'd no wish to speak the unspeakable. Also, I was happy to be reminded that Nathan's interests were never domestic.

As I've said, many things change, but some don't.

"Here, now," Nate said, lifting his canvas sack. "No more wild tales. If you'll boil us some water, you'll see what I have brought you here, and then you'll do anything I say."

He refused to show me what was in the bag until I had gone below with my oven mitts and come back with a metal pitcher in which water still boiled. He had taken the liberty to rummage in our cabinet, and had found two mugs. In the bottom of each he'd dumped a small handful of dark, aromatic stuff.

I squinted dubiously. "I like the smell, but it looks like dirt."

"Stow you and your chatter. Only wait." He steeped the brown dirt in the hot water, staring at the mixture intently and inhaling the steam. After several minutes he added some milk that, at his further command, I had brought out from our larder. "Now drink," he said.

I shook my head. "You first."

He drained half his mug at a gulp. He grinned. "'Tis heaven."

I sipped and made a face. "Will you not tell me what it is?"

"Essence of boiled java beans. They're brought from the East Indies. I've sunk fifty pounds in a Dutch venture—"

"Sunk them indeed, no doubt. Will you never learn you are no man of business, Nate?"

"I have always been a man of business, since the days I sold cast-off nails from the Globe playhouse."

"Not cast off. Stolen."

He waved a hand dismissively. "Words, words, words. But the java bean! 'Tis magical. 'Twill make you wise, and give you the strength of lions. We'll have the army brewing pots before battle, and . . . Have you sugar, dame?"

"Do I look like a thousand-pound heiress?" I took another cautious sip of the brew. It was bitter, but the milk sweetened the liquid enough to make the taste tolerable. At any rate, the stuff didn't seem to be poison.

From the stairs outside our rooms came the sound of climbing bootfalls and the hummed strains of "General Leslie's March to Marston Moor." Pearl ran back into our small parlor to open the door to the staircase. "Nate, take off the wig again," I said quickly. "I warn you, the one coming is no friend to players."

13.

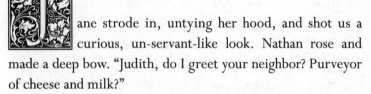ane strode in, untying her hood, and shot us a curious, un-servant-like look. Nathan rose and made a deep bow. "Judith, do I greet your neighbor? Purveyor of cheese and milk?"

"But no, Nate!" said I. Jane hung her cloak from a hook, keeping Nathan in her sights with a gaze now turned amused, and something disdainful. I gave him a playful half-box on the ear. "That neighbor is twice as old as our Jane. You should recall. You met our cheesewoman yesterday."

"Yesterday? Where?"

"Here, in the morning, nigh eight bells. When you first came to call, and we were abroad. Our neighbor told us a man had been here. I guessed you'd be back, and here you are. Not that I wanted to see you, of course—" I stopped. Nathan was shaking his head, his expression a mix of amusement and horror. "Was it not you?" I asked. This was puzzling. If not, then who? "Did you not call yestermorn?"

"At *eight bells*? I was abed. You have other admirers in London, it seems. Early risers." He wiggled his brows, and I rolled my eyes. "But your friend, Mistress Jane!" he said. He bowed again, still more deeply, in her direction. She snorted and put a hand to her mouth.

It was useless. Nathan's eyes and his gallantries had no power to charm Mistress Simcox. But, as it turned out, the special gift he'd brought us did the trick. When he kissed her dough-kneading fingers I thought she would pinch his nose, but then he winked and poured her a mug of his magical brew, and to my surprise, she loved it. She begged another cup. And strangely, when I looked down into my own mug, I saw that without knowing how, I had drained it to the bottom.

After pouring Jane's second java, Nate scribbled some words on a scrap of paper and pushed it at me. Then he picked up his diminished sack of beans, bowed a final time, and left. With Jane there, alternately sipping her brew and frantically scrubbing an already clean floor, and with Pricey awake, we could speak no more of his preposterous plot, which, to his credit, if he were telling truth, was not entirely his creation, but something dreamed up by mad Presbyterians with brains as whimsical as his own. And by the king, a famous romantic. It was well known in England that, like his father, James, and his mother, Anna, and his siblings and his Catholic wife, Charles Stuart loved plays. In his happier days, he had kept his own players. Nothing in his redesigned kingdom could have pleased him less than the enforced reformation of its entertainments. While describing his crazed king-freeing plot, with its twists and its multiple maskings, Nathan had told me our sovereign still kept dancers and musicians and comedians in Oxford, though they were poor fare compared to what he had enjoyed in his London palace of Whitehall, before plays were outlawed and the companies disbanded, and the great actors reduced to private performances in Royalist households, or furtive ones on

ill-maintained scaffolds in inn-yards. Some of the best actors
had gone abroad to play in France, or, in a different kind of
betrayal, turned Godster and joined the army.

Now Nathan had what he thought a better plan.

That night I lay awake for hours, listening to a dog bark
somewhere in the neighborhood, and to the creak of the house
in the wind. I was exhilarated by Nathan's visit, but also frightened by a new and mysterious question. If it wasn't Nathan
who'd come to call on me at eight of the clock the prior day,
who was it? It might have been one of my London patients,
but for the fact that, according to my neighbor, the caller had
mentioned Stratford. I'd told no one we hailed from there. No
one, that is, since that unhelpful city official had sniffed at my
papers the first week I'd arrived. So who? Had we been chased
the whole way south, by some poxy pursuivant bearing a sorcery charge? Had some enemy in Stratford intercepted one of
my letters to Quiney? Was I being hunted?

Perhaps we should shift our lodgings, I thought as I turned this
way and that and wound myself in the bedsheets. Or no. Perhaps
I should leave Jane and Pearl with the highwayman's gold, and
run off with Nate! I grinned in the dark. Pure fancy, of course.
Nate's presence and his ambitious idea had thrilled me—I
wouldn't lie to myself about that—but I could never join with
him, no matter what witchfinders were on my trail. To help
the king escape Oxford? To save the nation, as he'd put it? For
a laughter! To Nate the realm of the politic was like everything
else, a performance arena, with him in a plum rôle. He was
no Royalist. He was a Nathanist. His new grasp of statecraft
struck me with some admiration, but I saw that none of his
wider knowledge had changed who he was. Nathan was using
the fractured conditions of the realm to enhance his endless

game. All very grand, but if the game went awry, it might well result in hangings for all the players. Prison, anyway. And I? I had left my home for safety, not for adventure.

Had I not?

I heard Jane rise from the bed she shared with Pricey and go into the parlor. I heard the rasp of the tinderbox, and then saw the flicker of a candle through my open door. The bell of St. Clement's tolled three.

I rose and entered our common room. "Can you not sleep either, my Jane?"

She was seated at our table with paper and a stub of pencil. For an odd moment, I thought of my father.

"Nay," Jane said, without turning her head. She had long since abandoned the habit of rising and curtsying when I entered the room. She was never well-practiced in submissive gestures, and I was glad when she gave up the effort. "Mother Judith," she said now, still not looking up. "You should be abed."

"I am only tossing and turning there." I sat down by her. "What are you doing?"

She showed me the childish capitals with which she had carefully written, "NATHAN FIELD. SATAN FILTH DEN." Below that she had scrawled, "HALT, FIEND."

I laughed. "There is all kinds of cheating here, Jane. In this, you use the *T* twice, and there's no *S* in the name. And here—"

"No matter." She scratched it all out. "That old man is a fox. He is come to tempt you to sin."

"Me?" I blinked away the memory of Nathan's hands gripping mine hours earlier at the very table where now we sat. Quiney's hands were rough from lifting barrels and boxes and chopping wood, but Nathan's were still smooth and supple, with perfectly manicured nails. I shook my head. "What would he tempt me to? I'm sixty-one. I'm past vice."

"There is vice of the flesh, and vice of the spirit."

In the light of the candle her cheeks looked hollow, and her eyes were sunk in shadow. I felt a strange tingle throughout my frame, a prickling even beyond what Nathan's presence had aroused. What energy did Jane radiate? The night was more than half fled, and I'd not slept a wink, but next to her, I felt absolutely awake.

"You do not know Nathan," I said softly. "He's an old friend. Do you know, his father was John Field."

"Who?"

"You'd have liked the man. One of the hotter London Protestants, some forty years gone. Indeed, the most famous Puritan pastor of the first quarter of this century."

She frowned. "If such was your friend's family, then why is he not one of us?"

I sighed. "Jane, I do not know that *I* am one of you. I'm not a Royalist, but I don't know myself to be a Parliament woman. I'm a soul who tires of bearing witness to the fighting and the pain and the dying."

"Aye, you speak true. You're a *soul*."

The sharpness of her listening always surprised me. I held up my hand. "I know what you would say. *The flesh is a metaphor.* But it . . . The flesh makes claims." I laughed briefly. "Makes them much later than it has a right to." I spread my hands on the table and gazed down at the ridged, veiny backs of them. It was time to change the subject. "Jane. Will you never marry? And have children of your own?" I glanced at her shadowed profile. "Your sister had a sweetheart, you said. What of you? Have you never loved a man?"

"I have not, except in holy love."

"Do you not want a man to fall in love with you?"

"To fall *in* with me."

I smiled. "Clever! You're a fine young woman, Janic." I paused. In the candle flame I could not fully read her expression, though I could see that the muscles of her face were set and hard. She said, *"Man is born unto trouble, as the sparks fly upward."*

"I'll not argue with that," I said with a laugh. But I added, as softly as I could, "We are all born unto trouble. Man and woman alike. Yet even if you are no virgin, by some . . . accident . . . that's no barrier. A good man won't care."

She flattened her hands on the table, like mine. She said, "The flesh is as the grass."

"Aye, but even grass has its day and its uses." To my mind's eye came a brief vision of myself and Quiney in the days of our courtship, we almost as young then as Jane was now, lollygagging in the fields outside Stratford. Him holding my bonnet and laughing, and me chasing him, also laughing, and tackling him at the last. *The thing that was lost.* I shook my head, and went on. "I've seen how you care for Pearl. You'd make a good wife and mother, Jane."

She folded her hands, as though praying. "I have not yet been all I may be."

I leaned over and kissed her cheek. *"We know what we are but know not what we may be."*

She looked at me narrowly. "Not scripture, is't?"

"Nay."

"'Tis from another one of those plays of your father's."

"Ah, so you know of him!"

She nodded. "From Hannah. She heard stories. How your father would write in the middle of a ring of open books, and jump up to run first to this, then over to that, to read something quick, like the hands of a crazy clock."

This surprised me. The simile had been mine, and one I was proud of, but it was a mystery how Jane's sister could have heard it. I didn't remember sharing it with anyone at New Place, not John Hall or Susanna or Elizabeth. And I certainly wouldn't have wasted my wit on Master Nash. Him I avoided.

Jane toyed with her pencil. "I have heard that your father wrote a play of a man who lost his crown for pretending to be a god."

I smiled. "I know which you mean. *Richard the Second*. Perhaps you'd have liked that one."

"I would. What else did he say? Your father."

"What *else*? He said everything in the world."

Jane shook her head impatiently. "Nay. About not knowing what we might be. What was the rest of that saying?"

I thought. "Well. The greater part of it's nonsense. It's the speech of a mad girl in a tragedy. She says, *The owl was a baker's daughter. . . .*" I laughed. "But i'faith, that's you, Jane!"

"Not an owl."

"Not a wise owl?"

"Any wisdom of mine comes from scripture. And I am not mad."

"No," I said firmly. "You are odd, but you are sane. You'll not love."

"Perhaps in the time of peace."

I smiled. "The Millennium?"

"Scoff not. There are victories to be won in this land before a woman can live in peace in her own house. Before a man can."

This was true enough. More than half the young matrons of Stratford were doing the work of a husband as well as a wife, while their men tramped about the countryside in their breast-plates and axe-edged helmets. Or else the matrons were widows.

"But peace must come soon," I said. "The Parliament's all but won the war. The king's trapped like a rabbit. He'll have to submit to their terms." It felt a little deceitful to say so, after the hopes Nathan had shared with me. Nate's plot was sheer lunacy, of course. I didn't think Charles could sneak out of Oxford. But still, if the whole Scots Army and a body of London Presbyterians were indeed inclined toward a separate negotiation with the king, heedless of Cromwell, there was a chance, one way or another, that he'd be back on his throne in Whitehall before the year was out. This despite all the hopes of Jane and her radical ilk.

"The king is a tyrant," said Jane. "He has tried to rule England without England. To make the Parliament go away."

"Well. Aye. He has."

"He is an idol. He must not be put back in the basilica."

"Then where must he go, my night-owl?"

"To France, to join his queen and his son. Let him revel there. Or let him repent, and be a private English citizen. Let him humble himself to join our community of saints."

I shook my head. "Can you not see this is impossible? Even Parliament does not envision his abdication. Not even most of the Independents. They say Cromwell himself argues for the king's reinstatement, only under the terms of law."

Jane nodded. "General Cromwell is right about the law. Charles Stuart must bow to the will of the people, their will made law. He must confess God's people sovereign."

I thought of King Charles Stuart, proudly horsed in his portraits, and of Nathan, feigning to be the monarch, mounted on an imaginary steed, his fist on his hip, a regal look on his face.

"He won't," I said.

• • •

I FINALLY SLEPT BEFORE DAWN, badly. It seemed no time at all before the bellman's peal started me fully awake, and for the whole day that followed I felt groggy and confused. While treating our neighbor cheesemaker for a sliced finger, I rubbed the wound with essence of roses rather than witch hazel, and only noticed my mistake when his wife entered the kitchen and praised the scent. Back in our rooms, I splashed my face with cold water. I wanted to lie down, but, with barely a nod the prior day as Nathan went out the door, I seemed to have promised to meet him in the late afternoon.

I sensed a heightened, nervous liveliness on the streets. I saw it in the brisker movements of the passing soldiers, heard it in the quickened cadences of their voices and those of their officers. Something was afoot. I overheard someone say there'd been another Parliament victory, at Stow-on-the-Wold, and that London troops were massing outside Shoreditch, from whence they'd march north to meet with the victors on their eastward march to Oxford.

North.

I thought of the two letters I'd written Quiney since landing in London. It was now some ten days since I'd posted the second screed. I'd not had any message back from him at all. This didn't surprise me, since in this time of trouble, with regiments on the road, post-riders were hard to seek, and missives could go astray. But the lack of communication unsettled my stomach.

I stopped suddenly in my walk. Why hadn't I thought it? The same barriers Quiney's letters faced would have impeded my letters to him. Very like, they'd been lost, and he'd not gotten either of them.

Or else. I recalled my fearful thought of the night before. Or else one or both of them had been intercepted by someone in Stratford who meant me ill.

I thought again of the man who'd sought me in Milk Street, and who'd left no audible name behind him. He'd be back within the week, he'd said. Why? Who was he, and what did he want? Who had sent him?

Then I thought of my bedroom in Stratford, and our kitchen garden, and the little surgery where I doled out simples and stitched up wounds. I thought of Quiney, turning his worn cap in his hands, sitting alone in the dark in his sons' empty room.

I thought of myself, on a London adventure that—whatever good reason there'd been for my flight—was starting to seem like nothing more than extravagant hijinks. Why had I come here? Why *really* had I come?

I felt a sudden, aching hunger for home. But when I thought of the legal summons in Quiney's hand, and the hard, suspicious stares of those two dames in the marketplace, I felt cold fear again. Could I go back? Should I, without knowing what trials awaited me there? I was biding time in London, treading water, not knowing what I was waiting for.

On the other hand, was it not folly to return to a town that had seemingly sent huntsmen after my scent?

WE MET AT THE CROSS KEYS, which I thought safer than Nathan's own rooms for more than one reason, two being that its host turned a blind eye to unlicensed activities, and that the general chatter and bustle in the place masked private conversation in corners.

I lowered my hood, shook out my plain skirt, and sat. Nathan grinned at me. Before he could speak, I said, "Jane and I want more of those beans."

"If you'll ride to Oxford with me, you shall have java beans every day."

"Nathan, I cannot go. The Lord knows I've not much life ahead of me at my years, but I'll not put my head in a noose."

"Where's the noose? I do not even ask you to lie."

"What!"

"You may be Judith Quiney, apothecatrix and midwife, bearing an entry-pass to Oxford, that you may tend to all the lawless pregnancies there. And I promise you, there are many."

"All this so you may seize a kingly rôle and, in the end, be more famous than ever you were. But even if things go as you plan, how are you to get out? You'll have landed yourself in a city under siege, with the Roundheads pressing closer."

He held up a finger. "Twelvepence fine for saying 'Round-head.'"

"Stop thy fooling. Do you not see what goes on in the street? All the regiments are moving northward."

"They are. Things come to a head." He leaned closer to me. "I had a letter from the king's secretary this morning, through my French friend. We must act." He sat back and took a bite of the cod and mustard pie that sat cooling before him. After a moment of thoughtful chewing, during which I tapped a finger on the table, he said, "We must leave London by tomorrow night."

"But you've not answered my question, Nate. After . . . a certain person . . . escapes, if he does escape, and you strut about on a few balconies in your long wig, waving at the folk, what then? You will never fool Parliament's spies for more than a few days. Especially not if the . . . the . . ."

"Wise fellow? That hath two gowns, and everything handsome about him?"

"If the wise fellow is caught. Which he will be."

"Then off with the wig, and I shave the point off my beard. I'll go out as I came in."

I could see Nathan was so taken with the thought of himself in a royal rôle, not on a wooden scaffold but on the grand stage of the realm, that he'd barely given a thought to what might come after.

I looked at him hard. "My father was right about you. He liked to play kingly parts, too. But he knew better than to traffic with real monarchs any more than he had to."

"*Thy father*," he said, then stopped himself. He'd had his quarrels with my father, had Nate Field, the worst of them over a playbook he'd stolen and sold, which act had caused great scandal and hubbub in my father's company. Nate didn't know I knew the tale, but my father had told me the whole of it. I think he did it to show me my secret sweetheart was a rogue. Which I already knew, likely better than he did himself.

Nathan stayed quiet for a moment. He aimed his eyes at me, those smoky muskets. He didn't try to touch my hand again. He only gave me a half-smile and said, "Do you not know that I love you still?"

I wasn't prepared. I had thought my vanity fairly well dead, or at least stunned into submission by the bludgeoning force of reason. Now I looked back at him, looked hard at his scarred face, and without willing it I slackened my guard. I let myself remember that once I had kissed that mouth, and lain in those arms, and gazed into those sea-green eyes unspeaking, my young legs intertwined with his, during a fortnight when time slipped by us unnoticed.

Still holding my gaze, Nathan pulled a gold timepiece from a pocket of his jerkin, then glanced down to consult its face. "Four of the clock." He held the piece up to my view. "A gift to me from the sovereign, if my word's not enough." With a nail he tapped its engraved letters, a *C*, an *S*, and an *R* intertwined. "Charles Stuart Rex."

"I'll never doubt you again." I made my voice mocking, to hide my confusion.

He shook his head impatiently, and pocketed the timepiece. "I won't say I've never lied, Judy, but in this, I do *not*." Now he took my hand. "Come with me, friend! We'll brazen it out. We're quick-witted enough, you and I. We'll have a week in Oxford, and then we'll slip back to London, and live as merry as the day is long." He raised his eyebrows. "And the night."

I pulled away from him, hating the warmth of my cheeks. "I've a gold bauble, too." I pointed to the plain ring on my left hand. "I've a husband. He's the vintner."

"A fine trade. When the king's back on his throne and the fat bishops in their gold chairs, your husband's business will triple. He'll take himself a country wench, and he'll ne'er miss you at all. Has he ne'er had a country wench, save thee?"

I bit my lip and didn't answer.

"Ah." Nathan looked at me sharply. "I see he hath. So he may again. Come with me! Perhaps I'll take you to France."

Oh, the man could make me smile. Ducking my head, I stood and gathered my cape and my gloves, and raised my hood. "Nate, I'm too old for you now. Find you a young mistress and tell the fool you're forty. You may trust me with your plans, but I'll not follow you to Oxford, nor to France, nor to anyplace else under the sun." He stood, meaning to argue, but I put a finger to his lips. Only a brief touch, but with it, my voice softened in spite of myself. "In one thing you are right, my old dear. It is time for me to leave London. Jane and Pearl and I might welcome your false passes and your company on the road north, if you truly mean to go tomorrow. And if you bring the java bean."

Nathan's eyes lit up like fuses, and he grabbed my hand. "I told you the bean would make you my slave." From his broad smile I could see he thought he'd convinced me to do everything he wanted, or that he would have, by the time we reached Oxfordshire. I doubted it, as much as I doubted Jane would welcome his company on the road. But I meant to be practical. We would be safer in a man's company, especially if that man were a chameleon who could adopt any accents you'd care to name, for that is a skill that comes in handier than you might think.

A groom brought my horse at the front of the inn, and I began my ride home. But at the corner of Cheapside, I paused. Then I turned my horse's head toward Cloak Lane.

The Friends were already assembled and seated when I slipped into the small room at the tavern. In the two weeks since I'd first visited them, their numbers had grown from ten to fifteen. There yet reigned the silence, which was broken only five or six times in the hour by men and women standing to testify. Some of what was said was obscure. Some of it seemed a mere naming of actions all Christians knew themselves bound to perform, although hardly anyone in the world made a habit of doing them. We were to welcome the stranger in our midst. We were to love one another. We must turn the other cheek, and submit to our brethren in all charitable humility, and forgive our enemies. Some of what was said seemed pure whimsy to me. One man rose and proclaimed,

"The Grapes of Wrath are turned to the Wine of Wisdom, now that the gentle Fox is among the Chickens." At that several of the Friends smiled and glanced at Brother George, the clean-shaven, linen-scarved man who was their leader, if anyone was. I did not understand the jest.

Perhaps Jane was right. Maybe these people were simply off-kilter. It might be a fool's fancy to hold that any thought or word arising in a meeting of folk was the work of the Spirit. But yet, I found a cause to be here. There was still the silence. And as I sat in that quiet, between utterances, I heard, again, coming and going—whether from within or without, I could not say—a faint voice speaking. It sounded something like the voices in the wind that murmured to me under the trees by the Avon at home. It sounded something like my father's voice, and something like my own.

But I could not make out what it said.

As was his custom, Brother George took my hand as I left. "Come to us again, Sister Judith."

"Thank you. But I leave London on the morrow."

"Ah." He nodded, and declared, in the odd grammar that these folk used, "Thee must go where the Spirit sends thee."

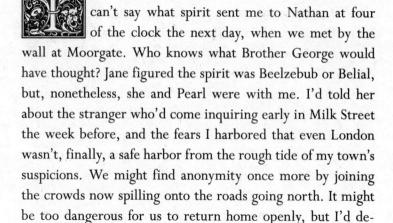can't say what spirit sent me to Nathan at four of the clock the next day, when we met by the wall at Moorgate. Who knows what Brother George would have thought? Jane figured the spirit was Beelzebub or Belial, but, nonetheless, she and Pearl were with me. I'd told her about the stranger who'd come inquiring early in Milk Street the week before, and the fears I harbored that even London wasn't, finally, a safe harbor from the rough tide of my town's suspicions. We might find anonymity once more by joining the crowds now spilling onto the roads going north. It might be too dangerous for us to return home openly, but I'd decided I must come near it. I needed to find out more about the pending case of Judith Quiney and her diabolical minions, Jane and Pearl Simcox.

Jane agreed that given the present state of the roads, all dotted with soldiers' garrisons and sticky with spring mud, we were unlikely, in London, to get any news from Stratford. And, she added shrewdly, Quiney might tire of pretending to neighbors that he knew where I was. She had dwelt in our house long enough to see that my husband was not a good liar (no

Shakespeare he). I also think—nay, I know—that Jane sensed the stir in the London air, and saw bands of men marching, and wanted to follow their holy track. At any rate, when Nathan's message had come late the prior night, stating our time of departure, she'd willingly packed her and Pricey's clothes and traps and rolled up the paper ballad that had been our only wall decoration. From the hole behind the ballad-sheet she'd pulled the highwayman's gold, and pushed it deep into my leather sack, under my son's useless jerkin. Now to Moorgate we came with our horses and bags and a new traveling trunk that fit behind a saddle.

Nathan whistled with admiration when he saw Glory, and looked entirely gleeful when Jane told him how we'd nabbed the stallion. He himself had a horse, a fine grey, which he'd bought or rented for the journey. He'd a short sword, which he kept strapped to his saddle, but no gun. He asked to see Jane's, but I held up my hand and hushed the pair of them. "If we are to go, let us go. Let's not be a knot of folk talking. We'll catch the eye of some officer. And, Nathan, have you no plain woolen hat?" He was dressed for the road in an apothecary's apron and cap, with a black-letter treatise on wart cures sticking up from his pocket. "What mad physician would wear this gear for traveling?"

"I only wanted to show you—"

"Off with it, or you ride alone."

"Well, then." Nathan disappointedly stowed his cap, apron, and treatise in a sack, and pulled out a more suitable bonnet. His horse nickered as Pearl leaned from her aunt's saddle and stroked its nose. As Nathan led the grey by the reins toward the city gate, he told us briefly that his forged papers named him a Doctor Caius Cornelius. ("*What!*" "Hush, the name pleases me, and they won't laugh. They know nothing of the old plays, these young fellows.") With his midwife assistant (me), he was bound for Abingdon. Such was his tale. If challenged, we were to say we went to attend a lady's childbed there, and that Jane and Pearl were my servants.

"I'll not bear false witness for your old fox," Jane whispered to me angrily as we approached the city gate.

"Then say nothing," I pleaded. "Let Nathan speak."

We had luck at the city gate. We were a few of a throng of people leaving London in the wake of the army, and the young guard barely glanced at our papers before wishing us fair traveling. Within a quarter of an hour we were well under-way, the high London wall and its outbuildings shrinking behind us.

As the sun sank behind the budding trees on the northern road, Nathan explained to us that new passes awaited us in Abingdon for the second leg of our journey, into Oxfordshire and thence into the spired city itself. I held up a hand. "That is where we'll part, Nathan. Not long after Abingdon. We're bound for Warwickshire. To Stratford."

"To be tried as a witch?"

"Nay, nay. I'll find out how things lie, first."

"How?"

"Never you mind."

I'd a plan, but I was loath to share it with Nathan, knowing he'd pick it full of holes in his effort to make me think my only path lay alongside his, to Oxford, there to play a part in his scheme of the century. But I'd told Jane my thought. As we packed, I'd let her know that despite her evident unwillingness to bring Pearl to New Place, we had little choice but to go there. Or in any case, I myself must go, to speak to Susanna. My sister would know what was what in Stratford, and whether dogs were on our trail. Perhaps we were hiding from shadows. Whatever had become of the poor jaundiced babe, perhaps I'd been a mere nine days' wonder, and might now come home and take up my odd, quiet life. But things might be otherwise. Susanna would warn me if I needed to prepare myself to be strapped onto a ducking stool.

THE ROADS WERE CHOKED WITH soldiers and folk fleeing northwest, and blocked by even more sentries than we'd met on our journey south the month before, so we made slow progress. I wondered how a king in disguise could ever hope to make his way through the many stops and questionings that would be imposed on him, even if he got out of Oxford. Nate's plot seemed more lunatic every hour. But I didn't share my thoughts with Nathan, for fear of being overheard by fellow travelers.

Our first meeting with a soldiers' roadblock increased my worry, not for the king, but for Nate. His papers caused no comment. It was his manner that raised eyebrows. When a red-bearded Parliament man looked at our documents, and asked who awaited our ministrations in Abingdon, Nathan was ready with the plausible-sounding common surname we'd finally agreed on. But he couldn't leave well alone. He then must wax apothecal, speaking a mix of Doctor Caius and Old Healer Cerimon, about the green box of simples he kept in his closet, and how he'd a powder that might the fire of life rekindle in a corpse not dead five hours, until I thought he'd be arrested for blasphemy or sorcery or both. Pressed though the private was with the stream of riding and walking travelers, he looked as though he might call over his sergeant to speak further with Nathan, but I intervened, saying milady So-and-So's time was near, and the doctor was wise, but we'd best on to Abingdon or our journey would be entirely wasted. We aimed to be at her house before the waters broke.

Puzzled, the young man looked at the sky. "I see no clouds."

"The *waters*." I gestured meaningfully toward my abdomen. The man looked alarmed, and in a trice we were through.

"*Ninny!*" I hissed to Nathan, once we were well past the garrison. "You doctor it well for the comic stage. Is this how you were caught before?"

"I did not *say* I was caught before. I said I almost was."

"Nathan, they spoke truly of you who called you a second Burbage. You are the best player I have ever seen on a stage—"

"Ah, you *said* it! You *said* it!"

"—but you're accustomed to playing for folk who know you're playing." I slapped away the finger he was waving in my face. "Try to recall that you don't want to be admired for how well you're doing it."

"I reckon you think you could play it better."

"I'm not *playing* it! I *am* it! I don't trot out prescriptions in verse! Most of the time I say nothing at all."

"Let's have this be one of those times."

"Well. Very well." I spurred my mare and rode ahead, gritting my teeth. How marvelous, if Nathan's playing skills were the thing that got us all thrown into the Clink as forgers! Could he even understand what it was to do, and not pretend to do? The times when I was most a doctor were the times when I thought least about being one. That meant simply performing the job of it: stitching a wound, measuring a powder, calming a patient, sawing a bone, if I had to.

I said as much to Nathan a half hour later, when I'd cooled down, and we'd stopped by a brook for a drink.

"God knows you'd not want me trying any of *those* things." He mopped his face with his cap, then put it back on his head and straightened it fussily with his fingertips. "I'm only trying to look the part."

"But this is just what I mean. On the stage, thou dost look the part, but on these roads, I fear for thee. *Truly* to look the part, thou'dst keep thy mouth shut. Or speak of the weather."

"Ah, Judy." He pinched my cheek fondly. "You are thee-ing and thou-ing. You love me still."

I cast a quick glance at Jane and Pearl. But Pearl was singing tunelessly and wading in the stream, and Jane was sitting entranced, as it seemed, with her back to an elm tree. Since we left London she'd been sunk in herself, as though buried in deep thought.

As I watched her now in the fading light, I saw her lips move. Was she praying? What was she saying?

Pearl waded to the side of the stream and splashed Nathan.

"Enough of you, vile puny!" he said, vexed. "I paid half a crown for these breeches. I'll not have them mud-stained."

We ate some cold eel pie and rode on for five miles, then stopped at a crowded roadside inn. Nathan presented my papers importantly, certain these documents would garner us fine treatment, since travelers' hosts are generally glad to have surgeons on the premises. Neither of us was prepared for the host's reaction to the sight of my name on the paper.

"Judith Quiney? You were asked after this very day."

I frowned. "How so?"

"A fellow came seeking a dame of your name of Stratford, said to be traveling with a woman and child. And . . ." He stared perplexedly at Nathan, who was still adjusting his apothecary cap.

"What was his name?" I tried to sound merely puzzled, and not fearful.

The man shook his head, but while he was still opening his mouth to answer, Nathan was guiding me out of the place by the elbow, saying, "No matter, good sir. Your fine house is bursting at the seams with folk; we'll lodge elsewhere." We remounted our horses as he whispered to me that this was not the kind of attention he craved on his northern journey.

"What do you mean?" I asked nervously as we rode on.

I hoped he'd not give voice to my own thought, but, naturally, he did. "God's councilmen are out looking for you, Jude. The agents of virtue. I tell you, you'd best *not* go home."

It was another four hours' ride, and the sun was well down, before we found another inn that had space for us, and this one barely did. Here we did not share my true name. Jane, Pearl, and I were shoehorned into a room containing two beds and, ensconced on one, a woman and her daughter, who were traveling with a cart to Stow-on-the-Wold to collect the lifeless body of a son who was also a husband. With the three of us—Jane, Pearl, and I—crammed into the other bed, I lay awake once more, my mind divided between sad thoughts of sympathy for our room-mates, and fearful wonderings about who might be trailing me, or trying to intercept my progress.

Nathan slept in the barn.

PEARL WAS FASCINATED BY NATHAN. All the following morning, it seemed that whenever I glanced at her she was staring at him, rather than surveying the folk on the road. This was no real surprise to me, since even in his grizzled state, he was a spectacle to catch the eye of any miss, of any age, as I have said before.

What puzzled me was Nathan's lack of interest in Pricey. Unless she was overtly bothering him, he studiously ignored her. I couldn't guess why until suddenly the truth dawned on me. He was jealous of her playing skills! In fact, it was Pearl who got us through the second garrison on the northern road, by launching into a troublesome whine just after a soldier, in all innocence, asked Nate what he should do for a bunion. Had Nate his instruments? Here, he'd take off his boot to show.

"Mama, I *can't* hold my water!" Pearl shrilled, tugging Jane's arm. "I *can't!*"

The soldier hastily straightened. "Go by, go by." I had just enough time to hunt through a bag for a packet of powdered red sage, and to thrust it at the man. "Boil it," I said. "The sage, not the toe. But put the whole foot in once it's done steaming. The water, not the foot." As soon as we'd gone fifty feet farther down the road, Pearl abruptly ceased her clamor.

"Do you really have to make water, Pricey?" I asked.

"Nay!" Her shout was triumphant.

"Good lass, then." I leaned over and gave her a kiss, which disturbed the horses.

Jane frowned at Pearl for lying. Nathan scowled at her, I guess, for thwarting his extemporaneous performance of a surgical fantasy, in rhyme.

WE WERE NEARLY TWO DAYS on the road to Abingdon. During those days Jane would sometimes ask passing soldiers for news about Midlands regiments, but only one thing stirred her to lengthy speech. That happened on the second morning, just after we'd drunk our boiled java. For Nathan had been as good as his word, and had brought his canvas bag of beans along, and a small mortar and pestle to grind them, though he warned us against more than a mug in a day, and that only before noon. Not long after we'd thrown the muddy sediment from our mugs and remounted, Nathan chose to trade godly chat with a wool-trader and his wife, Coventry-bound, who rode briefly alongside us. The husband was of a proselytizing turn, like so many folk in England's new day.

"And *you*, sir doctor," the wool-trader asked Nate, after one or two primary pleasantries. "Do you and your family walk in the way of the Lord?"

To forestall his attempts to convert us, or perhaps for his own entertainment, Nathan decided on the moment to out-zeal the fellow. "Aye!" He rapped his breast enthusiastically. "I am washed in the blood of the Lamb!"

"Praise God! And may this realm come to be so washed, from its commoners to its lords and its king. Have you taught your grandchild to pray for her soul's redemption?"

I looked nervously at all three of my "family." Any one of them might say anything. Anything at all. I opened my mouth to change our topic, but before I could choke out a word, Pearl broke into the Lord's Prayer, which she bellowed at the top of her lungs, making her voice deep and strange. At the same time, as if vying with her noise, Nathan raised his right arm heavenward and cried, "Ah, this child. Cleanse us, O Father, for the heart is deceitful above all things, and desperately wicked! Who can know it? Jeremiah seventeen nine."

"God bless you good people!" said the wool-trader. "We will pray for the girl, that she may be . . . That she . . ." His tongue failed him, and he raised his hat again, turning his wife onto an easterly bypath and looking perplexed as well as frightened by this lass, possessed by some demon who for some reason knew his King James. The couple seemed alarmed but somehow exalted by our encounter. We saw them talking with animation as they rattled away with their cart behind them.

"Christ be with you in the new kingdom!" Nathan called, then slapped his knee, laughing. "I'll tickle you for a Godster, i'faith."

"Mock on, rowdy." Jane's voice was cold iron, cutting through Nathan's mirth. "*I sat not in the assembly of the mockers, nor rejoiced; I sat alone.* Jeremiah fifteen seventeen."

"Ah, Mistress Simcox, I mean no harm."

Still she glowered. "You dishonor your father with your jests."

Nathan's smile fled. "What know you of me, or my father?"

"I have heard he was a godly pastor, and I see you are a fleering fool. *Children, obey your parents in the Lord.* Ephesians six one."

"*And ye fathers, provoke not your children to wrath.* Ephesians six four. I can match you verse for verse. I had it pounded into my head long years before you were born, wench."

In our youth, Nathan had told me tales of his life before he ran off to join the players. I knew he was not using metaphor, much. I spoke up. "Jane, Nathan, no rancor among us. I—"

"Shame!" Jane spoke past me to Nathan. "I pity the prodigal who leaves a godly home, girl or boy. Such a child will wallow in the mud with the pigs until struck by the light of repentance and salvation."

Nathan frowned. "Pigs, is it?" Pearl began to snort like a hog, and he raised his voice. "Look to your own house, mistress, and teach your cousin to act like a human child."

"My niece has the prophecies of Revelation by heart, and well she might let them fly, in a land of roisterers awaiting their Antichrist—"

"Jane!" I exclaimed. "Master Field is a greybeard nearly two score years older than thou."

Nathan didn't like that style of remonstrance, but it stopped Jane's mouth, so well she knew her duty to her elders. I'd never before seen or heard her rail at someone in the face, except, of course, for our highwayman, who more than deserved it. Jane didn't act the servant, as I've said, but before this, she'd spoken respectfully to me and to Quiney. She was always zealous, but rarely angry.

Still, I partly understood this lapse in courtesy. We were tired from our traveling, and it was very easy for anyone to forget Nathan's age. I know now there was more to it than this, for Jane. On this soldiers' road, she was wrestling with something that tuned her spirit to an almost unbearable pitch. But then, Nathan could crawl under anyone's skin. He was a sixty-three-year-old boy, and not a well-behaved one.

After a minute of silent riding Jane said in a humbled voice, "I beg your pardon, Father Field." Nathan liked this title less than her insults, I could tell, but he took her apology with a good grace. Then he rode along wordlessly for a time, humming a drinking song, and only I could see he was sulking.

This amused me very much.

We went along for a few minutes more in a silence broken only by the creaking of harness and the tweet of a robin building her nest in a hedgerow. The birdsong faded, and then I spoke. "Perhaps those java beans come from the Isle of Devils."

"Nay," he said. "They come from Java."

• • •

THAT MORNING WE PASSED THROUGH Abingdon without inci-
dent. Nathan made a mysterious exchange of documents with
a horseman at an inn, while we bought more food for our journey. Then we continued on our way. The sun was low on the
second day when the flat elms and oak trees of Oxfordshire
hove into view. We came to a crossroads, where Nathan reined
in his horse and looked at me seriously.

I spoke first. "Nathan, we've come this far. We have given
you some cover, and you've granted us protection. But here I
must bid you farewell." The night before, I'd entertained myself with the fancy of myself, instead of this, bidding the two
Simcoxes farewell, leaving our gold with them, and riding on
with Nathan to Oxford town. But in daylight, I could not seriously entertain the notion. I was bound to Pricey and Jane,
who both sat silent a-horseback, by my side. More than that, of
course, I was bound to Quiney, no matter what fate lay before
me in Stratford. I shuddered to contemplate what my husband
would think of my joining in Nathan's plot. For all Quiney's
loyalty to the king, he would never agree to place me in such
jeopardy.

There was danger at home as well, and on the road. But I
was determined to know just what that danger was. I could no
longer live by imagining.

"I must ride home," I said. I looked first at a cloud, and then
at the ground.

I expected and, against my will, hoped that Nathan would
urge me to avoid the lurking perils of Stratford. But this time
he didn't argue. "Then take this," he said. He fished a paper
from his jerkin and held it out. In a low voice he said, "That,
named there, is the farmhouse where I'll lie for two days. I
meet . . . ah, *friends* there, and we lay final plans. If you—"

"Hush." I stopped his mouth with two fingers. "Do not ask me again. I cannot. Nathan, 'tis . . ." I was gazing at him like a spent swimmer at a distant shore. Or no. He was nothing so safe as a shore. He was a pirate ship from whose deck I'd just jumped. Ah, but its hold held jewels. . . . I shook my head to clear my brain of moonbeams, and began anew. "Nate, it was the wildest of chances that we met again. Now . . ." My smile was brief and sad. "I think I may not see you more."

I took the paper he was holding out to me; took it, to stop him from stuffing it in my bodice. Then I stuffed it in my bodice myself.

Foolish water welled in my eyes as I watched him ride down the Oxford road, toward the pickets and the smoke of the soldiers' camps. Thirty yards along, he stopped and turned in his saddle. Bending his bearded, fox-like face in a grin, he held up the canvas bag with its store of java beans. He shook it, and I laughed through my tears.

Even Jane laughed.

15.

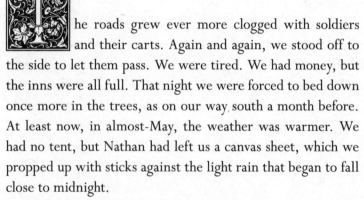he roads grew ever more clogged with soldiers and their carts. Again and again, we stood off to the side to let them pass. We were tired. We had money, but the inns were all full. That night we were forced to bed down once more in the trees, as on our way south a month before. At least now, in almost-May, the weather was warmer. We had no tent, but Nathan had left us a canvas sheet, which we propped up with sticks against the light rain that began to fall close to midnight.

The next morning dawned fresh and bright. Jane and I used our tinderbox to spark a fire, over which we brewed some ground pinches of the java Nathan had left with us. We drank it with our bread and cold bacon while the horses grazed. Then all three of us took off our smocks and petticoats and stockings and bathed shivering in the chilly river, which I knew for a branch of the Avon. We were coming close to home.

The rain had laid the dust in the road but had been too scant to make mud, and the morning riding was pleasant. Pricey was seated behind me on my horse. Three miles along the road she tightened an arm around my waist and pointed. "Look, Grand-mother Judith!" To the east, some ten miles off, in the direction of Oxford, a pillar of smoke towered high in the sky.

Jane nodded grimly, as though this were a sign she'd been seeking all along, on the road. I said, "'Tis Cromwell's soldiers." I felt ice in my stomach. "They're burning the barns of the Royalists."

Jane said nothing. But when we came to the next crossing, she reined in her horse and said, "Judith, my mother, our ways must part here."

I pulled my reins up short and glared at her. Behind me, I felt little Pearl stiffen. "Jane. What do you mean? You and Pearl need not come with me to New Place, if that's what you fear. I told you. We've coin enough to lodge you at some traveler's inn outside town, or in Shottery, while I play the intelligencer—"

"Take Pearl, and if things are well in the town, or e'en if they are not, leave her with your Quiney. She'll be safe with your man. I'll come back for her when the Assyrians are fled and their groves cut down. That time will not be long now." High on our purloined stallion, she sat proudly. "God calls me, and I go."

"Go where?" I pointed to the smoke rising into the sky. "*There?* Where men are burning poor folk out of house and home, only because they sent a few bushels of corn to succor Oxford town? Destroying their livings, like the Royalists did to your kin?" My voice sounded shrill in my own ears, and my mare shifted her feet nervously. Pearl said nothing, but she clasped my waist harder. "Jane," I said more quietly as I tried to loosen Pearl's grip. "We are told that God is a God of love. But this smacks of revenge."

"It smacks of justice." She tilted her head to the east. "My brothers' old regiment is mustered thereby. The men need succor, too, for the final battle."

I sat still and reflected. From what I had seen on the roads both north and south, this New Model Army dragged more than enough godly women in its wake, to stitch its clothes and bake its bread and bind its wounds after skirmishes. But Jane had watched me and helped me a score of times now, tending the sick and the wounded, and she'd learned some surgery by the way. Doubtless she could do more good than most, when things got hot. More to the point, I could see she was pulled to her holy war like metal filings to a lodestone. She'd been born to besiege. I could not stop her. She knew that I knew it.

So we dismounted and exchanged what was needful from our packs. A cooking kit, fresh small clothes, the near-empty sack of java beans, which I insisted she take, and as much money as I could press on her. We transferred Pearl's little abecedarium from Jane's bags to ours. Last, she carefully handed over the pouch containing Pearl's mother's one treasure, her engraved gold ring. Then we all hugged. Pearl cried a little, but didn't argue or whine. Jane held the child in a long embrace. Then she climbed back on Glory and rode east.

I CAME INTO STRATFORD BY way of an overgrown footpath through a neighbor's farm, where thorns tore my skirt and the branches grew so close they brushed against my mare's sides as she ambled. Once in town, I could not avoid the streets completely, but in the main I kept close to the river and trees, and I reached the stone wall that stretched along the gardens of New Place without being seen, or anyway hailed, by anyone I knew.

I hadn't known what to expect at New Place, my father's old house. When I'd left Stratford the dwelling had stood intact, but soldiers were camped and building fires in the orchard. Now I could see that the trees and bushes were a thought ragged, and the grass long, but almost all the soldiers were gone, and the place looked its old self. My heart eased a little.

But it began to beat fast again as I rang the bell.

A maidservant came to the gate. I did not know her, nor she me, and she regarded me and Pearl disdainfully. With the dust of the road on our cloaks, we must have seemed a beggar-woman and her brat, or her grand-brat. "The mistress has no bread to spare," said the girl.

"Indeed," said I. "The mistress is the richest woman in Stratford, and dresses her saucy maids in fresh starched aprons, but she's no bread to spare?"

The maid looked both affronted and confused, and I laughed. "Can you tell Mistress Susanna an old enemy has come to call? Tell her I've dug up one of her poppets from the yard in Henley Street, where I buried it a half-century past."

The maid scurried away, eyes wide.

"Grandmother Judith, did you really bury your sister's poppets?" Pearl's voice rang with admiration.

"Hush, child. Yes. Many times. Many, many—"

"*Jude!*"

And could that be my sister, black-gowned and limping from her arthritic leg, hastening with a cane down the walk, as quick as an old lass might, her face of weathered beauty all radiant with welcome and her arms spread wide? I hurried toward her. She embraced me as though she'd squeeze the life out of me, and I hugged her back. "*Little Jude, you're home!*"

For the second time that day, I wept.

• • •

A BLACK-AND-WHITE-TILED ENTRYWAY, VELVET DRAPES and tapestries, a Turkey rug, and silver candlesticks. Two plush settles, backed chairs, and everything in its place, including a portrait of my proud niece Elizabeth on the wall. Somehow the Nashes and Susanna Shakespeare Hall had managed to keep the bulk of their moveables to themselves, uncommandeered by either army.

With a chastened face, the housemaid served me a cup of something Susanna called "tay," a brown herb dissolved in hot water. It tasted passing weak in comparison to the boiled java I'd drunk just that morning. But I couldn't bear to say so and puncture the pride with which my sister said, "It comes from China." And it didn't taste bad. It didn't taste like much at all.

As I'd guessed, Susanna knew everything about my witchery case. "Yes, you were to be questioned," she said excitedly; indeed, a bit gleefully. "The woman wanted you hanged, and your mad maidservant, too."

I put a finger to my lips. Pearl was playing with a puppy in the next room, but I knew her ears were as sharp as her aunt's, whose last name I'd been careful not to reveal to Susanna. "My servant's not mad. A trifle overzealous, and as for the child . . . Well, she's no madder than I was once. But tell me of the chandler's babe. Did it live?"

"Recovered, and her silly wench, too. And then a fortnight later her man took sick, and at that, the woman railed against her next neighbor, old Mistress Aspinall. She said she'd seen the woman making signs in his direction."

"Belike she gave him the figo for being married to a shrew."

Susanna laughed, and I did, too, so light was my heart at that moment.

"At the second charge, the council sent Mistress Chandler home with a warning against false witness. And the next Sunday the pastor preached that folk can get sick or well or die without witchcraft."

"Did he so? What a wonder! Then reason may return to the land. But then, why did the town send an agent to hunt for me?"

She laughed. "For *you*! No one was hunting you. You are always trying to command attention." She took a sip from her cup, then set it down on a rosewood table. "I regret to say that no one in Stratford cares much about your foolish antics, when all's said and done."

I would not rise to this bait. I was too happy about not being a witch. "That pleases me, Susanna, more than you can tell. But I assure you, a man has been searching for me. He came to, ah . . . to the street where we bided, and followed me on the road——"

"Indeed, indeed. You were always full of fantasies."

I did not argue. It seemed the strange caller was not, in any case, a witch-finder, so I wouldn't worry the question at present. Instead, I looked down at my hands. "And . . . how is Quiney?"

She cocked her head and looked at me sharply. "I've barely seen him. He keeps to his garden and his shop. He'll be glad you're back from Banbury."

This was better than I'd hoped. No dunking stool in store, and whatever Quiney knew of the places I'd been, he'd kept the Banbury story alive for me. I could go home.

And why was it that a fact so gladsome could cause, ever so slightly, my spirit to sag?

With a rustle of skirts, my niece Elizabeth entered the room. It was only mid-day, but her hair was dressed with an emerald tiara, and she wore earrings to match. Her gown was of dark red muslin, cut low with lace at the bosom, and around her neck hung a string of pearls. In her left hand she held a pair of kidskin gloves.

"Aunt Judith," she said coolly. "You're back from Banbury."

I rose and kissed her lightly. "Elizabeth, where are you bound?"

"To Charlecote." She named the home of a rich squire and his lady, a mile outside Stratford.

"The roads are difficult. Soldiers are everywhere, massing near Oxford. You might be safer to stay—"

"My husband is there already, and I've plans to ride with Lady Lucy."

I watched her elegance leave the room, slightly heartened to know her husband, Nash, wasn't at home, and that we'd thus be spared any awkward meeting between him and a child said to be his daughter, even if none knew Jane's tale but Quiney and I.

Lizzy paused in the hallway. To return and give me a kiss of welcome? Nay. To put on her gloves, it must be. A moment later we heard the front door close. I looked at Susanna. "Why does she hate me, Susan?"

My sister sighed. "She doesn't hate you. But she's angry. If you truly want to know, she thinks you may have made her barren with your medicines."

"*Made* her barren! I tried to help her conceive. Why would I scheme against my niece?"

"First, because of Da's will. With her childless, New Place would have gone one day to your Rich."

"None of us cared about New Place. You Halls were welcome to it."

"Is that what Rich said? Or Quiney? Money's money, Judith. It's always meant little to you, or so you pretend, but it looms large in the thoughts of other folk. And then, when you lost your boys, Elizabeth thought you balked her hopes out of bitterness. I speak the whole truth."

I felt my face grow red. "I would *never* . . . Why, what a twisted—"

"Aye. She's wrong. But 'tis only her grief." Susanna leaned and patted my hand. "I told her she was unjust, and what's more, she's seen the proof of her problem, but I can't make her believe it."

I frowned. "What proof?"

"Do you remember John's double lenses? The little interlocking glasses he carried in his pockets, and would bring out, to watch the tiny fauna in the pond water?"

"Ah, yes. He showed me often."

"I have them still. I urged her to use them to view a sample of Nash's seed."

I gasped. "Susan!"

"I did! She thought me a strange old mother, but in the end, a year ago, she decided to try it. She used the trick you teach wives who want no more babies. She collected the seed in a vessel of lambskin. Then she rushed with it to my closet straightaway. I held the lamp, and we looked through the lenses." She shook her head wryly. "Nothing moved."

"Are you sure? Perhaps the homunculi went cold."

"I'm sure. I'd tried it with John's, out of curiosity, once. More than once. His stayed as lively as eels for a full thirty minutes. But Master Nash's . . ." She lay back in her chair and mimicked a corpse.

I stared at her in awe. "Susanna! You perverse hag. *You're* the witch."

"I thank you," she said, straightening and reaching for her tay-cup.

"Then it's not Lizzy's fault, which means it's not mine," I said. "But still she blames me. . . ." I stopped. My customary disdain for Lizzy was failing me. Of a sudden, I felt only pity. I'd known women who didn't want children. I'd known a cold-hearted wench or two who would have sold the ones they had into slavery, given a high-enough offer. But Lizzie had wanted a child fiercely, and it seemed now she'd never have the chance. Perhaps she'd found it difficult, when trying and failing, over years, to conceive, to listen to an aunt chatter and complain about her sons' scampishness and their wit. I felt ashamed.

Another thought, as well, was tugging at the corners of my brain. But I couldn't attend to it. Susanna was continuing. "She's lucky, though she'll never know it. When Tom died, and then Rich, I thought of our grandmother." She made a pained face. "Grim dame."

I knew her meaning. Mary Arden had lost so many young-lings to the plague that she'd learned not to love any child too much, even those who seemed to be thriving. That's why my father grew up thinking he was invisible, like a ghost, and why she paid little mind to any of us. So my mother had told us. But I'd not had the benefit of Mary Arden's lesson. God allowed me to keep two of mine until they were men, and I never learned how not to love them.

I sighed and shook my head to clear it, not of moonbeams this time, but of old griefs. "Might we find Lizzy an inamorato?" I asked. "Some dancing master, or—"

"Most of the ones I've known care little for women."

"Then a visiting captain, or—"

Susanna shushed me with a raised finger and a frown. She half rose, gripping her cane. "Are there *two* dogs in that room?"

"Nay, sit. 'Tis only Pricey, the child. She likes to . . ." I leaned forward and stared. "Marry, Susan, where did you find that?"

She followed my gaze, looking down at her hand as she settled back into her chair. "What, the ring? 'Tis Mama's. You know I gave it to Elizabeth, but she never wears it, so I do."

"But it must be mine, because . . ." I stopped, and pondered.

"'Tisn't yours, mistress," she sniffed. "You said you lost yours in your surgery."

"I thought I had. When I was treating a case of piles."

"Well, this was kept in Lizzy's jewel box. I didn't find it up your farmer's arse."

I laughed. "Susanna, you've some sparks of wit. I never thought it."

She shook the hook of her cane at me. "I only hope my wit's lively enough to keep us unsequestered. Elizabeth can be a fool. She's told everyone in Warwickshire we played host to Henrietta Maria, and she'll never stop boasting that her grandfather wrote plays for King James. *A King's Man!* You know what that sounds like nowadays. But everyone must know she's heir to the great William Shakespeare. She even spoke of it when General Fairfax came to call."

My jaw dropped. "General *Fairfax* was here?"

"Aye, three weeks past. Cromwell sent him to sound our sympathies. Nolly knew what they were, but thought we might have changed our minds, given his victories."

"A politic man."

She made a face. "A butcher. At any rate, I wouldn't lie to Fairfax, nor would Lizzy. My son-in-law was from home."

"Conveniently."

She gave a mirthless chuckle. "Perhaps. Better for us, though. Fairfax complimented Lizzy's eyes—"

"A gallant!"

"—and we served him tay. He was a courtly gentleman, and no Ranter. Nothing like what I expected. If he treats in his person with the king, we may see an end to this. . . ." She looked out on her garden, falling silent, but pointing with her cane toward a shattered ash tree, done in, it seemed, by musket fire. I'd seen sadder breakages in the past four years, of warmer limbs, and of bones and skulls, but I took her meaning. "And it will be worth bringing the gardeners back, to make it as it used to be," she concluded.

"Grandmother Judith? Can we go home to High Street?" Up from all fours, Pearl stood at the doorway. She curtsied to Susanna. Her head had looked as neat as I could make it when we rapped at the gate, but now her cap was askew. Susanna looked at her, then at me, then back at her, with a look of puzzlement. "She's not your grandmother, child. Where is your mother?"

I hadn't corrected Susanna's impression that Pearl was my servant's daughter. This was a question I'd feared. But Pearl answered precisely as I'd instructed. "Mistress Jane is my aunt, and she's following the army."

"The army!" Susanna glanced at me with a mixed look of shrewdness and pity. "And she's left you with Mistress Judith."

"Only until the molten calf—"

"Would you like to try tay, Pearl?" I interrupted.

Pearl tiptoed to my chair and took a sip from the proffered saucer. She licked her lips like a cat. "'Tis not so strong as java."

"Is it not? Hum." Jane and I had agreed that the last thing Pearl needed was a dose of the bean brew, but it seemed she'd sneaked a swallow.

"Java?" Susanna looked puzzled. "What is that?"

"Ah, sister mine." I set down my saucer and cup, stood, and fastened my cape. "You've much to learn."

16.

resh paint shone on the vintner's sign with its pictured green bush, and in Quiney's garden, the trees
were trimmed. Behind, in our stable, I unbuckled my horse's
saddle but left it on her back for Quiney to lift it to its rack later.
There were oats aplenty in the bin for the grateful mare, and
fresh straw on the ground. But inside the house, wooden plates
lay crusted on the kitchen table, the floor needed sweeping, and
dust blanketed the mantel in the parlor. With dread I peeked
into the larder, where lay only a pat of strange-colored butter
and a bran loaf that looked about as edible as Stonehenge.

I sent Pearl to work dumping fragments of dried egg and
old bread into a bowl for the cat, and found her a rag for wiping
the furniture. I hauled water from the pump to the scullery
and dumped the bucketful into a tub, along with a cup of river
sand from the jar that stood by the door. My arms aching already, I collected all the dirty dishes, bowls, and cups I could
find, rolled up my sleeves, and began to scrub and dry.

All this while I heard footsteps coming and going on the
floor of the shop above, and the sound of customers opening
and shutting the door up there, above the outer stair. I heard

animated voices, and occasional bursts of laughter, though I could make out no words. No wonder for the excitement. The vintner and tobacconist shop was a hub for news, and news there were aplenty at this moment, of the movements of troops to Oxfordshire, so close to our houses and farms. I heard war-excitement in the tones and cadences, but I also heard Quiney's low, measured replies to the words of his patrons, a steady refrain, like the burden of a song.

When he came down to the dooryard after some two hours, the house was in order, and so was I. I'd bathed Pearl with hot water and soap of Castile and put by both of our dusty traveling cloaks, and I'd braided and pinned my hair. Pearl's eyelids had begun drooping at the very sight of the old bed she'd shared with Jane in my boys' empty room, and I'd bid her put on her nightgown. Now she lay lost in her strange, childish dreams.

I'd washed my own face, neck, feet, and arms with the Castile soap, but, what with the time I'd spent cleaning every-thing else, including Pearl, I'd had no chance to change my bodice or my skirt before Quiney's step sounded at the door. He came in and shut it behind him. His face showed no sur-prise at my presence, and he gave no kiss of greeting. "Good day, mistress." He hung his hat on a hook. "I saw you come in from the road."

I felt my face fall. I'd thought to stage my re-entrance. Sweeping and scrubbing, I'd reckoned the tidied house would go a distance toward softening his manner toward me. He was often gruff, and he was like to be especially crusty-tempered after my long witch's flight. Truly Jane and Pearl and I had vanished like bubbles into the air.

Yet he'd known for two hours I was there, in the house below him, and he hadn't come down to greet me.

He sat in his chair and lit his pipe. He puffed and gazed at me, while I stood pleasantly by the window, hoping I looked passing fetching for an old dame, and a fair approximation of a dutiful wife. "Quiney, I'm home," I said at last, gently, when my winsome smile seemed to be having no effect. "Are you not glad? I wrote to tell you where I was, and why. Did my letters go astray?"

"One didn't."

That put a stick in my spokes. "Then . . . you had my message from thence?"

He puffed. "Aye. Your second, as it seemed."

"Then you know why we had to go there, though I . . ." I stopped. Had I scanted the explanation in the second letter, thinking he'd gotten the first? I started again. "In London, I'd no news from you." I could hear my voice growing sharper. I was feeling less repentant by the minute. "I could not tell whether I could come home freely, or whether I'd be pulled from the saddle and boiled in oil as soon as the horse set foot in the High Street."

"But they don't boil witches, nor burn them, nowadays. Only a quick snap of the rope."

I crossed the room and sat down hard on the settle. "Quiney, when did you get so clever? How can you jest about the matter? Marry, you were worried enough when you thrust me outdoor with a leather sack and a bag of coin. Eager for me to be on the road." I did not mean what I was saying, or not the tone in which I was saying it. Quiney had done what was wise, sending us off in haste, and many times since, I'd thought gratefully of his care. For all any of us knew at the time, he was saving my neck, and Jane's, and perhaps even the child's. But he was so vexing! I was disappointed. I'faith, I wanted to weep.

"I sent you to Banbury," he said.

"But if you had my letter, you know why I couldn't stop there. It would not have been safe. It was too close, and . . . Don't do that."

He was tapping his pipe on the table and spilling ash on the floor. Ignoring my complaint, he said, "So, has he joined the New Model Army, then, poxy bone-bag that he must be by now? Is that why you quit your gadding about and came back to Stratford?"

I stiffened and stared. My whole body changed temperature, on the instant. "What? Who?"

"The player whose head you dressed. The old acquaintance you met by wild chance. 'Twas he, was it not? Your friend of old?"

I could feel the blood drain from my face. How could Quiney have guessed what he'd guessed, from some casual scribbled sentence of mine about a player's accident, buried in a list of news of surgical visits and poor women's birthings? This was most unfair. I'd thought my very mention of Nate's and my encounter, set fairly down in a letter home, the proof of my virtue. Had I said nothing of the event, I'd have been acting as though I'd aught to conceal!

Well. Had I? After all, the thing hadn't entirely ended there at the Cross Keys, with Nathan's stitched head. I felt a deep stab of guilt, and the prickling of some nameless fear.

But no! I'd not escaped a witchery charge to be judged in the court of Quiney. He was being an idiot. I'd spoken no words of love to Nate. JesuMaryJoseph, I'd not have remembered how. The whole thing was nonsense. Quiney was casting me in the rôle of the wayward wife, a part that was ludicrous, for me. It felt like a mockery, and I hated him for it.

In my mind's eye I could see Nathan now, like as not hoisting a tankard among laughing Cavaliers in his Royalist farmhouse, some Doll Tearsheet on his knee. The vision made me angrier still. Had I not fled from the devil? And to be punished for my honesty!

Yes, there was that long gaze we'd exchanged across the table at the Cross Keys, and maybe one other, just before he rode off to his likely doom. But this was eyes only. I'd refused each temptation he'd offered or even hinted at (saving the java). Was I to be punished for old thoughts, held in a locked box in my heart?

"Did you think it was clever of you, not to write his name?" He pointed a finger at me in the way I hated, the way that made me want to eat his heart in the marketplace. "It was not clever at all. It gave your game away entirely."

"I wasn't *trying* to be . . . Ah, God!" I put my hands over my face, trying to banish the thought of Nathan's green eyes, and the sight of Quiney's finger of doom. "We're too old for this, Quiney."

"So would I have thought."

I dropped my hands and glared. "*You* said it when we pledged troth, long ago. The past is the past."

"And so I thought."

"Do you think I sought him out? That I went to London to find him?"

He said nothing. He only looked at me coldly and began tapping his pipe again.

I wanted to throw a chair at his head, but I restrained myself. I bit my tongue and kept back the crowd of insults that pressed against my lips. I held back *dolt*, and *weed-puffing geezer*, and *fat tippler*, and *Royalist slave*. But I couldn't restrain them all. Two words escaped. I spat them at him. "Margaret Wheeler."

He sat erect, struck the arm of his chair, and barked, "That was over and done with long ago, and well you know it!"

"Then *why* do you haunt her grave? I'faith, you wish you'd married her."

He stood up, knocking his pipe to the floor. "Do you shove by your vice with this excuse? I beg pardon of one long dead, while you—"

"Oh, you *do* pray to her, then, for the sin of marrying me. Perhaps we both should have married other than we did."

"If I *had* taken her, perhaps I'd not have been punished as I have been! With the loss of one, and then two, and then three. For all your craft, you couldn't save them!" I dropped back on the settle, my hands over my ears now. But he was shouting, and I couldn't block the words. "You with your oil of pansies and your monstrous bird mask and your spices. You could skill to save the chandler's brat, but not your own children!"

I screamed something at him then, not a word but a howl that tore loose from my throat. Then I ran. I stumbled through the house and out the door and, somehow, to the barn, where I fastened the saddle that still lay on my poor mare's back. No rest for her now. And none for me. I rode blindly from the yard, breaking through our bushes, scraping my legs against the hedge-thorns. When I came into the open I cantered down the High Street, where folk fled from my path as though they saw in me the Fourth Horseman of the Apocalypse, and neighbors stared from their door-yards. I must indeed have seemed a phenomenal apparition to earn those stares, after all the strange sights that had come and gone down that street in our four years of war. But I didn't care what I looked like. I kicked my mare into a gallop, and my pace did not slacken until I was past the border of town.

I was at the forest's edge before I felt the cold of the late-April evening and remembered I'd left my cloak on a hook in our hallway. Not only that, I'd left Pearl asleep in Tom and Rich's old bed. But I couldn't go back for it, or for her. Jane would fetch Pearl later, when done inspiring Cromwell's soldiers, and the girl would be safe with Quiney until then. However much he despised me, he could be trusted to feed and clothe an orphan child.

I came to the river in twilight. I dismounted and tramped through the trees to its bank. It was still light enough for me to see the vague outline of my reflection in the water, glimmering like a lost pearl, in a rock-bound place where the eddies pooled. I knelt and bent forward to look more closely. There I was, with my lined cheeks and my tired eyes and the locks of wild hair that had broken loose of their pins and fallen to my shoulders. I was a comical sight, and when I was done sobbing, I allowed myself a sad laugh. "Queen Elizabeth was wont to stuff balled linen in her cheeks when she reached my age," I told my ghost, aloud. "Should we do that, you and I?" Then I took a handkerchief from my bodice, not to stuff my cheeks, but to blow my nose.

I sat back on my heels and glanced left and right. No witch-hunters were about; at least, none that I could see. I bunched my hair and re-pinned it tightly behind my head. Then I leaned forward again. "Hamnet!" I whispered. "Is this how you would have looked?" I gazed for a long time. Then I added, slowly, still in the lowest of whispers, "Since the night we played here in the flood, my life has been a storm of error. Is fifty years enough of it? May I join you in there, at last?"

I kept my face still, and willed the image to answer.

Nothing happened, of course. No magic. The wind ruffled the water and the face disappeared.

I sat back on my heels with a sigh. *Why is my pain perpetual, and my wound incurable, which refuseth to be healed?* A voice reached my thought, and the voice was my own. *Wilt thou be altogether unto me as a liar, and as waters that fail?*

No one spoke but an owl on a branch overhead. It said, "Whoo?"

"The Prophet Jeremiah," I told it. "Chapter fourteen. Or anyhow, somewhere in the middle. Jane would know." I rose and stuffed my balled handkerchief back into my bodice. There my fingers met a paper, which I extricated and unfolded. I squinted at the spidery writing, and considered for a spell.

Well. Why not? I was either a witch or a woman to throw stones at, a scriptural outcast, a companion to dragons and owls. Where else should such a one go?

I had some local opportunities. New Place, of course. The house was still Susanna's, and she'd never turn me away. As for Lizzie, perhaps my niece and I might at last speak truth to one another in these latter days, given the chance. Could I offer her some comfort, in her brittle sadness? Her husband, Nash, disliked me as much as I did him, but he'd not challenge his mother-in-law in the house he only dwelt in by her good will. Indeed, my sister's humor was not to be braved in or out of New Place. I'd been present at a cousin's wedding, years past, when a family spat broke out and Nash, not too kindly, had called Susanna "old dame." She betrayed no sense of insult. She only said coolly, "This crone wears the crown in my manor, and speaking of manners, best mend yours. If you were as wise as you pretended, you'd treat me like a queen."

Dear Susanna.

Well. Crones might be crowned, and manor-manners mended, but even as I thought of New Place, my heart sagged a little. To leave my own house, to live there? What good would I be there, to anyone? Indeed, what now was the point of me? What were my powers? Quiney had given me too much credit this afternoon. I hadn't witched the chandler's baby, but neither had I saved him. The tyke had gotten better on his own, it seemed. Sometimes I thought most of my patients did the same, except, of course, the ones who didn't. So, who was I to sit in my sister's parlor, drinking tay and listening to war news and dispensing wise words about her arthritis? I would wither away from superfluousness. Why should I not instead disappear from the face of the earth? I would say to the mountains, fall on me, and to the hills, cover me, and as for the water . . . Well, that was an obstacle. The Avon had done my poor young brother in, but it was a river too shallow for me. I craved an ocean to dive down into, full fathom five.

"*Blessed are the barren,*" I whispered, "*and the wombs that never bare.*" I sat for a moment longer, and then added, "Luke twenty-three twenty-nine." Jane would have been pleased by my knowing the reference. And I did know it. Very well.

Deep dusk was settling around me. I heard a second owl hoot in the wood.

For reasons unknown, I still breathed. More strangely yet, there were those who still loved me, who perhaps even needed me in some wise, even if Quiney didn't. Self-slaughter wasn't in me. Silly fantasy! A thing for the tragic stage, to enliven a playgoing afternoon, once on a time. Good for Othello or Cleopatra, no doubt, but not for someone with her own handkerchief and a surname. It grieved me to think of putting Susanna to mourning, or Jane. Or Pearl.

Pearl was something to be thought of newly. A thing of great price.

And, too, an old question had been answered. Nathan was yet living.

I lay down on my back in the bracken, as was my wont when I was a girl pretending to cast a spell to make myself invisible. I moved slower, more gingerly, now than then. I closed my eyes, and clasped Nate's note in both my hands. The leaves and bark scratched my skin through my bodice. I welcomed the pain. I began to feel a jot more cheerful, remembering my young, wild, woodland self, and also thinking of roguish Nathan and his Biblical jest with the godly wool-trader on the Oxfordshire road. Or rather, his jest with himself, and then how Jane had boarded him afterward, and trounced him, and made him sulk. It had all been as good as a show.

I'd always prided myself on being deeper and wiser than Nathan, but perhaps I wasn't. Perhaps he knew the secret. Perhaps it was all for a laughter.

My mare nickered behind me. I opened my eyes, rose creakily, and patted her nose. "I saw what you ate in the stable, my greedy one. Oats enow for a day's journey. But best not drink here. There's a fresher stream eastward. Let's go."

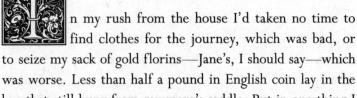n my rush from the house I'd taken no time to find clothes for the journey, which was bad, or to seize my sack of gold florins—Jane's, I should say—which was worse. Less than half a pound in English coin lay in the bag that still hung from my mare's saddle. But in one thing I had luck, if luck it can be called. The papers that proved me a midwife and a she-doctor were also in that bag, along with some few tools of my surgeon's kit.

I slept rough that night in a farmer's out-building, with the mare tied back in the trees. She ate grass, and I ate nothing. The next day I bought two dried pippins for a penny from a woman I passed on the road, going to market, and drank from a public well in the village of Headington. I am sure I looked like a beggar.

I was faint with hunger by mid-afternoon when I found what appeared to be the house Nathan had marked on his crude map. The fieldstone dwelling lay nestled in a fold of the river valley, shaded by two tall oaks, and was visible from the road. I reined in my horse. Steady puffs of grey smoke rose from the chimney.

I tied the mare to a tree and went down to the gate.

I put my ear to the door. From behind it I heard the murmur of men's conversation. The talk stopped the moment I knocked. After half a minute the door opened a few inches and a man peeped through. I could see right away that I hadn't guessed wrong about the looks of Nathan's companions. This one, anyway, a gallant of some thirty years, wore long locks and a cambric shirt that hung loose over his sword belt, and his lips were red with the grape.

"You're a pretty Cavalier, for a Midlands farmer," I said. "Did you not think to set a guard at the gate?"

The man's eyes went wide and he put his hand to his sword-hilt, but before he could push past me to see what short-haired soldiers had made me their cat's paw, he himself was pushed to the side by another man, who cried, "Judy!"

NATHAN'S WELCOME WAS AS WARM as Quiney's had been cold, though, of course, the circumstances were different. The first thing Nate asked after he'd hugged me hard was whether I'd brought my papers. When I showed them, he passed them around to his friends, who besides the gallant at the door were two older, unarmed gentlemen in plain woolen cloaks and breeches. (No jolly Nell lay sprawled on the floor, dumped from any gentleman's knee, to my relief. At least they hadn't made the place a bawdy house.)

All present scrutinized and admired the humble document affirming me to be a practicing midwife of Warwickshire, and bearing the signatures of John Hall and a county authority.

Nathan had clearly said something to these men, of a female collaborator who'd helped him come this far north. He seemed

to have embellished my commitment to the king's cause, for
they all crowded around me in the sparsely furnished, low-
ceilinged place, bowing and kissing my hand and vowing that
surely our august sovereign would reward my valor and hardi-
hood when he came back into the power of which he'd lately
been seditiously deprived by his pretended judges, and such
like. Much was said that evening about honor, a quality I knew
had never mattered much to Nathan, but he proved as loud in
its praise as anyone else. I wondered about his friends, who all
seemed, in an unlikely way, to have names that matched their
oratory and their manners. "Lieutenant Lovelace, at your service," said the Cavalier, making a leg, after begging my pardon
for his ungracious behavior at the door. The other two were
"Viscount Lord Queensfoil Worthy" and "Keeper of the Privy
Seal Lord Chalice." I make free with these names now because
I am sure not a one of them was real.

"Where's your Scotsman?" I asked.

"General MacKilty has gone back to Newark."

To my faint disappointment, Nathan showed little interest
in knowing where I had stowed myself in the two days since I'd
seen him last, or what I had done with Pearl and Jane. "Tell me
nothing," he said. "You are here, and so well you convince, in
your rôle of apothecatrix—"

"Rôle?"

"—that I cannot fail with you by my side. Enough that I
have you again, and that you spoke to no one of our plan."

"How do you know I kept mum?"

"Judy." He looked at me fondly. "Judy, Judy. I know thee."
He cocked his head and scrutinized me. "You are so bonny
still!"

I laughed shortly. "So bony, you mean."

"And you've a terrible wit to match your father's. I guessed you could not stay away."

I pinched his arm hard with two bonny, bony fingers. "You speak true. You kept most of the java."

WE MOVED THAT VERY NIGHT, after a brief meal of capon and radishes which I somehow found myself roasting and serving. I barely had time to wash, and was still clad in the dusty bodice and skirt I'd traveled in for days, but Nathan said it was well enough, since I looked my part (part, again!), and he'd buy me what I needed later, in the town. Our farmhouse lay some five miles north of the city wall, where General Fairfax's pickets were spaced wide, so we had no great trouble snaking through a wood on a horse path down to the banks of the Cherwell, though my heart was beating fiercely the whole time. Lieutenant Lovelace rode with me and Nathan, after he'd donned a nondescript cloak, and tied back his hair, and pushed it up under a cap. A laconic boatman waited for us at the riverside. Code words were exchanged, and then the long-haired lieutenant, if such he truly were, bowed deeply, praised our valor once more, and turned to lead our three horses back to the farmhouse. I was glad to see the back of him. His company was pleasant enough, but dangerous. Now that we were truly on the move, I was starting to fear we'd be easily caught and I'd spend all the years I had left in a dim jail. It might be satisfying to die a martyr to the king's cause, since it could lead Quiney to think I was not an utter failure, but I'd rather be shot than shut up in a cell.

Perhaps I'd get *that* wish. At any rate, I felt safer out of Lieutenant Lovelace's gallant company. The boatman in homespun was bound to slip more easily past the pickets.

Though I still worried about what Nathan might say or do.

The sun was nearly down, and there were few craft on the river. Borne by the current, we passed a great new fort on a hill, a stronghold alive with soldiers, and I shuddered to see its cannon pointed straight at the walls of the town we were fast approaching. On both sides of the water lay the camps of Fairfax's men, with their fires and their tents and their crowds of followers. I wondered if Jane had found her regiment.

The river gate was in view when we met the blockade, a line of boats that stretched across the narrow Cherwell. "Halt!" came a voice across the water. In the last light of the sun I could see the glint of flintlocks pointed at us. I wanted to throw up my arms in immediate surrender, and Nathan put his hand on my wrist as though he feared I might. *Calm*, I thought, and reminded myself that I was practiced in half-lies.

Two soldiers wearing the familiar double-axe-pointed helmets were rowing vigorously toward us as we sat stalled in the river, our boatman paddling backwards against the current. He'd not said a thing since the men had traded passwords at the bankside, upriver. The soldiers reached our boat. A torch in a bracket lit the water that lay between us, spangling the surface with diamonds. "What make ye on this river?"

Fools of ourselves, I thought as Nathan bent forward to hand the man his forged pass and my real papers. The soldier scanned them. The silence was a torment. I waited in panic and dread for Nate to destroy the tension with a speech from *Cymbeline* or *The Merry Wives of Windsor*.

But he had listened to me. He said nothing, until the soldier looked up and asked, "You be a man-midwife?"

Nathan pointed at me. "She is the midwife. I am a surgeon. In Christian charity, let us pass. We serve the citizens of this county, who need help in childbed and sickbed, whatever betide. There are plain folk in Oxford who have no great say in what passes between king and Parliament."

"Before they need surgeons in earnest, they had better get out."

"Some of them cannot."

The man nodded almost imperceptibly. His fellow said something to him in a low voice, and the first handed the papers back to Nathan. "Pass."

We were a quarter-mile down the river before I trusted myself even to whisper. "Marry, Nate, *I* thought you were a doctor. You even thought to say 'county' instead of 'parish'! Well done."

"No fear," he said. "The second soldier in the boat was a king's man. We were expected. He made sure they were first out to meet us."

I was flabbergasted. "But—"

"But me no buts, my mistress. Cromwell keeps spies on the inside, and Charles keeps spies on the out."

And then we were through the river gate, and into the city.

OXFORD.

If I'd needed more proof that the world had turned topsy-turvy, I found it there, and straightaway. As our boatman steered our small craft toward the quay, I stared at the torch-bearing pleasure boats on the water, and at the sworded gallants and silk-clad ladies strolling the walkways along the banks, past taverns alight and resounding with song. All the colorful roistering that had vanished from the lanes of

Southwark and Cheapside, that had gone underground, was here, on full display.

I'd been to Oxford a handful of times before Charles fled north to make it his war capital. But as for the black-gowned, book-bearing scholars I'd then seen swarming everywhere, like two-legged beetles, they must now have been hiding in their colleges—that is to say, the few colleges that still remained in their ancient function, without guns on their greenswards, unoccupied by billeting Cavaliers with their blades and their silks and their high-crowned, feathered hats. And here the knights walked, not drilling, but drinking and drabbing. Were the half-clad women who hung from house windows expensive prostitutes, or merely the saucy dames of Charles's new court? Half the riverside establishments had gone from eating houses for bookmen to what seemed to be brothels. All was changed. London was now Oxford, and Oxford was London.

I wished my father could see it. In his youth he'd longed to study at university, but my grandfather couldn't send him, for lack of money. He'd had to content himself with borrowing books from his uncle's library and gazing worshipfully up at the college spires on his journeyings between London and Stratford. His disappointment at not taking a degree had never wholly left him, even when he was known by the queen, and had money enough to have started a college of his own.

How would you like this, old Da? I thought. *Your court's come to the Midlands, and this town's a stage.*

We disembarked, stiff-leggedly, at a dock, and bid our boatman thanks and farewell. He touched his cap and disappeared into the watery shadows. Nathan took my elbow and steered me through a crowd of well-dressed revelers, to whom the pair of us might well have been invisible, to judge from the attention they paid us. Nate seemed to know just where he was going. He brought me to an inn called Charles's Wain, which stood in a quieter part of town, some ten minutes' walk from the quay. A sign painted with a crown and a wagon made of stars hung over its entrance. We went in, and I stood aside as Nate spoke to the innkeeper. I wondered exactly what lies he was telling about who we were, but felt too tired to try to wield influence. His performance in the boat with the soldiers had been devilish good, and besides, this was a distinctly un-Puritan city, in more ways than one. Was he claiming, with a wink, that we were married? I still do not know, because, after bargaining with the host, and paying him, too, he came back to where I was standing and said he'd not stay at the Wain, he'd a meeting at the Duke of Richmond's apartments with a man named John Ashburnham. Despite Nathan's claim to have faith in me, he hadn't trusted me with many of the names of his new friends. But I thought, and have since had the proof, that Ashburnham's name was a real one. I'd heard Susanna and Elizabeth speak well of the man. He was a member of the House of Commons who in the early days of the war had made himself unpopular defending, in session, the ancient rights of the king. He still held his seat in Parliament, but by now he'd openly left its cause for Charles's.

Nathan passed me some coins. "I'll be back to fetch you at noon tomorrow."

"Fetch me for what? You're in, and I'm the baggage."

"You shall see. Whatever betide, I will need to get out. You can help me there. And we must sport."

"Sport. I see. And what am I to do until noon tomorrow?"

He kissed my cheek. "You'll find stalls that sell ladies' attire in the lanes hard by Cornmarket Street."

"*Ladies'* attire?"

"Nothing in cloth of gold. Nothing like what you borrowed when you came to me in the tiring house at the Fortune when you were a fresh, budding virgin."

"You forget that I wasn't, because—"

"Oh, no. I remember every detail of what passed between me and you. As a poet, I speak metaphorically. You flipped my young heart like a pancake, then. Now, recall that you be an ancient midwife, for this adventure."

He gave his old wolf's grin, and I pretended to laugh.

18.

he next morning I went early into the lanes of
Oxford, as Nate had advised, and purchased a
sober smock and skirt, bodice, apron, and hood, as well as
a cloak and a second-hand trunk to pack the garb in. These
were items befitting my age and my calling. But I'd money
left, and in the afternoon I bought pins for my hair, a gown of
blue satin, and a stick of kohl to line my eyes. When I tried
the gear on in the dressmaker's shop, and gazed in a glass, I
saw I looked years younger. I might have been the elder sister
of my niece Elizabeth. I'd never before noticed our likeness.

There were fine items of clothing and jewelry enough to
be found in the Oxford stalls, though already I could tell,
from the prices, that the town's food supplies were growing
pinched. I marveled at the names of the shops, most of which,
like my inn, paid some tribute to the royal family. I bought a
half-loaf of bread at the King's Bakery, and washed it down
with a tankard of ale at a place I recalled as the Saracen's Head,
now rechristened the Charles Goes A-Hawking. Josiah Bain-
bridge, Printer, where my father had used to browse among
drying sheets of black-letter, was now the Ball and Sceptre

Press. I wished Nathan were with me to laugh at a sign that read HENRIETTA MARIA'S CHOPPED EELS. I thought I must show him later. Then I recalled his morning's message, and thought, with vexation but no amazement, that I might not have the chance. Nate might have abandoned me entirely.

Ah, well.

"No royal eel pie?" I asked the fishmonger with a wink.

He looked at me sadly, his hands clasped before his slime-spattered apron. "Nay. Since last week, I can get no flour for the crust." Something in my face must have inspired his trust, because he leaned toward me and said, "Eels half-price today, dame. I'll be shuttered by the end of the week."

I'd no use for eels, live and wriggling or chopped, but I might well have use for an exit from this town. "How will you go?" I whispered.

He looked cagily about him, then said, "There's low spots enow in the south wall, for those who lack the governor's by-your-leave. By Sheep Street, for instance."

I smiled innocently and, for this intelligence, bought a live eel, which I dropped in the Cherwell. *Sheep Street.* I thought of the pillar of fire Jane and I had seen rising from the burning farms in the countryside. In the daylight I sensed, as I hadn't the night before, the current of fear that underlay the gaiety of the town. No siege had begun in earnest, but the common citizens were leaving. If Charles did escape, when the fact became known, perhaps Cromwell's army would abandon Oxford, but they might, again, not. Would they not wish to punish the town for its insolence, in trading its scholar-ants for a grasshopper king? And speaking of insects, Oxford was, after all, the central nest of Parliament's chief enemies, Charles's nobles, who could not all be escaping with Charles. And then there was Charles's army.

For those who lack the governor's by-your-leave. Thinking of the fishmonger's words, I was struck by a new worry. Belike this common eel-man had heard a rumor that the king meant to escape with the town governor's help. And if he knew, might Cromwell's spies not know, too, and have signaled their compatriots outside the wall?

In London, it had truly astonished me that Nathan Field had survived into his sixties. But abetting Charles was no petty crime: no theft of a play-script, or flouting of London morality laws. If Nate got through this escapade with his head still on his shoulders, I'd be ready to believe in unicorns.

I was not five minutes back in my room at Charles's Wain when I heard a tumult and babble outside my window, and went to look out. I drew in a breath, and stared. There, passing through the street not twenty feet below me, was the sovereign himself—it could be no other—astride a tall white horse, followed by a glittering chain of lords. His left hand held the reins. His right gripped a gold-headed cane. He sat tall and straight, fully matching the grandeur of his portraits. The daylight shone bright on the yellow silk sash that crossed his breast, and on his velvet-clad arms, and on his high hat dressed with so many feathers it looked like the crown it almost was, or like the nimbus of a saint. His cape was tipped with ermine. As the people cheered he bowed to them, regally, formally, raising and tipping his cane like a sceptre or like Aaron's rod, in blessing. His gaze was serene and remote.

He looked like a king.

• • •

NATHAN DIDN'T COME FOR ME at noon. He sent a messenger, a young boy bearing a sealed letter. This missive explained, in Nate's fine playwright's scrawl, that another meeting was toward, this one with a Person who had Two Gowns and Everything Handsome About Him, and that I was to lie low at the Charles's Wain. He would be there anon, perhaps this evening, perhaps on the morrow.

I crumpled the letter, then straightened it out and tore it to bits, which was a measure for safety, and also an expression of my feelings. Then I brushed those bits into the jordan beneath the bed, and went again into the street. I'd imitate my father, and browse the bookstalls.

THE MESSENGER CAME BACK AT nightfall. I'd grown tired of reading the bound copy of *Tales of King Arthur* I'd bought at the Ball and Sceptre Press. To pass the time, I'd put on my satin gown and was admiring myself in the pier glass in my room. I had fastened my hair with the new jeweled pins, and was administering just the least bit of kohl to the rims of my eyes, and wondering how Queen Elizabeth had managed to talk with her cheeks stuffed full of linen, when the host of the inn knocked on my door to tell me that same boy waited below. I seized my cloak and went down to him.

This time the lad passed me no letter. He only said I was to bring all my gear and my papers and money and he would guide me to my "friends." A part of my brain advised me to send him away, go back to my room, put on my crone's weeds, grab my skeletal surgeon's kit and the silver I had left, and sneak down to Sheep Street to climb that low wall. I still had good muscles in my arms and legs. Once on the other side, I'd somehow find my way to Jane's brothers' old regiment and to Jane herself, and there I would stitch up Roundheads bleeding from the battle, when it came, while she baked them bread.

I did none of this. I did as the boy directed, and followed him into the evening streets.

We walked perhaps half a mile, saying very little. Then we entered a courtyard. It seemed to belong to one of the colleges, though it was too dark to see the letters engraved on the arch under which we came in, after the lad had murmured a password to the group of armed guards outside the gate. The boy led me through another archway and up a stair and down a hallway and knocked on a heavy door.

"The word?" came a voice from inside.

"Sacrament."

The door was opened by an elderly man, dressed as fine as a lord, who dropped a coin in the lad's hand and watched him disappear down the stairwell. The man then scanned me up and down, looking dubious. "Mistress Judith Quiney, midwife?"

"That is I, milord."

He bent his waist in the deep bow the Royalists were so fond of making, and ushered me in with a sweeping arm-gesture.

The room was richly appointed and filled with glinting objects, which were mostly cups half-filled with wine. The place also held several other people. A pair of plainly dressed men played cards at a small table by the window, and near them another man, clad in velvet breeches like the gentleman at the door, examined some papers at a desk.

At the window stood a gentleman. He was looking out at the black night, his hands behind his back, the right fist clasping a gold-headed stick. His long, curled black hair reached the middle of his back. He wore high leather boots, dark breeches, and a blue coat lined with a gold thread that glittered against the scalloped white cuffs of his sleeves.

He turned to face me, and I drew in my breath. Strangely, unexpectedly, I was tempted to sink to my knees and bow my head before him. I had seen kings enough on the stage, and I had seen this very one today, passing below me on the street as though in a pageant. But I had never looked a king in the face. What must I do? I made a deep curtsy, then straightened, and said, "Your Majesty."

He smiled distractedly, tugged at his pearl earring, and said in a soft voice, "Sit, Madam." I stood there in confusion, until he allayed my distress by lowering himself in a stately way onto one of a pair of green-backed chairs, holding his cane before him like a symbol of office as he did so. I sat down to face him, stiffly, my hands on my knees.

The others in the room had barely glanced at me when I entered, and didn't look at me now. The two men at the table still traded their cards. The lord who'd opened the door had joined the fourth man in examining papers.

"Are you indeed a midwife, and a surgeon?" said the king, in his soft voice.

I nodded speechlessly.

He poured me a goblet of wine from a bottle that stood by him, atop a harpsichord. "Here." He held the glass aloft, almost ceremoniously. "Drink." I accepted the wine, and tasted it, though I could barely swallow.

"Do you see," he said, filling a cup for himself and sipping thoughtfully, "it is only that you were to spend my hard-earned coin on an old dame's second-hand apron, and here you turn up, with your hair in gold pins, gowned like Lady Politic Would-be. God's small clothes, Judy, is there any money left?"

The slap of cards on the table had ceased, as had the rustling of the attendants' papers. I stared at this gamesome monarch. He raised his eyebrows and wiggled them. Then I clapped a hand to my mouth and said, in a strangled voice, "*Nathan!*" Laughter and applause came from the corners of the room.

Nathan stroked his pointed beard. "A nice job of dyeing, would you not say?"

"I . . . But where . . . But who . . ." I could not take my eyes from him. The uncanny likeness to the portraits of Charles lay not in any facial resemblance to the sovereign. The wig, and the beard, cut to a point, did their work, of course, as did the fine array. But as in our spare London rooms, Nate's resemblance to Charles came from something less definable. It was a certain regal posture, and a formal way of holding his goblet, like a priest with a vessel of communion wine. It was the haughty set of his face.

Nathan stood and raised me to my feet. He gestured with his head to the side of the room. "You may make your curtsy this way, Lady Judith. *There* sits your sovereign, Charles Stuart."

One of the card-players rose, smiled, and bowed briefly. His hair was of middling length, barely touching his shoulders, and his beard was short and brown. He wore plain woolen breeches, a red cloth cap with a round crown, brimmed in the front, and a jacket and jerkin of leather. I stared at him, unbelieving, until Nathan elbowed me in the back and I dropped into a curtsy. "Your Majesty?" I said, feeling foolish, and unable to keep the questioning lilt from my word.

"I answer to that title," the fellow said mildly. "Please, lady, sit. Thus far you are a perfect audience. Master Field, you said your friend was a handsome dame and almost the chameleon *you* are. If she is indeed this Midlands housewife, you told no lie. Now, if you would be so good as to hand me my cane."

Nathan bowed and surrendered the walking stick. As the king grasped it, the gold knob at its end came off and dropped to the floor. A candle flickered in a draft that came from somewhere, and I felt a sudden chill. "It does that," Charles said, watching the knob roll. Then he shocked me further, if I'd had any more space in my mind for amazement, by stooping and picking up the gold ball himself. He screwed it back on. "Comes loose. But there's no time to fix it. And besides, I must leave it with you, John." He smiled at his partner in card-playing. Then he gestured at the bottle on the harpsichord. "Have more wine, Mistress Judith. Once I've lost *this* game, we shall plot the other, and hope for better luck."

I stood perplexed. I looked back at Nathan. "Then 'twas *you* who rode through town this morning on the white horse, holding the cane—"

"No," said Charles. "Your friend was asleep at that hour. That was I."

THE SIX OF US STAYED in the room until well past midnight. I learned that the king's partner at primero was John Ashburnham, that rare Royalist member of Parliament, and that the man who had welcomed me at the door was the Duke of Richmond, whose well-furnished rooms these were. The other was Sir Thomas Glemham, the governor of the town. Nathan showed me the scissors he himself had used that very evening to blunt the king's beard and to cut Charles's tresses and lovelock. "I might sell this for a relic," he said, holding up a shorn lock. I darted nervous eyes at the sovereign. But Charles only laughed.

In the hours that followed it was easy to forget that the King of England, the centerpiece of the decade's wars, was among us in the room. He looked like anyone and no one. He played a card, sipped wine, blew his nose, scratched his ear, and listened to others speak. Meanwhile, Nathan and the lord, the knight, and the governor debated, sometimes laughingly, sometimes tensely, sometimes heatedly, as they finalized the plan for his escape. At length they all agreed on the particulars of getting him out. Charles would take on the name of Harry Folkes, Ashburnham's servant, and pass through Parliament garrisons with the aid of the forged safe-conduct of a Royalist scout, who would disguise himself in scarlet as a Parliament military bearer. Nathan would remain in Oxford several days, appearing as the king at several strategically plotted locations and times.

Nathan had done it. He'd nabbed himself the rôle of a lifetime. Having acted his way into Charles's good graces, he'd convinced the king's closest advisers to trust the wisdom of his outrageous proposal. He, the pastor's son, the player Nathan Field, would "perform" Charles so well in front of his Oxford supporters, not even the shrewdest spy would suspect that the real king had slipped the net.

As for where Charles would go, once he was outside the city walls, that was a sticking point. Should he indeed proceed to the Scots at Newark-on-Trent, or ride south, to meet friends north of London? Or bypass London, heading for Portsmouth and the Channel, to find succor in France?

"France," said Charles Stuart, softly and longingly, looking down at his beringed hands.

"Indeed, the Continent might be the safest destination." This from Richmond.

But Nathan shook his head vigorously. "There are sixteen of Cromwell's garrisons lying between this town and the southern coast." I was pretty sure he had pulled this figure out of the air. "Majesty, my Scottish friends are awaiting you with open arms at Newark. Stay in your kingdom!" His tone was startlingly peremptory, no more so than the duke's, and yet, the sauce of it! Nathan was no peer. A hired player, and to speak thus to a king! And for a further wonder, Charles hearkened to him. Not submissively, yet with no air of offended majesty. The sovereign's manner was bland and neutral, like that of an actor who'd no mind for anything but to listen for his cue.

All in all, my hours spent in Richmond's apartments were sufficient to show me that the man Charles Stuart, at his ease, and despite his claim to the contrary, was not the man I'd seen passing below me that day in the street, for all that the two of them shared a skin. I do not mean that the rider was Nate. I mean that Charles was himself a double person. He was no negligible fellow; not only handsome, even in his plain-clad and shorn state, but also good-humored, friendly, and observant. These, however, were qualities he displayed in private, only among his intimates, seemingly. Those casual and private aspects formed nothing of his royalty. That royalty was another thing: an icon for display, all frozen into manner and symbol. I had seen him astride his horse, holding his gold-tipped cane like a sceptre, making his mount his throne. His posture then was formal, his gestures weighty, his look haughty and commanding, his whole being translated to monarch.

• • •

CHARLES AND HIS MINISTERS AND Nathan reached no conclusion that night about which track the sovereign should take,
beyond his immediate escape through the town gates, and
the first leg of the journey beyond Oxford. The options were
clearly several, and in the end they'd decided not to decide. Or
rather, they'd wait on their observation of the dangers of the
roads—on the numbers of Old Noll's troops thereon.

Yet they plotted and argued long. There among them, in
that room, I sat amazed by the freedom the king allowed to
the debate. I saw the deference he paid even to servants, much
more to his ministers, and even to Nate. Charles listened,
and made a suggestion or two. He was an intelligent fellow,
possessed of a dry wit. But he didn't seem to grasp that this
dry, listening fellow—call him Harry or Charles—was who,
in his essence, he was. He seemed to think what that fellow
said didn't matter. He wasn't kinging it, so it wasn't real.
The king, like his subjects, was waiting to discover what the
king would do, or what would be done to protect that august entity. He was a prized chess piece, and the others were
knights and bishops and pawns. Again and again, watching
him, I thought of a man idling, standing off stage until called
upon to assume his true self, before the crowd. No wonder
Nathan could play him.

"*His ceremonies laid by, he is but a man, as I am,*" Nathan whispered to me, when, at long last, all the plans were laid that
could at that moment be laid, and "Harry Folkes" slipped with
Ashburnham out the door.

That's when I knew Jane was a prophetess, or that she was
right in one thing, at least. This idol must be kept from the
basilica. For Charles as king *was* an idol, not a man but a thing,
a gaudy spectacle to be set before his subjects and adored. I see

now that this was a tragedy because Charles himself was caught in the lie. His soul was fettered to the golden calf. He could not let go of its horns, any more than he could, in public, put down his gold cane. For all their harshness, for their zeal that, at times, bordered on madness, the Parliamentarians were right. It was Charles who'd turned the world upside down.

Some of these thoughts passed through my head that night as I lay sleepless, staring up at a high ceiling from a wide couch in a room in Richmond's apartments. Nathan breathed evenly at my side. The sovereign was fled, the servants had retired, and I was alone with the mock king.

The owl of Minerva flies at dusk. Who had said it? My father, once, though he'd seemed to be quoting some distant oracle. I shifted uncomfortably, thinking of my old da and his tense relations with the man who now rested beside me. And I thought of my father's doings with kings.

In his life as a playwright, the hired servant of two royal courts, he had met three monarchs, two English, and one Danish. Of all of these, he'd once said to my mother, "One of them knew that a prince was human, and two did not." Now I laughed through my nose, remembering. Nathan murmured something in his sleep, but he didn't wake.

It was better so.

I stared at the high, darkened ceiling, feeling suddenly weary of rulers, on the stage or off it . . . and of the confusion between them. It was clear to me that the time for a god-king was past. Now the commoners read books, and carried guns.

And Nate. I'm sure he also sensed that in mimicking Charles, he was performing a kind of history play. But he didn't care. He craved the game.

And I could no longer play it with him.

• • •

NATHAN ASKED ME TO RUN away with him, that night. Not in jest this time, but in earnest. "When this week is past, we'll make a life in London," he said, softly, privately, to me, once the others had departed. "And if Charles's hopes come to naught, there is, indeed, France. Judy . . ." But I was shaking my head. "Judy."

"Nay."

"Judy!" He took my chin in his hands. "I have never loved anyone as I love you."

Feeling the touch of his hands on my face, to say "No" this time took all the reason I possessed. I knew he was telling the truth. But I also knew he had no real power to fulfill anything he claimed or promised. I'd always known it. Nate was like Charles, also, in that, although with this difference. Charles thought, wrongly, that he was the source of his power. Nathan thought, also wrongly, that no such power existed.

So, hours later, as the old twin of my heart slept in Lord Richmond's rooms, his costume laid by, dreaming of the kingly ride he'd make down Cornmarket Street on the morrow, I kissed his cheek, and I left him. I changed into the plain clothes and cloak Nate had asked me to bring, and took my papers and the bag with my kit, and a part of the money. I had helped Nathan get into Oxford. He would have to get out by himself.

I left the blue satin gown hanging from the king's empty chair, and closed the door softly behind me.

In the quiet of the night, as Charles Stuart crossed the Magdalen Bridge with his small party, and the governor unlocked the north gate, I walked southward, alone, to Sheep Street. I found it by the lowing of lambs and ewes, some of which were penned near the entrance. At this point the wall was yet ten feet high at its lowest point, but ill-maintained. I spotted a place where its highest stones had fallen away, and where some of the masonry below jutted outward. With care, I could find a foothold. I tossed my bag over. Then I tied up my skirts and climbed.

At the top of the wall, I stopped for breath, and put a hand to my head. Although there was none to see me, I allowed myself a moment to tidy my hair, for the pleasure of touching my new jeweled hairpins. I'd kept these gauds not for vanity, but as a token to convince myself, if I lived, that the events of this day and night had truly happened.

Though the things that would pass in the week to come would seem madder still.

19.

I never recovered my mare.

I might have. I could have wended my way back to the farmhouse and Nate's henchmen in the country north of Oxford, creeping along in my old mother's weeds, asking a question here, showing a paper there, looking bewildered and lost or officious by turns, depending on the air of my questioner. Simply being in Nathan's company had renewed all my old player's instincts. I'd been his rival on the stage, for a fortnight, long ago, after all. But I calculated the difficulties and the risks, and the worth of the horse, and found the sum of it all much outweighed by other considerations. To rejoin those Kingsmen, even if they were still there, would further entangle me in Royalist plotting, and I was at that moment less a Royalist than I had ever been in my life. Also, Colonel Love-Doodle and the Duke of Silkbottom and the other one might suspect me of double-dealing if I came back by myself, without Nathan. The plan, after all, had never been that I'd strike out from Oxford on my own. The mare was a good mare, but I'd seen that the elegant Royalist colonel knew horses, and was kind to them, and I didn't fear for her. I could buy another mount if I needed to.

And I wanted to find Jane.

IT WAS NO LIGHT TASK to do so. I weathered days in the search. By now I was used to sleeping in fields and woods with naught but a cloak for a blanket. On the high cusp of May, the weather was warming. And in the daylight I found there were so many ordinary citizens on the roads, fleeing Oxford and its nearby villages while they could, that no one especially marked me. My questions about the whereabouts of the regiment from Newark-on-Trent, the one to which Jane's brothers had belonged, sounded commonplace from an old dame seeking her lost sons, which was what I seemed. But even among the massing soldiers there was much confusion and partial knowledge, and I wasted many weary steps following wrong reports. At length, I had the luck to find a seat in a wagon full of blankets, boots, and linen pulled by a carter who was supplying several regiments, one of which seemed to be the one I sought. We jogged along for a couple of hours, and I fell asleep to the rhythmic motion of the roofless cart and the smell of boot leather and fuller's soap. High above me, I saw stars shining in heaven's vault like bits of shattered masonry. Among them the round, white moon had punched a sizeable hole in the black sky. No Oberon was in it.

I slept fitfully. I kept waking to memories of the late scene in the duke's apartments. It was all way beyond curious. I thought of all the times in the past few years when, in the heat of argument, Quiney had called me traitor for speaking against the king's cause. Now, contrary to Quiney's thinking, I had gone some way toward helping that cause, though more out of reckless despair than from any ancient devotion. Once in the room with the king—once it was discovered to me who *was* the king—I had said little to him or to anyone. I had only sipped a little wine, and listened, and even napped for part of the time in the next room. But there had been a moment when, on impulse, I spoke.

It happened when Charles Stuart was at last preparing to leave. I'd watched him surrender his gold-tipped cane to Nathan after extracting a promise from the city governor that when Nate was done kinging it, the governor himself would keep it safe for Charles, whatever betide. But then, as the sovereign turned toward the door, I saw him lift a beaded rosary from under a cloth on a table and slip it into his pocket. Without thinking, I said, "Your Majesty, it would look ill were you to be caught with that on your person."

He stopped with his hand still in his pocket, his expression startled and guilty, like that of a child caught with a stolen sweet. Ashburnham and the others looked at me, then at the king, then at the king's fist, now drawing out the beads. He stood motionless, clutching the thing, looking nowhere, while all the men shot looks at each other. "Heavenly God, heed what she says, Your Grace," Richmond said. "Leave that bauble with me."

Charles handed the rosary to the duke, looking resigned and a little embarrassed. "You are right, Mistress Judith," he said, darting his eyes at me and wearing a rueful expression. "A superstition merely." As the king bent to pick up his own cloak bag, Richmond glanced over the king's royal head at me and mouthed the words *Thank you.*

Then Ashburnham and Oxford's governor ushered "Harry" out the door.

• • •

WHAT IS A TRAITOR? I wondered now. If our king wasn't a papist, he might as well be. This for all his royal claims to stand for True Protestantism, and calling his enemies in Parliament a sort of impious hypocrites facing-out rebellion and murder with the appearance of religion. Charles had always seemed too close to Old Religion for the taste of English folk. I cared nothing for Charles's faith, insofar as it concerned Charles, the man. But wasn't this just the issue? Charles made no distinction between his own soul and the royal rôle by which he embodied a nation. And his was a nation that had long since freed itself from the dominion of Rome. For his love of arrogant bishops, as well as for mounting an army in defense of his right to call Parliament only when *he* chose, the king was a traitor. So thought Cromwell, so thought the Commons. And in my small way I had helped this traitor escape, if escape he had and would, even though I had now abandoned the project, and was going to Jane, if I could find her, and, even if I couldn't, was bound for the Parliament side, where I'd patch up whatever broken bones and bullet holes I could when the siege broke.

What *was* a traitor? What was I?

I am one tired of death, who craves peace, I thought, for the thousandth time in four years.

I WOKE TO THE WELCOME, homelike smells of bacon and hot bread, and the sounds of women chattering and splashing as they washed clothes and dishes in a stream. From a distance came the rumble of wheels turning and the shouts of men. I sat up. I was still ensconced in the supply wagon, which had stopped on the outskirts of a soldiers' camp.

I jumped to the ground with my gear in my arms, dizzying myself with the motion. I stood still till the weakness passed. Then I looked around. "What regiment is this, miss?" I asked a young woman who stood with a sleeping babe strapped to her back. She was holding an iron bread-toaster over a fire. "Is't Zion of Newark?"

With a strong North Country accent, she said, "Nay, mother. This be Castleton men, the Lions of Judah." She pointed toward a thin column of smoke that rose above the trees downriver, some distance away. "If ye're from Newark, ye may find your son there."

The camp was pitched next to a bend in a stream, and the vigorous women had hung blankets from branches to create some privacy for bathing. So I washed the road dust off my body and my garments, and changed into my one set of fresh clothes, while I washed the others, then hung my skirt and bodice and sleeves on a line to dry. Then I joined the females, and heard their stories. Some of them, like the lass with the babe, were wives following their men. Others were seamstresses and cooks, some of these homeless and displaced by the war's hurly-burly, selling their labor for the crumbs from the soldiers' messes. Some might have been punks, I suppose, though none claimed that office, and though by this year most of the whores had rightly reckoned that business was better with the Royalists. All of them were kind to me, thinking me a homeless old Rachel seeking her children, as, indeed, more than one of them was. Among them they collected for me not only some bread and bacon but a pair of stockings and some linen underclothing, much-patched but clean. They were surprised and grateful when I insisted on paying for these gifts.

I described Jane Simcox to them, and was told by one nearly toothless dame that she sounded much like a woman who'd worked by her side baking bread for the Zion two days past, or perhaps it were three, aye, a sturdy woman well-versed in the Chronicles.

I shook my head. "The woman I seek knows something of Magna Carta, and of Richard the Second, but she cannot have read Hall or Holinshed, or Samuel Daniel."

The old woman looked puzzled. "I know not these names, save something of Daniel, and aught of Samuel. This woman spoke of Sennacherib King of Assyria, and that we are to take away his high places and cut down his groves—"

"Ah!" I smiled. "*Those* Chronicles. This may be she."

With a hopeful heart, I made my way toward the plume of smoke downriver.

There, among the Zion of Newark, I seemed to have reached my goal, or what, at any rate, had been Jane's. I spoke to soldiers and camp followers who knew the name Simcox; who remembered Jane's brothers and who knew or had heard of their father, the baker. But none knew Jane. And here, among the mustering men, I found fewer souls with the patience to entertain my questions and help my search. For during the hours of my downriver trudge, something had happened. Some rumor of impending battle, or of some movement toward a final siege, was racing through the camp. I could sense all around me the heightened vigor and excitement, like the feeling in the streets on the day we'd left London. Tents were being folded, flintlocks and wheel locks and long muskets loaded, horses harnessed, boots tightened, and women kept well in the rear. Camp was being struck.

"There is a John Simcox," one private told me as he hurriedly strapped armor on his back. He gestured widely. "He lay yonder last night, in a tent by the water. He may know aught of your friend."

Following his gesture, I noted, by the stream, a small tent, still standing while the others around it were being folded and stowed behind saddles or in carts. It might yet be occupied. Jane had mentioned no other brother. Some cousin, perhaps, from whom I might glean a bit more intelligence than I now possessed. I went to the tent and stood outside, hesitant. I could hear the sounds of a soldier dressing within; the creak of boots being pulled on, the knock of a hand against armor. Hesitantly, I called, "Private Simcox?"

There was a pause, and then the tent flap flew open.

For a moment, I stood blinded by the glare from a polished helmet. Then the head beneath it tilted, and sunlight shone on the face of the warrior.

I took in my breath.

Rather than tie back her hair, she had cut it shorter than a Roundhead's. It barely showed in a tiny fringe below the iron edge of her helm. She was clad in a scarred breastplate and backplate, a leather jerkin, thick wool breeches, and soldier's boots. Her hands were bare. From a belt at her waist hung a powder bag, and another that looked to be filled with shot.

I stood mute, but she spoke in a low voice. "You have found me, mother. And you'll not betray me." She grinned and gestured. "Come in, then."

I obeyed. The tent flap dropped behind me, leaving us in a greenish half-light. "No doubt you think I look like a fool," she said.

I shook my head. "*Nay.* You are . . ." I had words, words in my head, but I could not find the one I wanted. *Magnificent? Sublime? Perfect?* I swallowed. "Holy."

Her disguise was no disguise, but her true raiment. Even in the dim light, she was radiant. She was Joan of Arc, and Minerva, and Bellona, Goddess of War. She held her head high. Her feet, in men's boots, were planted solidly on the earth.

"Forgive me for staring," I heard myself say. Then I uttered the strangest sentence. "I have never seen a real woman before."

That, of course, was nonsense. My mother, my grand-mother, my sister Susanna, the chandler's wife, the young miss with her babe strapped to her back by the stream this morning, the toothless bread-baking beldam—we were women, all. So, now, I cannot tell quite what I meant. As then, I grapple for words. I can only say that in that long moment I spent gazing at Jane, something came back to me from my own buried past. I remembered my own self, striding through the lanes of Southwark at the age of fourteen with my hair chopped short, clad in the clothes of my dead brother, my hands in my pockets, whistling and kicking stones, masquerading as a boy, and feeling, somehow, more like myself than I ever had in my life. What I'd tried to be then, Jane was.

But then I saw the barrel of the musket slung over her shoulder, and my stomach went cold.

"I must be off," she said. "We are mustering."

I shook my head. "Jane, you spoke true. I'll not betray you. And I will not tell you that you have no right to fight. You have any English citizen's right to fight. But I beg you. Don't!"

"Why?"

"You lack training, you—"

"Stop!" She held up her hand. "Remember the thief on the London road? I shot him, and my aim was true. I told you. David and Mordecai taught me."

"You did well. You were a hero that night. But, Jane, I fear for you on the battlefield. In the din and the smoke—"

"I've been through a skirmish already, only yesterday. To the north. A farmhouse full of pagans was routed."

"Ahhhh." I let my breath out slowly.

"They went off riding, but chase was given, and they were joined by confederates, and in the hills, three of Prince Rupert's captains fell." She smiled. "I was there. Proved less green than some of the lads, I will say."

"Marry, this is another point, Jane. You don't look like a lad, even in that gear."

"I know."

"Your *fellows* will know."

"I stay by myself. Some of them guess. They smile, but say nothing."

"You're a young woman among men, and you're not uncomely."

She shook her head fiercely. "The flesh is nothing. Daniel went in among lions and was not harmed."

"Hmm. Well, at least you have a gun."

"I have two. Besides, I fight alongside my brethren. The righteous will not harm me."

"I wouldn't trust that thought too far, Jane." She was looking away from me now, her mouth twisting as at a painful memory. What did she see? An ungallant Cavalier, some insolent sir unleashed on the townsfolk of Newark, pot-valiant from ale or wine, firing roofs, slitting noses, ruining shops? What had she felt? Hands, perhaps, soft but ungracious, breaking into barns and kitchens, beating down the doors of bedrooms, grabbing the wives and daughters of the leather-aproned men, the women without swords or guns to fight them off.

I spoke as softly as I could. "It wasn't Hannah, was it, Jane?"

"I know not your meaning." Still avoiding my eye, she leaned to pick up a short sword that lay at her feet. Where had she got all this weaponry? Had she plucked it from a fallen Cavalier? Bought it with the highwayman's gold? Well, it was her money.

She kept her face averted as she examined the short sword.

I said, "You don't truly know whether your sister was ravished. But you know you were."

She began to polish her blade on her breeches. Outside the tent came the shouts of men, yelling, *Hi, hi, fall in! Foot soldiers to the rear, and horses to Headington!* Jane stuck the dagger in her belt and pushed the tent flap open. Sunlight spilled in, hurting my eyes.

"Say nothing, then," I said to her back. "Only listen." I followed her out and touched her shoulder as she knelt to pull up a tent peg. I whispered, "Let men kill each other. We need not do it, too." I looked at her strong fingers, busy with the tent's fastenings. "Your hands were made to bake bread, to dry the tears of children—"

"*And* to slay the wicked." The tent collapsed, and she rolled it up quickly.

"Jane—"

"John, so please you." She picked up the tent-roll and stood.

"*John*, then. Whatever name you choose." What could I say? I knew the woman could fight. She'd manage herself on the field as well as most of the mother's sons in the regiment. She knew it, too.

She held out her hand like a man would to a man. "I must leave you. I must stow this canvas, and saddle my horse, and not know you, Mother Judith, until the battling is done."

"But I promised I would not betray you," I said in a low voice.

She smiled. "You would not try to, but you will. You'll call me Jane."

"What then of Pearl?"

Even this could not sway her. "'Tis for such as she that I fight," she said.

I wasn't sure what that meant, but I knew she knew Pearl was well, wherever I'd stowed her. She trusted me to have found her safe lodging. Searching, my brain found its last weapon, perhaps the single tool that could stop her from riding off to deal death to other English folk. It seemed a flimsy enough tool to me, but with her, it might serve. I whispered fiercely, "A woman shall not wear what belongs to a man! So says Deuteronomy. Is it not an abomination?"

But Jane shook her head. She looked around to make sure none were in earshot. Then she said softly, "I know the text. But this"—she tapped her breastplate—"no longer belongs to a man. It was Mordecai's armor, and he's a soul in bliss. The arms of the fallen shall go to the house of the fallen. So 'tis mine."

She'd out-Bibled me. I stood no chance with her on this holy ground. "Ah, Jane. John!" I laughed sadly. "What a lawyer you'd make!"

She smiled and tapped her helmet. "*We know not what we may be.*"

"And the things you remember!"

I trailed her all the way to Glory. There were plenty of soldiers standing and walking and riding around us, but none heeded the old woman wringing her hands worriedly, beseeching her young man to be careful, to fire from behind a wall or a tree, to come home at the end of it all. I knew Jane wanted me gone, but I followed her like the plague, stuck like a burr, not to be shook off. "Riding off with a dream in your head!" I chided, even as I held her foot to help her mount. "You are like my father. In another day, you might have been a player."

She did not even deign to answer me. And I knew, even as I said it, that it was a lie. Jane was never a player. She was what players pretended to be.

20.

t fell a grim May Day outside Oxford. Poles and ribbons and dancing youths were things of memory, and not even that for the youngest around me. Theirs was a new merriment, and a deadlier. Cart after cart now rolled into the camps, bearing guns and barrels of powder. With the traffic and the bustle and the predictable confusion and accidents, there was work enough for me even before any big battle broke out, as the regiments drew ever closer together, setting the trap, tightening their net, beginning the third great siege of the city of Oxford.

The last, nearly two years before, had ended in a draw, with the king still in possession of his royal seat. Then he'd still had a hope. Now the Royalists were vastly outnumbered. Bands of them yet scuffled valiantly with Roundheads in fields outside town, but the bulk of the king's army was sequestered behind city walls, awaiting a command to engage that might never come. I knew, from the men's talk in Richmond's apartment, that the king's ministers and commanders trusted the siege would be aborted once the king's escape were known. Why knock down the hive when the honey was gone?

They were wrong.

The thrill racing through the camps on the morning I found Jane, the cause of the bustle and mustering, was in fact the news of the king's escape. I had it that afternoon from a captain whose bandage I was changing. His arm had been wounded in the late set-to Jane had mentioned, wherein some remnant of Prince Rupert's Royalist forces had been challenged and routed. The news was hot. The king was no longer in Oxford. He was with the Scots at Newark-on-Trent.

So! Charles had slipped the first net. And who remained in Oxford? Only the king's private troops, and the lords and magistrates who, traitors to their Parliament, had fed his defiance for years. Why should God leave them be? Let them treat with God's generals, or suffer His punishment.

Where is Nathan? I wondered. From the king's own mouth, I knew that harboring with the Scottish Covenanters had not been the sovereign's first choice, but Nathan's own. The king had wanted to flee to France, to head a new rebellion, even if foreign troops must be purchased to field it. He wished to be a leader, a potentate, not a politician and supplicant bargaining with (as he'd put it) lunatic Presbyterians and still madder Independents. Something, then, had happened to persuade him he could make no progress southward. Something had sent him east, to the Scottish Army. But this had been foreseen by Ashburnham, and wished by the London Presbyterians with whom Nathan had plotted, so it could not be said that the king's plan had failed. As wool-capped Harry he'd passed through garrisons and arrived at a place where, dividing his enemy's army, he might find a ground for a compact with the nation. Might, if it were in him to compromise publicly.

Which, of course, it wouldn't be.

But what of Nate? He must have succeeded at impersonating the king, for a pair of days, anyway, else Charles's escape would have been known before this. Fairfax's spies would have sent word of it at lightning speed to their allies outside the city, and Charles would have been apprehended at some checkpoint. Nathan had bought Charles time. And now, where was Nathan? Had he escaped as easily as he'd gotten in? That was what I'd hoped for, and what I'd vaguely expected when I climbed the wall by Sheep Street to make my own timely exit. But suddenly Nate's escape seemed fearfully unlikely. Against all expectation, the news of Charles's flight, unlike the knowledge of his presence in the city, had brought down the hammer of the siege. Orders from the House of Commons had been swiftly ridden northward. No person now was allowed to leave Oxford even by safe-conduct pass, unless upon parley surrendering the town. How was this absolute blockade received in the city? What did its governor think Parliament knew?

In the first week of May I had my answer. I didn't guess it would come in a form that would threaten my life.

LIKE THE OTHER WOMEN WHO rode and walked with the army, I stayed far to the side and the rear. On May the third I went to fetch unfouled water from the highest point of a brook that ran down a rise near the very town gates that, I knew, had closed behind the disguised king the week before. The siege was now in full force. The fields below the gate were a mass of men, moving like ants to their places, amid a forest of pikes and cannon, the men in scarlet, the waiting guns black, fifty flags marking the divisions. I recognized the St. Edward Cross, gold on a blue field, surrounded by falcons, and the Red George's

Cross and green field of the Hertfordshire militia. From up in the town flew the rival banners, highest among them the black-and-red crest of the Duke of York, with its own George's Cross. And, of course, the royal banner of the king.

As I bent to draw water from the brook, the great bustling noise of the army began to die down into silence. The sudden quiet struck my ears. I stood and turned my eyes back to the massed men, some five thousand strong there at the gate, and a shock ran through my frame.

They were all kneeling. Every jack of them had bent his sinews to the ground and lowered his head in prayer. Most had removed their helmets. Even the horsemen had dismounted to kneel. Among them, ringed by their steel, a single soldier sat still on horseback, his own helmet under his arm, his head lowered with the rest. Then he raised his chin. His eyes looked to be closed—it was hard to tell from a distance, from the hillside—but his countenance shone like the face of a lion as he lifted it to the sky. The wind brought me his words.

"O Lord of battles, with him is an arm of flesh, but with us is the Lord our God to help us, and to fight for us. Humble our hearts to make them strong and courageous. Cleanse our sins to make us mighty men of valor, that we may take away his high places and his altars."

The man raised an arm. No sound came from any throat. I could hear the snapping of flags in the wind. Even the enemy was still, the halves of their helmets just visible as their eyes peeped over the city wall. Like me, they were regarding the New Model Army, whose like had not been seen on this earth for four centuries, since the days of the Crusades.

Now the praying general lowered his arm. "Amen." The many-throated multitude echoed his word in one voice, like thunder. "Amen."

The men got to their feet, and the babble of voices gradually swelled once more. The general spurred his horse and rode off. I watched him disappear beyond the edge of the crowd, skirting the soldiers, circling the city.

When I looked back at the great bulk and mass of the army, I saw some men on its front edge pointing to the city gate. Then more of them began pointing. A ripple of excited talk spread through the divisions. I followed their joined gaze.

There, above the gate, on a platform the defenders had erected, on the wall just to the right of the barricaded entrance, stood a solitary figure. He wore a cloth-of-gold cape that glittered in the fitful sun, and he bore a gold-tipped cane. He went uncapped, and his long, dark hair blew in the wind.

I didn't think a single thought. I dropped my bucket and ran, stumbling down the hill, pushing through the infantrymen who were now crowding to the front of their lines, closer to the wall, yelling and jeering at the player pretending to be Charles Stuart.

I knew what Nathan was doing. He and the king's ministers might know Charles's escape was known by Parliament, and by Cromwell and Fairfax. But they were gambling on the common soldiers massed outside the wall. If the most these infantrymen had heard was a rumor, then their king's living, breathing image might compel them to disband. No doubt Nathan had convinced the ministers of this. I could well imagine his spirited persuadings. *Most of these silly folk have never seen a king. And then there he stands before them, anointed by God and potent* in majesty, *the blood of Plantagenets in his veins, or a few drops of it, at any rate. There he is, the very nation incarnate, and he rebukes them.* Something of this sort. Nathan would have convinced them. The lords who revered their sovereign would have believed him, could do nothing but believe that in the face of monarchy itself, even the most fervent of God's new soldiers would throw down his arms, or turn them in favor of the man who was England.

Even if *that* Englishman was not really here, but in Newark-on-Trent, hobnobbing with Scotsmen, sporting a clipped beard and a montero cap.

I'm a hale old hag, and I know how to get where I'm going. I pushed past armed men half again as big as myself in my quest to arrive within hearing distance of the shining figure on the wall. When I reached the front of the line, I could hear the rich, formal voice of my old King's Man as he called from above. "I do not treat with a sort of traitors. *Show us the hand of God, that hath dismissed us from our stewardship!*"

Don't, Nathan, I thought helplessly. *They don't know who you are, but you're wrong if you think they don't know who you're not. Don't stand there and quote from old plays. Get down!*

And yet, though I knew him for a ninny, I couldn't help but admire him. His gamble wasn't entirely lunatic. For here he was, on a nation's stage instead of a scaffold in Southwark, and indeed, he was majestic! Though my voice was lost in the soldiers' noise, I murmured, "*Yet looks he like a king.*" And he did. Indeed, he looked even more like a king than the king did, now.

But here was a paradox, and the hell and the riddle of it. The quality that in Nate's younger days had subdued rowdy London playgoers had no power over the soldiers he now faced.

To this day I don't know whether they all knew he was an impostor, or whether some of them thought they were looking
up at the face of the real sovereign. I only know they didn't
care. That was Nathan's miscalculation. He braved the army's
guns hazarding that even the king's enemies would fear to slay
his image and figure, yea, even if those enemies guessed the
real monarch was elsewhere. But these men had discarded the
old reverences. To them, Charles was a statue to be toppled,
and if, by chance, report were mistaken and the regal man
on the battlements happened to be the king himself, then so
much more the false image was he, and so much more worthy
of toppling. There was a reason the king's wiser counselors had
disguised him as plain Harry to move him through the Parliament's garrisons, and that reason was not just to keep him from
capture. It was to keep him alive.

"By Saint George, disband! Go home to your wives!"
Nathan's voice rang with counterfeit authority. But the men
below him only shook their pikes at him, calling out, "Nebu-
chadnezzar!" and "Assyrian king!" and "Useless!" and, in one
case, startlingly, "*Poor player, that struts and frets his hour upon the
stage!*" "Down with *you*, Pharaoh!" one man yelled. "Let your
people go!"

Behind them I could see a captain riding pell-mell through
the lines, yelling out some command, calling for discipline.
But he couldn't be heard up here, amid the jeers and hoots of
the men mocking the idol on the gates.

And then, to my left, I saw a soldier aiming his musket.

What is a traitor? Did I fear that a king's murder enacted in
brutal jest, before an army of Englishmen, would soon make
the real thing inevitable? Or that such a rehearsal's effect would
be opposite, and spur a horrified people, finally, to turn back

the Parliament juggernaut, and repudiate their own lawmakers just to have the real Charles back? I feared both outcomes, I think. But neither fear was uppermost in my mind or heart when I acted. I cared nothing for statecraft. I only wanted to save my friend.

And so, as the soldier steadied his gun, I darted forward and yelled up to Nathan at the top of my lungs, gesturing wildly for him to lower himself. "*Ho! Ho, Hermia! They KNOW you're a fake! Get you DOWN!*"

The things that followed all happened at once, or in too quick a succession for sequence to be gauged, however many times in my mind I have tried to do it. The soldier fired just as Nathan turned to look at me, and in almost the same motion, as he looked, Nate was dropping (was dropped?) from his perch, and was lost from sight beyond the wall. The musketeer swore some wholesome oath, such as "H-E-Double Toothpicks!" or "Saint Bunghole!" and I thought he'd missed his man. But I couldn't be sure. Nor could I stay to discover what there was to be known, because just then rough hands gripped my arms, and I was dragged from the place.

GENERAL CROMWELL'S QUARTERS ON HEADINGTON Hill were as Spartan as I might have expected. When the guards dumped me before him, without as much respect for my age as I thought proper, he was seated behind a desk, holding a pair of spectacles in one hand and a paper in another.

I had heard much of Old Noll. That he was Julius Caesar, or Hell's own bloody slaughterman, or a visionary prophet. That he held an axe in his fist for every crowned monarch, or that, to the contrary, he strove against the zealots in Parliament to

keep the king unharmed. I had heard that he stood for absolute liberty of worship, and thought Europe's Jews should be
allowed back into England, partly to speed the arrival of the
Millennium, as was prophesied somewhere in Revelation, but
mostly so the House of Commons could borrow their money.
So I was prepared to see, now at close range, either a fearsome
ogre or a haloed saint.

However, off his horse, he looked like a man of business,
if an unusually vigorous one. Though of late middle age, he
went beardless, like so many in his army. His hair did not
reach to his shoulder, nor even his collar. He was of middling
height, and had a fleshy, prominent nose. I had heard he was
wealthy, but the sole mark I saw of money was his shirt. A
thing of fine, plain cambric, its buttons were pearl. Yet he
was careless in his dress, or preoccupied; the shirt hung open
at the front. His armor, I saw, was propped against a far wall,
next to his sword. Next to his right hand on the desk sat a
carafe, and beside it, a bowl filled with buttercups.

The guards dropped my arms, and the general dropped
the paper, which I took to be my midwife's certification. It
had been removed from me outside the fort by a soldier, by
means, again, of an over-rough rifling through my clothing.
The commander stood and dismissed the men. He ducked his
head to me, and in a pleasant tone said, "So, my good dame."

The audacity I'd felt before the Oxford city gates was
somehow still with me, or perhaps I was only angry at being
manhandled by Roundheads half my age, as well as in a state of
excitement and worry over Nate. Still, a curtsy seemed called
for, and I made it. "Lord General Cromwell."

"I'm not a lord, mother."

"And I'm not your mother, General." Had I said that? I had.

He shot me a look of faint warning, but his eyes were amused. "Well. Mistress Judith Quiney, then, of Stratford way. You have served as a surgeon to the troops, on several occasions, since Edgehill Fight. So my lieutenants tell me."

"Aye, sir. I did not lie to them."

"I applaud your knowledge of the healing arts and, more, your charity. I am told also of this mad interlude at the city gates. What compelled you to intervene?"

I seized on one of his own words. "Charity, my lor— General, I would say. Mere charity. The king's known by all to have fled. Why should a poor, deluded fool lose his life for his fantasies and his loyalty? And no order to fire was given. I saw the soldier aim his gun, and, i'faith, I did not think. I acted to save the fellow. After all, I am a healer." I swallowed. "Was . . . was he hit, think you, sir?"

Cromwell looked at me keenly. "Who can tell? The man who fired has been disciplined." *Though this is not your business*, his face said. He gestured toward a chair. "Will you not sit? And have some wine?"

I cleared my throat. "I'd rather drink water, so please you. Or java."

He laughed. "Now, *that* is strong spirits. Something new, from our Dutch friends. I fear we've no beans in the fort now. My captains grind and drink them as fast as the supply sergeants can bring them in. It gives them the strength of lions. Or so they think." He stood and poured me a cup of water from the carafe on his desk. I took it gratefully, and lowered myself into the hard-backed chair he'd gestured me toward. I thought of the bucket of water I'd dropped on the hillside. The morning seemed days ago.

Cromwell reseated himself, still looking at me intently. I was calm, though my heart was beating fast. Yet I wasn't afraid. I see now that I was past caring what happened to me, and that fact imparted to my thoughts a kind of stillness, and to my words a clarity. Also, most strangely, I was less dazed and confused in the company of this man of real power than I'd been before Nathan Field back in the Duke of Richmond's apartments, when I'd believed, for a few minutes, that Nate was the king. The general had no aura, real or imaginary. He had prayed with the voice of a zealous pastor from his horse by the gates in the morning, and now his voice was quiet and conversational. Yet somehow the voice was the same. I don't know how to say it. He seemed like an Englishman. That's all.

He continued gazing at me with an interest I couldn't quite fathom until he said, "I know families in Stratford. I once met Doctor John Hall, and I know some Quineys. William Shakespeare was your father, was he not?"

I had faced this question scores of times in my life, but I hadn't expected it here. It was impossible to know what a safe answer might be. Still, it was useless to lie about it. "Aye, sir."

The general tapped his desk with his spectacles. "Do you know, the men who brought you here seemed to think you knew that impostor on the wall."

I shook my head vigorously. This, I would lie about.

"Nay, truly?"

I cleared my throat, then took a sip of water. "Nay, sir. Though in my father's day, to be sure, I'd seen that type of person." This was half-true. I'd met players, but never another quite like Nathan Field.

He looked at me unblinking, and I returned his look in the same way. I smiled. He narrowed his eyes as I sipped again. "*Show us the hand of God, that hath dismissed us from our steward-ship,*" he said softly.

I nearly choked. "I beg your pardon?"

"It's what your king-player said, up high on his wall. I was told. A fair imitation of our real sovereign's views! Some know not where to look for the hand of God. In truth, that power works from below."

I nodded sagely and, I hoped, seriously.

"That power moves through meetings, *tedious* committee meetings, and shifting assemblies of men. Yea, even of women!"

I ducked my head to express gratitude for this addition.

"Dames in mobs, dames like yourself, signing petitions, practicing trades, speaking in churches, demanding their say. The hand of God reaches upward from village guildhalls and country kirks and town congregations spread throughout our nation. And do you know where else God's hand is found?"

I chose not to hazard a guess. "Where, sir?"

"God shows His hand in bargaining corporations. On His palm lies silver for java and pepper and muslin. His hand pokes its fingers into foreign lands across the seven seas." The general gave a mirthless laugh. "King Charles is no ordinary fool. He holds stock in the Dutch East India Company. But he is a fool, nonetheless, because he is his own chief investment. And his stock is fallen. What say you to that, Mistress Shakespeare Quiney?"

"I have never been more inclined to agree with any statement pronounced by human tongue."

He stared at me shrewdly. Then he leaned forward suddenly, in a quick movement, like the arm of a sprung trap. "Tell me, Mistress Quiney, why did your father write plays? Was it to glorify God?"

This was a strange form of interrogation, partaking of both the mildly menacing political and the religio-philosophical. He put me greatly on my guard, but the experience, as I have always since said, was more clarifying than dreadful. I thought for a moment. "He didn't intend it so," I said slowly. "Not at first. Perhaps not ever."

"Then what *was* his reason?"

I sipped again from my cup. "Well. When he spoke to me of his work, he gave many reasons." I frowned, still pondering. "But one seemed truer than the rest."

"How did it seem truer?"

"It matched what I saw."

"A good proof. Continue. He said?"

Was this chat merely the calming prologue to some more forceful discipline? Was I shortly to be clapped in irons? It was a sin to write plays in England's brave new world, or the part of it this man controlled, and that was the greater part. Was it now also a crime to have had a parent who wrote plays? The sins of the fathers are visited on the young. I know it. I have seen it. God had poured me out like milk and curdled me like a cheese. Nothing now would have surprised me, female Job that I was.

Yet from his questions, Cromwell seemed truly to hold my father's achievements in some regard. And I recalled Susanna's favorable judgment of General Fairfax, Cromwell's chief lieutenant. Fairfax had proved the gallant at New Place. He'd refrained from seizing it wholly. I'd thought it must have been Susanna's charm that stayed his hand, but perhaps it were simply good to be Shakespeare's daughter. It might be good even if you were the crazy daughter. It had often been the sport of kings—and one queen—to guess at my father's politics. It was only his family that knew the truth: at bottom, he had none.

I could, at any rate, answer Cromwell's question. "He said he wrote because he could not control the world he was in, and so he fashioned others. In Illyria, or Bohemia, or on some magic island, it was he who decided who lived or died and what was said or not said, and who timed all the exits and entrances."

He smiled. "Like a little tin god."

"I grant ye." I smiled back. "He'd have applauded your simile, sir. But he told me that after the writing, when the thing was done and went up on the stage, it all slipped from his grasp, and he found he could control nothing: not the players, nor the audience, nor the queen's applause or, after her, the king's, nor the censorships, nor all the accidents that troubled the performances."

The general nodded soberly. "The thousand natural shocks."

"Aye!" I laughed. "All was unruly. And then he saw that he must either throw down his pen, or else simply do his own part and let the rest run its course."

Cromwell nodded, gazing at his armor and sword by the wall.

"But 'twas never an easy thing," I added.

He raised his eyes to the window, looking out at the fluttering flags on the plain. "Nay," he said. "'Tis not."

21

I don't know whether Oliver Cromwell believed I was only what I seemed, the odd duck daughter of that odd duck William Shakespeare, and therefore a woman who simply had a warm heart for players; or a party to some wild plot to help the king's chances. I am certain his soldiers mistrusted me. But whatever Old Noll thought, he let me go.

"I hope we will have small need of your skills here at Oxford," he said as he bowed again. "But your attendance will be welcome, in any event. Only God knows how it will go." He returned me my papers, and gave me an escort back to the skirts of the Nottinghamshire regiment where I had landed several days past.

There were men from all parts of England forming part of the siege, including units from Warwickshire. I knew that somewhere about were men, and perhaps women, of Stratford. But I felt a tightness in my heart when I thought of my town, and on instinct I shied away from its citizens. Home was a thing to be thought of anon. Not today.

• • •

NOW THE NOOSE AROUND OXFORD drew tighter. There was small fighting in the first week of May, but there were also, indeed, the ordinary infections and sores and strains to be found among soldiers who'd tramped twenty miles afoot in a single day, sometimes in ill-fitting boots; and the usual diseases passed among men who dwelt massed in close quarters. And there were, too, the women, some of whom brought with them small fry, and some of whom were pregnant. One lass from Maidstone gave birth in the camp, to a healthy son she named Persistence Broadchurch.

I attended at the birth, and overlaid the child. Indeed, I was sent to do it. I'd made myself known to whatever apothecary men and women I found attending on the regiment and those nearby. I felt a kinship with these healers, who sought only to repair wounds and temper suffering, and I lived in quiet dread of human damages to come. The other surgeons and midwives shared with me what medical supplies they had, but I also replenished our stores in the meadows and woods in Oxford's vicinity. I was challenged many times to display my credentials when wandering too close to officers' tents. So many times, indeed, were my poor papers folded and unfolded that they threatened to fall apart, and their lettering became hard to read. Nevertheless, being an actual apothecary instead of a pretended one is a great help in convincing others that you are what you say you are. This is what I'd told Nathan, and so it proved in my case.

Though I hated the war as I ever had, and feared what might happen any day at Oxford, I began to feel a calmness each morning as I awoke in a tent of women, some young wives of soldiers, some mothers, some cooks, some midwives. I even prayed with them, though more and more it seemed that my real prayers were those that welled up in my heart when I walked apart in the woods and meadows, examining grasses and flowers and berries and herbs, sometimes holding a canvas cloth over my head to shield myself from the rain. The din of the camps and the shouts of the siege would fade to a dim babble behind the trees. If I did indeed pray as I walked through the woods, it was a new sort of prayer. A kind of listening. I asked God for nothing. Instead of the words, words, words I had poured out to heaven for years, I kept silence. I paid attention.

And this attentiveness, I found, I could bring to the men and women in whose company I found myself in the camps. I heard their stories. These folk were indeed all sorts. One of the dames who had followed her husband to war was a titled lady of Staffordshire, her husband a captain, and she as zealous a Puritan as any butcher's wife from East Anglia. She led Bible readings in her tent, which sheltered six others, all of whom solicited me for medical advice for ills real and imaginary. I visited both sexes, but mainly the soldiers. I treated a Yorkshire private's eyestrain, and quarantined a Cornish farmer who'd contracted purple fever, and pulled the tooth of a Sheffield corporal of whose language I kenned not a word, though I gave it an earnest ear, and thought perhaps it might be English. I marveled at its music. I cauterized a festering wound in the arm of a Coventry man who knew my cousins. A week after that I stitched up a gash in the leg of a stout sergeant whose speech perplexed me utterly, it was so outlandish and barbarian.

"How did you come by this ball?" I asked him. I held the bullet up to his view with my forceps.

He took it in his palm, rubbed it, and pocketed it proudly. He gestured with a thumb. "Set upon by king's horsemen at Cowley, yonder."

I write these words with *r*'s in them, but I swear he never voiced a one. "Yondah" was his term.

"JesuMaryJoseph," I said, and watched him wince, not in pain, but at my oath. "Is Old Noll recruiting the men in the moon? From whence in God's name hail you?"

He bristled. "You may vainly swear, mother"—this, I think, was meant by his "sweah, muthah"—"but in God's name I do come, across an ocean, to help in this great turn of the tide. New England's Tears for Old England's Fears! In a blessed ship from Boston we sailed, and landed at Portsmouth." *Potsmuth*, this was. Indignantly, he concluded, "Have you not heard of us?"

I hadn't, but I raised my hand in a grand salute, which mollified the fellow. As I bandaged his calf, he prattled on about graven images in the sanctuary and how executing archbishops was one thing, but to rid ourselves forever of all kings was next, because there was one king, and one only, and He reigned in Heaven and not on Earth, and now that Charles was caught like a rabbit by the Scots he would be gutted like a rabbit by the English, and blessed be the righteous, and something about a New Jerusalem.

"Are you married?" I asked, securing his bandage.

"Nay, good dame." His face brightened. "Have you a daughter?"

"A friend." I noted his name and regiment.

THAT AMERICAN SEEMED LIKE A wild man to me, and it was the same with the several other Massachusettsers, those "New England's Teahs fah Old England's Feahs," whom I met in the weeks that followed. And yet there was a method to their madness. They were cocksure in their prophecies about the fate of the king, and though, to myself, I scoffed at their ideas, still, bit by bit, as the days slipped by, their foretellings began to come true.

This started with the action of the Scots. Charles had trusted to their army at Newark-on-Trent to side with him in some subtle, private compromise, and thereby to strengthen his hand with the English Parliament. But by the middle of May everyone knew naught had come of that trust. Within days of treating with Charles, the Covenanters seemed to have decided that as a monarch, he was impossible. Too, they felt strongly the tie of their old accord with our Parliament. All of them, in the end, were some kind of hot Protestant, and so were as far from Charles's thinking as west is from east. And so, within weeks, the king's plan was foiled. The Scots sold him to the English.

But the punishment of Oxford continued.

Now, as May wore on, the sky above some parts of the old university city grew dark with smoke. It was said that Charles's Privy Council was burning the records of his government. All books, all papers, all trace of his parliamentary proceedings— his mock parliamentary proceedings, said the besiegers with scorn—were being consigned to the flames. The full siege was two weeks old, and no large battles had yet erupted. But neither had the lords of the town shown any signs of giving in, despite a letter sent them by General Fairfax, in the name of the true English Parliament, insisting that the city surrender. Insanely, the lords and their garrisons seemed to think the town was defensible. Yet no supplies had been permitted to enter it in weeks. The towns in Oxford's vicinity were fully blockaded, and three thousand of Cromwell's foot troops were concentrated at its northern gates.

By the end of May, the great guns of Headington Hill were hurling shot into the city. This insult was answered by a barrage of defensive cannon fire, with some balls landing in the fort on the hill. A Parliament colonel was killed. The return blasts from the fort were terrible. Volley after volley of Parliament shot thundered over the walls of the town. I cringed to think of the damage being wrought on the inn Charles's Wain, and the Royal Haberdashery, and Henrietta Maria's Chopped Eels, let alone on the poor of the city, or those hospital-bound, who'd had no means of leaving. But still, the town stood firm.

And then, on the third of June, the east gates of the city swung open. Yet those gates did not gape in obedience to the besiegers. Not a whit of it. For out of the city, their plumed helmets bright in the morning, swept one hundred Cavaliers all a-horseback, riding fast with their swords held high.

They rode for the king's doomed cause, though by then they must have known its hopelessness. They rode for the ancient right of Alfred the Great and Richard Plantagenet and Elizabeth Regina. They were willing to die in defense of that right, to perish, even as that regal and sacred authority faded into history. They fought for a dream.

But in another way, the motive that drove their sortie was as practical, and as timeless, as that of any British border raid. They wanted cattle. Their aim was soon clear. They planned to hold off the enemy long enough to herd the dumb beasts in through the gates, to help the city assuage its hunger. So they rode through the fields of Cowley.

There they were beset by Fairfax's own horse soldiers, who rode down from the fort to meet them. The fighting was bloody and brief. At the end of it, two score Cavaliers and Parliament men lay scattered, gasping and bleeding or dead, in the eastern fields.

News of the skirmish spread quickly through the camps. I was lent a horse, its saddle loaded with leathern bags of clean water, and I rode to the place with two other surgeons and a chaplain. We threaded our way through plodding cows who, having huddled together in alarm at the noise, were returning to their placid grazing. We tied our horses together, a soldiers' custom where no trees were to be found, and set to work to help those we could. I am glad to say none of us bothered to ask on which side any of the wounded had fought. I do not think any such question entered our heads. With some the answer would have been clear, from the cut of the hair or the color of the sash. With most, as they lay spent and dirty in the field, it was impossible to tell without putting the poor souls to speech, which would have exhausted them. And it didn't matter to us. I remember hoping, after cleaning, suturing, and bandaging a bullet wound in one man's shoulder, that the fellow would simply rest a while, then rise, beg some food at a camp, and make his way home. But when I voiced my wish, he looked affronted. The gleam of the fanatic was in his eye. I know not which type of fanatic he was, but I sighed to think my healing labor might, in the end, be wasted.

We were three hours in the field, hoping mightily the whole time that the big cannon and the culverin from Headington Fort would stay silent until we had done all we could do. I wiped stinging sweat from my eyes, and splinted arms, and sewed up sword-gashes, and dug out bullets, and in more than one case I simply gave sips of water to men who were hopelessly bleeding into the English earth. "Leave me," begged one fellow, a lad with a strong Yorkshire accent and a terrible hole in his belly. As I so often had on these fields, kneeling next to dying young men, I had to struggle against the memories of my own sons in their death throes. This man looked, with his shaven face, to be a Parliament fellow, though perhaps he was beardless only because of his youth. A pike poked from the earth beside him, where it had stuck when he fell and loosed his grip on its shaft. He could have been any Englishman, as he closed his eyes, holding his wound with his left hand and gesturing weakly with his right. "Over there," he said. "There's one over there to be helped."

His voice trailed off. His hand fell slack and he bled apace, his guts spilling from the unbreachable gash. I covered him with his coat and folded his arms over his chest. Then I looked where he had pointed, at the edge of the field.

I jumped to my feet, and my old legs ran.

SHE SAT WHERE SHE HAD dragged herself, with her back propped against a stone wall. Her heavy gun lay beside her. She had laid her helmet to the side, or perhaps it had tumbled from her head, and her hair had spilled out, longer by at least an inch than when I'd last been with her, weeks before, when I'd seen it cropped close like the Roundhead brothers in whose memory she fought. Now the dark locks reached well below her ears.

She cried out in pain when I touched her, but I could not forbear doing so. With my knife I cut the straps of her breastplate and moved its stiff bulk aside. I pulled her clothing from her, and there I saw a gash in her side half again as long as the dying youth's had been wide, and as deep. Her breeches and shirt were soaked with blood.

I couldn't fix her. I took her by the shoulders. Slowly and gently, I laid her down flat on the earth. She groaned, and then was quiet.

"Jane." I could barely speak for sobbing. "Jane."

Her eyes fluttered. She whispered, "John."

"John, then. Be whom thou wilt. Do you know me?"

"Aye," she breathed weakly, if her word were not only a long sigh. But then she said, in a stronger voice, "Mother."

"Aye, 'tis I, 'tis Judith."

She took a painful breath. "I . . . slew him. In God's justice, I . . ." She fluttered her hand a little. "He wore three feathers on his helm, and he grabbed for my breastplate and in . . . the pride of his heart, I shot him down."

"Excellent, Janie. You did well." I stroked her cheek.

She struggled to speak. "In . . . the battle, Glory said *Haaaa!*" The last word was an exhalation, as though her spirit were fleeing her body. Yet she still breathed, slowly, and her face wore the ghost of a smile. "Glory," she faintly whispered.

What was I to do? Pray to some deaf saint? Or, worse, to God? I no longer doubted He existed. I had come again to believe—in some ways, to fear—that He did. But He disposed according to the fitness of His purposes, and what Judith Shakespeare Quiney might wish for, on this day or that, meant nothing to those.

I pushed Jane's gun to the side. I lowered myself to stretch out next to her on the ground, and laid my head by hers. My skirt was sodden with her blood, and I wet her cheek with my tears. "Janie. Daughter, sister, friend." I stroked her hair. Uselessly, I pleaded, "Do not die."

"I am not . . . dying. This . . ." She touched my arm with a finger, and I felt her smile. "Not real."

Her bleeding flesh seemed real enough to me, but I wouldn't argue. "Thee are a lioness," I said instead. "And I love thee. Now, thee will leave me alone!"

Her eyes remained shut, but she smiled, a brief flicker at the corners of her mouth. "Th'art never alone." She spoke not, as I had, in the speech of the Friends, but in her usual King James. "Lo, he is with you always, even unto the end of the world."

I buried my head in her shoulder. "That is what I fear. Can we never get away?"

But she lay still, and didn't answer. I lay long at her side, my eyes closed, hearing only the wind in the grass.

WE QUICK-BURIED THE BODIES, SPRINKLING lime brought in on a cart, to prevent the spread of disease. I walked away when the soldiers came to Jane with their spades. They could hardly have missed seeing that she was a woman, but none of them said aught about it, at least in my hearing.

We recovered the combatants' horses, Glory among them, from the edges of the field. Afterward, the other surgeons and I hastened back to camp to leach our bloody garments and wash our needles and thread and medicaments and surgical instruments, expecting to be called again on the instant, to stitch wounds or close eyes in other fields around the city.

But this has not happened. The men are held back. And today, a parleying party came forth through the gates. They were not dressed in bright armor, with plumed helmets, but modestly, like sober townsmen. Rumor now runs through the camps that the governor and men of Oxford have denied the lords' and their generals' right to treat on behalf of the city. Now, Fairfax and Cromwell deal with the common citizenry, instead. And this means there will be no second Naseby, no final field of slaughter. The word running from mouth to

mouth, from sergeant to private to carter to wife, is cessation
of English arms.

So the Royalist garrison will soon march forth, two thousand strong, to be disarmed and dispersed by their short-haired
English fellows, and all ports and gates of the town will be
opened to peaceful commerce. The game will move south, to
London, and its end will be played between the fox and the
hare, which is to say, between Noll and Harry, or, speaking
plainer still, between Cromwell's Commons and the king.

THIS EVENING A SOLDIER CAME to the flap of the women's tent.
By his accents I knew him to be a man of the Midlands. I heard
him ask for me, and when I stepped outside, he ducked his
head. "Cousin, do you know me?"

I squinted at him. His hair was cut short, he had a scrape
on his cheek, and in the crook of his arm he held the axe-blade
helmet of Cromwell's army. I'd never seen him in this guise,
but after a moment I knew. He was Quiney's nephew, my
father's godson, who ten years ago had moved himself and his
family from Shottery to London, to serve as a wool-trading
agent there. "Philip Quiney!" I said. "Good cousin, have you
joined the fight?"

He smiled proudly. "Before all's done, I have. I was told a
lady surgeon from Stratford was hereabouts, and I guessed it
were you! I meant to see that you were well. It was my charge."

"Your charge?" For a moment I had the mad thought that
General Cromwell had sent this man after me, in an act of
surveillance.

But he said, "Aye. I'd a letter from Stratford to look in on ye
in London, and then ye were gone from Milk Street, and then I

left to join the Parliament men, and I thought I might catch you on the road north, and——"

"You!" I placed my hands on my hips. "You left no name, and you caused me a fright!"

"Indeed, I said who I was, in London. I called my name through the top of the door, but the woman couldn't listen. Her house was all clatter and ruckus, so——"

"JesuMaryJoseph! I thought you had come to arrest me, but you were only Quiney's man!"

"Aye, well, he was worried——"

"Worried, yes. I know about his worries." Impulsively, I kissed Philip on the cheek. "Cousin, you are fine in your English armor."

The man positively beamed.

SO THE ARMED BATTLE DRAWS to a close, to give way to the battle of words and laws and precedents. And what, then, of Shakespeare's youngest daughter? I write of her now, by the light of a lantern in the women's tent, in a nearly blank commonplace book I found in a dead man's luggage. I write of her as though she were one of my father's characters. If all the world be truly a stage, what now must this ancient child do?

Audacious beldam that she is, she might do much. The army has laid claim to Private John Simcox's stallion, and I've no credible argument by which that fine steed might be made mine. Still, a daughter of crafty Will might beg or barter for some more humble horse, and chop off her own hair like Jane did, and ride south with the large mass of soldiers who are now starting to mutter that they will march on London to demand their pay. And then, she might board a ship to New England, and cross the wide sea, and find a new world for her surgical practices, among painted red Indians, and men and women who cannot pronounce the letter R.

Or she might make her way back into Oxford town, among the home-bound citizens who are even now streaming toward the gates and ports. There she might seek a lost friend, an old player, a part of herself that may yet be alive. *Ho, ho, Hermia! 'Tis I, Viola, who speaks. That was a poxy brave part you played on the wall, you old ass, but know you this, and know it always: I could have done it better.*

Ah, yes. I am Viola, forever. A woman plays many parts in her time, and that one will not be taken from me.

But another path waits, weed-grown, long neglected, and strewn with thorns. It stretches behind and before me.

To the north lies the thing that was lost.

22.

ast week I came back to Stratford. As it happened, I neither begged nor bought, nor stole, any horse for the journey. Instead, I rode west and then north in a miller's cart, on the first dry day after four of drenching rain, when the sun came forth and the dew sparkled on the wild lilies, and the world was charged with the grandeur of God. I crowded in among sacks of meal and discarded armors and two soldiers from Shottery. Both were farmers, and both were young. I noted their scars and bruises, and asked them where they'd served before Oxford. They counted Edgehill, Newbury, Naseby, and Langport between them. For a while we traded stories of lances and pikes and the gunfire that left a man half-deaf for a day, or a woman, as the case might be. Hours passed. Night hobbled in like a cripple. As the darkness fell over our faces, the men's talk turned to their families. One spoke worriedly of a daughter he'd left in her sickbed, last summer, when called to join his regiment. The other was anxious for his wife, big with child when he'd first marched away. A son, she had written soon after, but he'd had no message for months. *And she lost her first, two years ago, in the birthing* bed, and that leaves a kind of . . . There was nothing to say, so I stayed mum. They, soon abashed by their own disclosures, turned their topic to late spring planting. I huddled in a blanket and slept.

I dreamed, reliving my ride north with Nate, Pearl, and Jane, and my days in the field. In the clamor of night-birds I heard the din of battle and the whimpers of the wounded. I saw the sprawled, dark-clad bodies blotting the green leas outside Oxford, and the warhorses running riderless. I saw the limping of the weakened and halt from the field, and Jane's dying face, anguished, but alight with glory. When a road-stone glanced off a cartwheel, my eyes flew open and I started, hearing in its sharp report the fateful musket shot at the Oxford gate. My ears rang with that shot, and my mind's eye was stamped with the sight of Nathan, King Nathan, my Nathan, hunching and dropping, his right hand raised to the sky. Vanished from view. Had he also gone out in glory?

The farmers snored gently in their corners of our bumping cart, their bodies slumped and slack.

I lay darkling in my blanket, wide awake now, picturing Nate high on the wall in the sun. I told myself I could have changed nothing. Playing the thing he wasn't, Nate had been himself, full and complete. If my shout hadn't saved him, if I'd not warned him in time, well, then, what of that? If he was gone, he'd died playing a part he'd longed for and relished to the full, and what better way to exit a life? The more I thought about it in this way, the more right that probable outcome seemed, and the more comforting.

The same might be said of Jane and her death, in its way. But when I thought of her face and voice, and the loss of her, I was again awash in sorrow.

• • •

THE CARTER WOKE ME AT the muddy crossroads, at the turn between Stratford and Shottery. The two farmers were still asleep, fresh-faced like boys, for all their stubble and scars. They looked too young to be fathers. I blessed them each with a hand to the forehead before the cart rumbled off.

In the quiet of the dawn I stooped to pick some violets that were growing wild by the side of the road. Then I set out for home. My legs were stiff, and though I'd bathed in the cold spring by the camp before setting forth, I couldn't remember when I'd last seen a comb. I knew I must look like the witch some folk hereabouts had been pleased to think me. But despite all that, this time I came into town the main way.

There was bustle enough by the Market Cross. Among the milling soldiers and other citizens I heard snippets of news about the king and his battles, and the fate of Oxford. I wasn't the first to return from the siege, and rumor had taken its course. Passing by the busy stalls and shops, I'd not gone a hundred yards before I heard that the king was in Cromwell's custody, or else he'd been shot off a wall at Oxford, or else he'd eluded his captors and sailed to the Isle of Wight. Oxford was victorious, or Oxford had fallen, or the city had opened its gates peaceably, or Cromwell's foot soldiers had stormed in and reduced twenty ancient colleges to flames. From the corner of my eye I saw neighbors I knew, who looked at me in surprise, as though they would speak, but could see that for now, I would not be spoken to. Not yet.

I walked straight through the center of the town without hindrance. But a woman caught up with me as I stopped at the churchyard gate. "Mistress Quiney." She was breathless. "Please stop."

I turned. Red-faced with exertion, or with something else, the chandler's wife stood before me.

"Well!" I smiled. "Hocus-pocus to you, madam."

She looked uncomfortable, and a little fearful. But she said, "I am glad to see you."

"And how is thy babe?"

"He's well, God be praised. A mite colicky, at times, but he eats, and he flourishes."

"I am glad to hear it."

She put a hand to her cap and straightened it. "I must get home, or the punies will tear up the kitchen looking for treacle. But I wished to tell you. 'Twas the black hellebore that saw him through the jaundice. I thank you for that."

I frowned. "Hellebore helps. But I do not recall giving you any. Though I would have, given the chance." I strove to keep the edge from my voice. "I hadn't the time."

She nodded, blushing more deeply. "Nay. I know it. But 'twas Master Quiney. He stopped me at church and urged it. He said you had said so, that you'd named the very plant, and that you'd used it for your own child, once. It was a kindness, especially when . . ." She looked uncomfortable. "Do you know, until then, I'd not known you were a mother."

I nodded.

"And indeed, it matched a thing my own mother had told me, and so, I mean to say, what I wish to say is, it did help. And then I knew you had not witched any of us." She took a breath, and looked me in the eye. "I'faith, I should have known it. You are a midwife in good standing."

"And an apothecary. And a surgeon, too."

She nodded. Pleading, but a little defiantly, twisting her apron in her hands, she said, "I do beg pardon, but . . . have you a notion how fearful it can be, the worry that a child of your body might die?"

"Aye."

"I was frantic. But it wasn't you or your servants."

"I know."

"It was that black dame Aspinall, with her muttering and her—"

"Good day, Mistress Chandler." I turned. "And . . ." I half turned back. "Thank you."

I opened the gate to the churchyard, and crossed to its far corner, where I laid my wild violets on Margaret Wheeler's stone.

IT WAS MID-AFTERNOON NOW, AND warm, and the blue sky was dappled with clouds. At the edge of town the fields were green. I went in through the cow gate. I found the old footpath my brother and I had used to walk as children. My boys in their turn had raced down this path, when school and chores ended and they were freed to rampage through the countryside. A breeze was blowing. Around me, the new wheat rippled like the sea.

I walked for some minutes, then stopped. I stretched my arms out wide on either side and stood with my eyes closed, hearing the silence. On my face and deep in my body I felt the sun, and the wind, and the grief that was everywhere.

I stood so, unmoving, for I know not how long, thinking of the tragedy that Time is and the comedy that God is. I thought of every life my life had touched, of those who were dead and those still living. I felt a word welling up in my heart. It was a note such as a musician might sound, plucking the bass string of his viola da gamba. It was a precious and heavy word, but I raised it to my lips and offered it to the breeze.

It occurred to me that to anyone passing, I'd look like a scarecrow.

I'd make a good one, I thought. *I might hire myself out.* "Off, scavengers!" I cried, with my eyes still shut. But a bird came and settled on my palm. From my throat burst a sob that was also a laugh. I opened my eyes and dropped my arms, and the bird flew away.

I put a hand to my brow, under my bonnet, to shade my face from the brightness. Then I squinted.

They were walking toward me across the fields. In the sunlight the child's hair shone like ripe corn. At first I thought I, faint from hunger, was dreaming, and that it was Brother George from the London meeting who held Pearl by the hand. That is because Quiney had on the broad-brimmed hat he wore to pull garden weeds, and had shaved off his beard. When I narrowed my eyes further, I could see them both clear. As they came closer I noted that Pearl was carrying Rich's old hornbook in her hand. Quiney's voice was carried to me on the wind. "*C-a-t*," he was saying. "*Cat. C-o-w. Cow.*"

When they were still some twenty yards away Pearl broke from him, but she didn't run toward me. Instead, she gave me a cheery wave, dropped the hornbook, and raced to a shade tree. She jumped for its lower branch, but proved too short to catch it. After a few fruitless tries she dropped to her knees and began to examine something on the ground.

Quiney stooped for the hornbook, then came up to me.

"Are you in the fashion, i'faith?" I asked. "You look like a courting youth."

He took off his hat and examined it, in the way that he had. "The child put honey in my beard as I slept in the garden. She did it to bring bees, so she might look at them. Or so she said."

"Did you tell her bees make honey, and don't eat it?"

"Aye, I did, after." He replaced his hat. "Though I think she had known it already."

I laughed. "Well. I met your spy."

"Who?"

"Philip Quiney of Stratford and London. Now of Cromwell's army."

"Ah. Yes. What? So he found you at last." He took my hand. "Wife, I knew not where you went, this time. I don't know now."

"You'd not believe me if I told you."

"Then perhaps you'd best not. Or tell me only what parts you will. But, for God's love, stop running away. Though I do not blame you for bolting, after what I said. I am sorry. 'Twas cruel of me. Nay, 'twas . . ." He wrinkled his brow, seeking the true word. "Unjust. None could have staved off the plague, or healed it when it came. I know it. All know it."

I sighed and patted his sturdy shoulder. "Perhaps I saved myself from Tom's sickness so I could give water to Rich, at the last, and tell him I loved him. Perhaps we should all have worn plague masks stuffed with spices."

"I think none of that does anything much, for good or for ill." I am sure I looked pained at this, because he added quickly, "Still, you are a good midwife."

"I thank you for that." I half smiled, thinking of my recent chat with the chandler's wife. Then I looked again at Pearl, and turned fully sober. "I must tell you, Quiney, Jane Simcox has died."

"Ah! How? I am very sorry!"

"I don't think she was. Sorry, I mean to say. The tale's long. It can't be told in an hour." I stopped, my eyes still pinned to

Pearl. Now seated beneath her tree, she appeared to be con-
versing with a stick. I pointed to her. "Who do you think of,
when you look on her?"

"The devil."

"Let's not jest that way."

"Right." Quiney gazed at the girl for a moment, then said,
"You."

I laughed. "Perhaps. That's not for me to say. I can never see
me from outside, only from in. Who else, then?"

Now both of us watched Pearl for a long, silent minute.
Unaware of us, she suddenly jumped to her feet and began
running madly around the shade tree, waving her stick like
a sword. From where we stood we could hear her yelling,
"*AHHHHHHHHHHH!!!!!!*" Then, as quickly as she'd risen, she
collapsed to the earth like one struck by lightning. A moment
later she sat up and resumed her dialogue with the stick.

"Ah, I see it. Your father. No question." Quiney turned to
me with a quizzical look. "But why, Judy? She isn't—"

"She's Tom's."

"Tom's!" He stared again at Pearl, unbelieving. Wanting to
believe. "She resembles him in the face. I had thought it before.
Then, Tom chased the Simcox maid?"

Like father, like son, I did not say. "I believe they chased each
other."

"But how can you be sure?"

I put an arm around my husband's waist and squeezed. "I
couldn't prove it in a court of law, nor would I if I could, for all
the tapestries in New Place. Anyway, it does not matter. Does it?"

"Nay," he said slowly.

But I saw the wonder in his face, and the yearning, and I
pinched his arm. "You lie. It surely would have mattered to my

father. Believe it, then, if you like. She's that thieving rascal Tom's. *I* believe it. I'll tell you later why I think it. I'll build my case like a lawyer, Grandfather Quiney."

"Ah-*huh*." He stroked his beardless chin. "I will need to grow this again." He smiled. "I mean, to be a proper grandfer."

I grinned. "I will miss my courting youth, then. I'faith, I wondered where he'd gone."

He hugged me so hard his hat fell off. He said, "I am still here."

THE THREE OF US WALKED back to town hand in hand, with me in the middle. Pearl chattered on about insects and horses and Armageddon, but I said little, thinking, with sadness, of what I had to tell Pearl. In time, I'd give her the ring Tom had found in my surgery long ago and nabbed for his sweetheart, Hannah; the ring Jane had kept for her niece all her life. On my last, brief return home, I'd placed that ring in the boys' old bedroom. There it sat now, in a drawer, in the pouch Jane had left with me, when our ways had parted on the road from London, and like Joan of Arc she'd ridden to her war.

PEARL WEPT WHEN SHE FINALLY understood that her aunt would not be riding back to her on Glory, not now, not ever. But by early evening, her tears were mostly out. She wasn't hungry for supper, and we did not make her come to the table. At my bidding, however, when her sobs had diminished to sniffles, she washed her face and her hands and her swollen eyes. Now she squatted in the garden near the ripening strawberry plants. Their perfume reached me on the breeze.

As in the afternoon, under the shade tree, Pearl was examining something in the grass. When I came down to the garden bottom and squatted next to her, I saw she was addressing a grasshopper. The green thing stood, big-eyed, long-legged, alert, and motionless, next to a fat red berry.

"I will bring you to book!" Pearl was telling it sternly. "I will bring you to book!"

I kissed her head. "What do you think that means, Pricey Pearl?"

"I will teach him to read."

"Ah!" I laughed. "Very good. Teach him to read the Petition of Right."

She looked up at my face. Released from her spell, the insect hopped jauntily away. "What is the Pishon of Right?"

"That, you will learn after *you* are brought to book. And look, I've something to the purpose. 'Tis a remembrance, but a useful thing, too." I sat back and opened the abecedarium in my lap. "My boy's old hornbook is all very well, but you'll like this better, I warrant. The images are brave. Look." I tapped the page. "*A* is for *Athena*. See her armor and her owl?"

Pearl touched the picture gently. "She looks like Aunt Janie."

"Aye, so she does. And here is *B*, for *Boudica*."

"BO-DAY-SHA. Was she a queen?"

"Oh, yes. And a warrior, too."

Pearl looked up into my face. "Will I be a soldier, like auntie, and my uncle Mordecai?"

I hugged her. "I hope not. We've too many soldiers in England as 'tis. But who can tell? I know not what you may be."

Pearl looked down at the book again. "Will you show me *P*? Is *P* for *Pearl*?"

"For *Pearl*, and *Perdita*, but most, and best, of all, *P* is for *Portia*."

"Who's Portia?"

"A very wise lady who knew the law."

Pearl knit her brow, thinking. "Did she drink java?"

"How else could she have gotten so wise? She drank three mugs a day."

"May I drink java?"

"You do not need to, Pearl. When you are old, you may." On the morrow, I thought, I must compel Quiney to send to London for my drink of the gods. I'd no doubt the java bean was medicinal. And as for the cost, I had some of our highwayman's gold left.

I'd much to tell Quiney.

With two fingers Pearl caressed the etched face of stern, proud Boudica. She was not a shy girl, but she was capable of awe, and I think it was reverence that made her fear to turn the fine vellum leaves of the book by herself. Still, she could not look away from them. The better to effect her will, she placed my hand on the paper. "Please, Grandmother, come to *Portia*."

"In good time, sweetheart. Portia will wait for us."

The thing to do was to turn the page. So I did, and then laughed as her eyes went as wide as apple rings. I went on. "Now, *C* is for *Cleopatra*. . . ."

ACKNOWLEDGMENTS

For the completion of this work, I owe a debt to my husband, Tom, who read everything I asked him to read and laughed at the funny parts. Many thanks are also due to Harper's Sara Nelson and Shelly Perron for their wonderful editing and thoughtful insights. Most of all I thank my agent, Julia Livshin, for her dauntless faith in the worth of this story.

ABOUT THE AUTHOR

GRACE TIFFANY is a professor of Shakespeare and Renaissance drama at Western Michigan University, an editor of Shakespeare's *The Tempest*, a translator of Jorge Luis Borges's writings on Shakespeare, and the author of six other novels, including *My Father Had a Daughter*, a predecessor to *The Owl Was a Baker's Daughter*.